*I had become a creature of the dark, of the night. Never again did I walk the earth during the day.*

## UNTIL NIGHTFALL

Kittredge followed, slowly, not caring if the human escaped. He stepped into the doorway, paused, as if the clouds might suddenly part. He stared through the deep gray twilight to where he *knew* the sun had to be, but there was no searing pain. With his instincts screaming for him to take cover, he took a single step outside. For the first time in over a century he was free to walk outside in daytime, alongside the living.

To feed.

Nightfall had come upon the earth!

### VAMPIRE WINTER

**BLOOD BEAST**          (17-096, $3.95)
by Don D'Ammassa

No one knew where the gargoyle had come from. It was just an ugly stone creature high up on the walls of the old Sheffield Library. Little Jimmy Nicholson liked to go and stare at the gargoyle. It seemed to look straight at him, as if it knew his most secret desires. And he knew that it would give him everything he'd ever wanted. But first he had to do its bidding, no matter how evil.

**LIFE BLOOD**          (17-110, $3.95)
by Lee Duigon

Millboro, New Jersey was just the kind of place Dr. Winslow Emerson had in mind. A small township of Yuppie couples who spent little time at home. Children shuttled between an overburdened school system and every kind of after-school activity. A town ripe for the kind of evil Dr. Emerson specialized in. For Emerson was no ordinary doctor, and no ordinary mortal. He was a creature of ancient legend of mankind's darkest nightmare. And for the citizens of Millboro, he had arrived where they least expected it: in their own backyards.

**DARK ADVENT**          (17-088, $3.95)
by Brian Hodge

A plague of unknown origin swept through modern civilization almost overnight, destroying good and evil alike. Leaving only a handful of survivors to make their way through an empty landscape, and face the unknown horrors that lay hidden in a savage new world. In a deserted midwestern department store, a few people banded together for survival. Beyond their temporary haven, an evil was stirring. Soon all that would stand between the world and a reign of insanity was this unlikely fortress of humanity, armed with what could be found on a department store shelf and what courage they could muster to battle a monstrous, merciless scourge.

*Available wherever paperbacks are sold, or order direct from the Publisher. Send cover price plus 50¢ per copy for mailing and handling to Pinnacle Books, Dept. 17-450, 475 Park Avenue South, New York, N.Y. 10016. Residents of New York, New Jersey and Pennsylvania must include sales tax. DO NOT SEND CASH.*

# VAMPIRE WINTER

## LOIS TILTON

**PINNACLE BOOKS**
**WINDSOR PUBLISHING CORP.**

PINNACLE BOOKS

are published by

Windsor Publishing Corp.
475 Park Avenue South
New York, NY 10016

First printing: December, 1990

Printed in the United States of America

> *. . . Did I solicit thee*
> *From darkness to promote me?*
> Milton
> *Paradise Lost*

# 1833

At the very first, I feared the dark. It was utter, lightless, airless black, the dark of the grave, and I was in terror that I had been buried alive.

My power of movement had not yet returned. I could only lie there in the midnight heart of the earth, alone with the pulse of my heart. I would have shed tears, but that I was unable. Nor can I to this day.

Gradually I became conscious of the earth's slow rotation. Above me, beyond the cold earth pressing down upon my coffin, beyond the warm blue of the sky, shone the sun. My flesh tingled with the awareness, and I *knew*, beyond all mortal certainty, that I could never again endure its touch. Yet even at that moment the earth was turning, and soon would come the night, the safety of the dark. I must wait.

By this time I understood that I had passed through death and beyond, to what state I did not yet know. Nor how long it had been, whether merely hours, or days. Did Eleanora stand at that moment above me, at my graveside, veiled in widow's black? Did she weep the tears that I could not?

*Eleanora!* The sharp pain of my longing for her made me cry out aloud, but the sound was absorbed by the earth.

It had been a quarrel between us that sent me out into that fatal night. I agonized there in the darkness — why could I not have allowed her to win that final game of chess? Did mere victory mean so much to me? But I had not, and she swept the pieces from the chessboard and swore that she could not learn the game, would never attempt it again.

I left the house to walk away my anger. There was the soft, warm touch of a summer mist on my face, dissipating my ill humor. I had already turned back toward home when the attack came, and I was seized with a strength beyond my power to break free. Chill breath made me shudder as fangs found my throat and bit down, bringing blood.

My life was ebbing away with each heartbeat, and as my terror mounted, so did my killer's pleasure. I could feel it, more acutely than the pain, his ecstasy growing as he drained my life away.

And now, stirring within me, was something new: a void, a need. As my strength returned, I recognized it as hunger. With each pulse of my heart in the close confines of the coffin, the compulsion within me grew. I reached up, shattering the lid. With my bare hands, I clawed my way through the earth of my grave up into the welcoming night. By the time I reached the open, the hunger was a frenzied, raging mania. My reason could not question what I was doing, what I was. It was instinct that led me as I caught the scent of human blood, tracked it, seized it, as my fangs tore into the flesh.

Now I knew the bloodlust I had felt in my killer as he drained my life. I sought the ecstasy again that night, and again. Yet, all too soon, the night had to end. The earth's ceaseless rotation was bringing the dawn. At last, sated, I broke free of the frenzy, only barely ahead of the sun. Its light was already brightening the eastern horizon by the time I found shelter for the day.

From that time, I became a creature of the dark, of the night. Never again did I walk the earth during the day.

Until Nightfall.

# Nightfall

## 1

The destroyer of worlds had come in a firestorm, in a whirlwind. The city's substance was being consumed in an immense blast furnace, the draft howling like a demon in agony.

Blaine Kittredge felt the earthshock within his vault more than an hour before dusk. Cracks appeared in the reinforced concrete walls, and the steel slab of door warped as if it had been melted.

Alarmed, he exerted all his strength to force it open. Rubble blocked the door and the stairs, broken slabs of concrete. He could hear the sound of water running from ruptured pipes. Above him, the whole building had to be in ruins. He could only imagine the extent of the devastation.

Waiting for sunset to release him from hiding, his greatest fear at first was that firefighters would discover his resting place and expose him to the light. But the air grew heated, and his concern mounted. Fire could destroy him as painfully as the sun. Yet while the temperature rose within the vault, he was kept from escape by the deeply embedded instinct by which he _knew_ that the earth had not yet turned away from the sun. His sanctuary had become a trap.

The time came at last, and he released the latch on

the outer door. When it opened inward, jagged chunks of rubble fell through.

Kittredge emerged into hell.

The firestorm made his pupils contract in pain as it lit up what had once been the Chicago skyline to the north. The whole landscape was flame. Around him the scale of the destruction was overwhelming. Buildings had been smashed, trees uprooted and splintered, cars crumpled as if they were made of foil. For an instant, he stood awestruck before the magnitude of the force that humanity had finally let loose upon the earth.

*What have they done?*

But the heat was already blistering his face, and, like a mortal being, he ran in panic and terror to save himself. Although his resting place was beyond the limits of the firestorm, lesser conflagrations were consuming whole blocks of the South Side. Bodies lay in the streets, ruptured, charred, not even recognizably human. The scent of their burning was thick in the smoke-blackened air.

And from beneath the wreckage, he could hear the cries of living humans buried, trapped, waiting for the fires. How many of them had sought shelter below ground as the civil defense sirens sounded their warning? If they were lucky, the smoke would kill them before the flames, combustion would suck the oxygen from the air and asphyxiate them kindly. There was no such mercy for his kind, Kittredge knew. Horror clutched at him as he ran, thinking how he had almost shared the fate of those humans being burned alive. How many minutes until it would have been too late to escape, the firestorm overrunning his vault as he waited below for the dark?

For miles, the streets held only the dead and dying. Any humans escaping the holocaust had already fled.

But there were the cars, backed up and abandoned by the hundreds, the thousands, where the overpasses and bridges had collapsed. Kittredge, on foot, with more-than-human abilities, could bypass those obstacles as he made his way out of the zone of devastation.

Finally into the safety of the suburbs beyond the Tri-State Tollway, he looked back at the burning city illuminating the night with its flames. Of all the millions of humans, how many had escaped? How many were on the roads, fleeing in panic ahead of him, on foot, terrified and vulnerable?

Kittredge's heartbeat quickened slightly at the thought of potential victims, but for once his bloodlust did not rise. He had been as overcome by the disaster as the humans he was accustomed to hunt.

But after a few more hours, once he was out of the suburbs into the Will County farmland, the demands of hunger were becoming too strong to ignore. Its incessant pulse throbbed through his brain, his whole system. He glanced back again at the city, obscured by a black pall of smoke. It was unlikely that the fires would spread this far.

With a predator's caution, he began to observe his surroundings. Here, the destruction from the blast seemed limited to a few shattered windows. The houses he could see were all dark, without electricity. The only light came from the distant glow of the city. But not all the humans had fled. Even with the smoke filling the air, he could still detect their scent, terror-filled, drawing him on. He stopped. Someone was pounding on a door, crying, pleading, begging for refuge from the holocaust. Other voices replied, cursing, threatening. Kittredge moved faster, silent in the dark, coming closer to his victims.

But he had to remember one thing, and his glance

10

darted nervously toward the eastern horizon. Although the sky was still dark, the year's shortest night was only a few weeks away. Even if the world were coming to an end, he must make sure he was not caught out in the open at sunrise.

A gunshot cracked, startling him. Fear-scent flooded the air, and the hunger surged through him, undeniable, each heartbeat an urgent pulse of need. His vision was edged with the red tinge of bloodlust. He craved it, the savor of terror in the blood, the more so tonight, when he had fallen victim to dread and panic as much as any mortal human. Now he wanted desperately to exorcise that memory of his own weakness.

Striking from behind, he seized his victim, cutting off her cries of panic. His fangs struck the artery and lifeblood gushed, warm and thick, salt and iron and oxygen and the sharp rich tang of fear.

The ecstasy was intense, obliterating all thought of the nuclear horror behind him. For a moment, as the heartbeat gave out, he trembled on the edge of frenzy. But his will won out over the bloodlust. It was time to take shelter, and here, with the humans beginning to fight among themselves, was no safe shelter for any being.

Miles away, off the main road, he found a deserted farmhouse with a good, deep, cool cellar. He lay down there on the dirt floor, craving rest.

His kind do not sleep or dream, not as the living do. Kittredge had always spent the days in a semidormant state, fully conscious. But the events of that night had been too traumatic to allow him rest. He was unable to slow his heartbeat. The cool must of the cellar's dirt floor seemed tainted with smoke, with burning flesh, and a strange, noxious bitterness.

It was the Apocalypse.

The words came back to him from distant memories of life, Eleanora reading from the Bible in a century when no one could have conceived that man himself would bring about the end of the world.

> So shall her plagues come in a single day,
> pestilence and mourning and famine,
> and she shall be burned with fire;
> for mighty is the Lord God who judges her.
> And the kings of the Earth, who committed fornication and were wanton with her, will weep and wail over her when they see the smoke of her burning.
> Hallelujah! The smoke from her goes up for ever and ever.

Oh, Eleanora . . .

A sound interrupted his memory, brought him to full alertness. Floorboards groaned with the weight of footsteps overhead.

*Caught!* Kittredge cursed silently. The years had taught him just how vulnerable he could be during the daylight hours. Now, made careless by the horror of the night before, he had trapped himself!

He jumped up at the thud of the cellar door falling open. A thin flashlight beam shot down the stairs, darted over the shelves, illuminating the rows of Ball jars and cans.

A voice— *"Down here, Greg!"*

They were looters, two of them. The stairs creaked as a man descended, flashlight in one hand, a shotgun under the other arm. Silent, Kittredge retreated to the darkness behind the stairs, wondering if he could pass for human in the cellar's darkness, a refugee seeking shelter. But considering the shotgun, he recalled the violence of the night before. Humans killed their own kind. This man was an intruder as much as he was.

Then he must kill, even though it was day. Yet he hesitated. There was something—the lingering taste of bitterness, a heavy, uneasy sensation in his gut. The man reached the bottom stair, was about to turn, and Kittredge struck from behind. There was no hunger in it, only the need for self-preservation. His hands, with all their strength, closed around the man's neck, crushing it. The man was dead by the time his gun hit the dirt floor.

At the sound, Kittredge froze. This one had been armed. The other would be, too. He did not want to risk the effects of a shotgun at close range. The flashlight had rolled into a corner, yellow beam still shining. He bent down and switched it off, knowing his advantage lay in the dark.

Glancing up to the top of the stairs, he could see a brief flickering of light. Another flashlight. Then he blinked, looked again. A flashlight, to light the way around a house in the middle of the day? And he *knew*, as he always knew the sun's position, that it was the middle of the day. *Darkness at noon,* at the end of the world?

*"Dad? Hey, is everything all right down there?"*

Kittredge's instincts told him to wait, to take this one as he had the other, in the lightless safety of the cellar. But his instinct to remain hiding in his vault until sunset had almost left him trapped as the firestorm swept over him. And he was curious now. Why was it so dark? Still, the risk made him hesitate as he went soundlessly up the stairs, ready to retreat instantly at the first glimmer of sunlight.

But the house lay in twilight, a murky gloom that brought back memories of times when the smoke from coal fires had been so dense in some cities that people in daytime would light their way with torches

13

through the streets.

Like a torch, the flashlight beam hit his eyes.

*"Dad?"*

Kittredge flinched back from it. But the man was fumbling in panic with the safety of his shotgun, and Kittredge sprang, just as the human managed to get it up between them.

Face to face they stood motionless for an instant, each of them gripping the length of the barrel. With the scent of human fear so close, Kittredge's eyes shone red in the nearly lightless house. Exerting his strength, he ripped the gun away, jerking the other down to all fours, where he knelt, staring at the apparition above him, mouth open in disbelief and paralyzing terror.

The man was young, with a light stubble of beard on a tanned face. His hands were rough from outdoor work — a farmer. His eyes were open wide, pupils dilated and black. Then, a choking cry coming from his throat, he turned around and fled, stumbling, half crawling, through the open door of the house.

Kittredge followed, slowly, not caring if the human escaped. He stepped into the doorway, paused, as if the clouds might suddenly part. He stared through the deep gray twilight to where he *knew* the sun had to be, but there was no searing pain. With his instincts screaming for him to take cover, he took a single step outside. For the first time in over a century he was free to walk outside in daytime, alongside the living.

Nightfall had come upon the earth!

## 2

Greg Reichler ran from the Wallace farmhouse with his own terror giving chase at his heels. He ran blindly. The dark gray overcast made it hard to see where he was going, and he tripped over a rusted truck muffler and lay on the ground gasping, his arms thrown up over his face to fend off an attack. It seemed like hours until he could hear, over the sound of his own sobbing breath—silence.

He made himself lie still. He had seen death in that house, in those eyes, gleaming red, right up next to his own. Was it—whatever he had seen—slowly, soundlessly stalking him through the farmyard? Oh, God, behind him right now? Or was it still inside?

*Inside there with Dad!*

Reichler's hands clawed the dirt in powerless guilt. He had run away, leaving his father to face that . . . alone! Common sense told him that Ernest Reichler must already be dead, that the intruder in the farmhouse had killed him down there in the cellar. But he couldn't leave his dad there, not knowing for sure whether he was dead or alive, not knowing what that *thing* might be doing to him.

The Wallace house was a dim dark shape across the yard. Near the back Reichler could make out the shape of the pickup where they had parked it. The Wallaces had driven by their place last night, on their way to escape the nuclear disaster. Everyone had to get out, they warned. There was going to be radiation, fallout.

The Reichlers thought about it after the Wallaces left. They were less than thirty miles from Chicago. Maybe that wasn't far enough to be safe. But who could know what conditions would be like someplace else? Hell, the Wallaces didn't really know where they were going. And this was the Reichlers' land. It had been their home for five generations. How could they leave, without knowing what they might be coming back to?

Maybe they should have gone when they had the chance, Greg Reichler told himself now. Maybe it wasn't even too late—for the rest of them, anyway. *Oh, God, Dad!* But you didn't *know*, that was the trouble. There was no TV, no radio anymore to tell you what to do. What was this fallout, how dangerous was it, really? How long would it last? Would they be safe in the basement? And what about supplies—food, water?

He and Dad had finally decided to take the pickup over to the Wallace place to see what they'd left behind. Better that neighbors should have the stuff than looters from the city. Dad had been more worried about the looters, blacks coming out from Chicago, than about the fallout. Reichler remembered now—the women and children were back at the house alone—his mother, his wife Frieda, and their kids.

He let out a small sob, not knowing what to do. Dad was still in there! And their guns, too. Whoever—whatever—it was in there had jerked the gun

16

right out of his hands! He could still feel the stinging in his palms.

He froze. There was movement. Someone coming out of the door of the house!

Reichler flattened himself against the ground as the stranger turned his way. It looked like a man, carrying a shotgun, as far as he could tell in this light. The shape walked over to the pickup, and Reichler tensed, ready to cry out. *No, let him take it and just get out of here!* But the stranger turned away from the truck. Suddenly, like a ghost, he was gone.

Reichler shuddered. Forcing himself to move, he got up to his feet and went back to the farmhouse. He was sweating with fear. *Something* could still be in there. But he made himself go inside through the kitchen door. The house was empty. The cellar door was standing open. Step by slow step, he went down those stairs.

He found Ernest Reichler's body by touch, there on the dirt floor, at the foot of the stairs. And, next to it, his hands encountered the flashlight. He switched it on. The shelves of the cellar were well stocked. There was enough here to feed his family for at least a month. That was what Dad had called out to him, the last thing. And his shotgun, just a few feet away.

Reichler got to his feet and took his father's body under the shoulders, started to haul it up the stairs.

After he had gotten it into the truck, he came back down to the cellar and started to carry up the food. They were waiting, back at the house. He had to get back to them. The work took over an hour, emptying the Wallaces' cellar and kitchen. When they came back, he thought, he would settle it with them. Or, maybe they would think it had been looters. From the city, yes.

He drove back to their own place with his father's

body propped in the seat of the pickup next to him. He kept his eyes from it. Jesus, what was he going to tell Mom?

Suddenly, he braked the pickup to a stop, the truck sliding sideways on the gravel. His breath caught in his chest. *Oh, God!* That gate had been shut when they left!

His fingers felt numb with dread as he switched off the engine and cut the lights. Shaking, he took the shotgun from its rack and reached across his father's body for the ammunition.

*Damn!* The full box of shells was gone! The stranger by the truck—he must have taken it!

Reichler put the last half dozen shells into his pockets and got out of the truck, went silently up the driveway to his own house, weak-kneed with fear. A car was parked out front, a rusted-out black Ford. The front door of the house was kicked in.

*They must have seen us drive off! They came right after we left.*

"Lock the door," was the last thing he and his father had told them before getting into the pickup. "Lock the door, stay down in the basement, and don't let anyone in."

*God,* Reichler cursed bitterly, *we didn't even think to leave them a gun!*

And shaking no longer, numb, knowing somehow what he would find inside, he walked around to the side of the house, to the outside entrance of the storm cellar. A few minutes later, the blast of a shotgun came from the house, repeated twice, three times.

When Reichler finally came out, he was alone.

He buried his dead in a single grave in their own yard, digging it out by hand. Afterward, he could not go back into the house. He sat for a long time on the ground, wishing that the world would finally get

18

around to ending so he wouldn't have to hurt anymore. But all that happened was the sky kept getting darker.

They hadn't just killed them, of course. Not the women, Frieda and his mother. But the thing that made it even worse, somehow — they were white guys had done it. Their own kind. He just couldn't understand.

Finally, a car passed on the highway, visible by its lights. It slowed. Reichler stood in his driveway, holding the shotgun ready, not caring that it was empty. If they came and killed him, that was all right with him. The headlights caught him. The car stopped, backed up, and went away.

The sky darkened to black. Reichler finally made himself think what he was going to do. He couldn't stay here, couldn't go back into that house. After a long time, he got up, drove the pickup a half mile down the road to the Duchon place. Their house was closed up and dark, the way his own had been. He pounded on the door, pounded again, louder, when there was no answer.

He knew they were down there in the cellar, taking shelter from the fallout. Their cars and truck were still parked outside.

He called out, "Al, it's me, Greg Reichler!"

After a minute, he heard footsteps from inside the house. The curtain at the door moved aside. Then the lock clicked and the door opened a crack. Al Duchon looked out. He was carrying a gun, pointed at Reichler.

Reichler nodded grimly. Al was ready to protect his own. The way it should be. The way he should have been.

The gun barrel lowered. "Greg. Hey, what is it? God, don't you know there's been some kind of nuclear attack? You shouldn't be out in the open!"

"I know. Al, they're all dead. Killed."

"What?"

"My dad, Frieda, Mom . . . It was looters. They must of waited for Dad and me to leave, then they broke into the house." Reichler's voice shook. He hadn't been able to cry, before, but now that he had someone to tell it to, he couldn't hold it back. The Duchons and the Reichlers had been neighbors for years, gone to church together. He could think of nobody else. Nowhere else to go.

Al Duchon's face showed shock and pity. Reichler tried to stop himself from crying. "Al," he said, choking on his own tears, "I can't stay there. Not alone. I can't."

The look of sympathy on Duchon's face hardened. "Christ, Greg, I'm sorry. You know I am. But I'll tell you, there's not all that much room, what with all of us in here."

"I know what you mean, Al," Reichler broke in quickly, before he was turned down. He didn't want to have to break down and beg. "But I've got the pickup outside, loaded up with supplies. Canned goods and all. I wouldn't be a burden."

Duchon's glance went past Greg Reichler to the truck parked by his door. He considered. You take care of your own. That comes first. But charity to your neighbors, that matters, too. Al Duchon had never turned down a neighbor in need. Already today he had sent away two families, strangers, asking for shelter—he *had* to. Now Greg Reichler, a real neighbor, comes looking for help. . . .

"All right," he decided. "I'll call Jake and Matt to help get your stuff downstairs."

Reichler nodded, grateful tears forming in his eyes. There would be people here, warmth and light. He

20

said nothing about taking the food from the Wallace place. No need for Al Duchon to know about that. Here, he would be safe. Safe from things that hid in empty houses in the dark.

## 3

The looter had run out of the house and fallen down somewhere close to an old truck parked in the farmyard. Blaine Kittredge could scent the sharp edge of his terror, could hear his harsh gasps of breath. But his hunger was dormant. The chance to explore this new world, this Nightfall world, was more compelling.

He glanced up at the dark gray sky. How long would it last? How long would the humans have to wander, lost, in his own element, the night? Twilight, rather, he corrected himself, turning practical.

Through the long years, he had learned the value of protective coloration, to appear as human and inconspicuous as he could. Now he stopped to consider for a moment the kind of world he would be entering. The men who had come into the house to loot had carried guns, were wearing work boots. His own clothes, fashionably urban, would no longer do.

He went back into the farmhouse and up the stairs to the bedrooms, where a search of the closets provided jeans slim enough to fit him, a plaid shirt, denim jacket, and heavy, scuffed boots. He dressed in the rough clothing without a sidewise glance into the mirror over the dresser. More than a century of his existence had finally cured him of that habit.

The Blaine Kittredge who was not reflected back to himself appeared to be in his late twenties, a pale, blond man of less than medium build with a thin-bridged nose and high forehead. *Patrician,* they had called his features when he was alive, in days when he wore broadcloth and the finest linen. Days irretrievably gone. He could only judge his appearance now from human reactions. At a distance, when there was not enough light to see too clearly, he could usually pass for human. But how much he would give to *know* how the metamorphosis had altered him! The image of some fanged, leering horror haunted his imagination.

Hanging on a hook in the closet, a backpack. He held it thoughtfully. The looters had been looking for food. Food might become valuable, the currency of the times. It would be best to possess it, then. Slinging one of the straps over his shoulder, he went back down the stairs.

The looter's shotgun was still on the floor. That was another thing he had better possess for the sake of the appearance. Though he hated the things intensely, he could recall other times when a man had to carry a gun.

A few moments later, he went out the door of the house with the shotgun and the pack full of canned food. He glanced across the yard. The looter was still there, trying to press himself into the ground. Kittredge ignored him, went to the truck parked outside the house, and took out a box of ammunition for the shotgun. There was nothing else of interest. He walked away into the twilight.

His instincts were beginning to adapt to his new circumstances. Already the impulse to seek shelter was fading. Kittredge looked up to the noontime position

23

of the unseen sun and bared his teeth in a grim, lupine smile that wiped the humanity from his features. His greatest vulnerability was gone. No more need to seek shelter for the day, from the sun, from the humans who hunted him. As long as the Nightfall lasted, he would be the hunter now both day and night. The prospect thrilled him.

When he came back to the main roads, he began to encounter refugee humans on foot, pitiful specimens—harried, hysterical men and women, whining children. Some still clung to possessions, huddling inside cars that had run out of gas. A few called out to him for help, but others, seeing his gun, shrank down and grew quiet. Weak and strong were already sorting each other out.

Farther down the road was a congestion of cars, and a mob of screaming humans beyond. Curious, Kittredge threaded his way through the crowd until an angry-faced man almost bumped into him. The man glared at him in quick assessment: enemy or neutral?

Then he said, "Forget it! They're not letting any of us in!"

Kittredge glanced past him and got a brief sight of barricades, men in uniforms carrying weapons, holding back the press of the mob. A hoarse, amplified voice broke through the unintelligible clamor. *Go back! We can't take any more of you!*

"Shelter's full?" Kittredge asked, grasping the situation.

"They *say*," the man said bitterly.

"Anybody killed yet?"

"I don't know." The man looked again at Kittredge, again at the gun he was carrying. It was too dark for human sight to make out clearly the details of a face. "You on foot?"

Kittredge said so.

"Look," the man offered, "I've got nearly a full tank of gas in my van. Plus a few gallons extra," he added. Kittredge heard a tone of guilt in this admission. The gas must be stolen, then. "Enough to get us someplace farther away from here. What I could use is a gun. How would you like a ride?"

Kittredge considered it. *Why not?* He agreed.

"My name's Will Jirsa." Jirsa held out his hand.

"Blaine Kittredge," he answered, pretending not to notice the gesture. The chill touch of his flesh was something he was unable to conceal.

The two of them went back to where Jirsa had parked his van. "Will?" came a woman's anxious voice at their approach.

"It's me."

"Oh, thank God! There was some man, sneaking around."

Jirsa's face went tight. "Are you all right?"

"Yes, but I was worried!"

Jirsa looked back over his shoulder. "My wife, Cathy. This is Blaine Kittredge," he told her. "I've asked him to ride with us. He has a gun."

"Oh."

Jirsa opened the door as she unlocked it. "Let's get in."

Kittredge took his seat, setting his pack on the floor.

Cathy Jirsa was in the back with a toddler in a car seat. "We're leaving?" she asked.

Her husband explained as he started the van, "They've got cops with guns blocking the way into town. They say they've already got more people than their shelter can hold. We can find someplace else."

"But what if they won't let us in anywhere?"

*"We'll find someplace else!"* Will Jirsa shouted, his voice near breaking. The van was moving slowly. It

was hard to maneuver through the cars blocking the way.

"Couldn't we even stop to buy diapers?"

"I suspect," Kittredge told her when her husband was silent, "that you wouldn't find any for sale."

She started to cry then, and the toddler woke up, wailing. Will Jirsa gunned the van's engine, lurching it forward. His knuckles, gripping the steering wheel, were white.

Kittredge shifted uncomfortably on his seat. Human emotions disturbed him, threatened his control. He did not know how long he could stand to be closed in with so much confusion, grief, fear.

To take his mind off it, he asked Jirsa, "Do you know what really happened? What kind of attack it was? Was it only Chicago?"

In answer, the man snapped on the car radio. It emitted nothing but an occasional hiss of static. "It looks like maybe they hit everyplace! I don't know. You tell me!"

Kittredge looked out the window at the dark sky. "Then this isn't something local," he said thoughtfully. "Conditions will be the same everywhere."

Jirsa ground his teeth and uttered an inarticulate curse. They drove on in silence, back up the road. The van's headlights picked up one of the groups on foot that Kittredge had passed earlier, who still hadn't made their way as far as the welcome at the town limits. He glanced at the space in the van, estimating it could easily hold six more. Jirsa drove past without seeming to notice them.

It was slow going. They encountered more than one roadblock, had to detour again. Gradually Kittredge got as much information as possible from the humans, mostly from Cathy Jirsa. She wanted to talk, to try to come to grips with what had happened to

26

them.

The first warnings had come during the 5:00 p.m. rush hour—sirens, and emergency broadcast on the radio. *Take shelter,* they said, *don't try to leave your homes.* They had, maybe, fifteen minutes warning before the blast.

She started to cry again, talking through it. "It shook the whole house, worse than a tornado. Trees were down, windows broken. . . . I waited in the basement with the baby until Will got home. He had to leave the car on the expressway and walk for miles. By then the radio was out, the electricity, everything. We couldn't stay. We were lucky we had the van. We had to drive off the roads sometimes, but we finally made it out of town."

The Jirsas were only one family of many, all spreading out into a countryside unprepared and unwilling to absorb them. *They don't even know where they're headed,* Kittredge said to himself. *When we start to meet them coming from the other direction, from Springfield or Indianapolis, then what?* He wondered if the attacks had hit places like Springfield and Indianapolis.

Jirsa got increasingly irritable as the van started to run low on gas. He stopped more often to check gas pumps and abandoned cars, but someone else had always been there ahead of him. The emotional level inside the van, the close proximity of the humans, was having its effect on Kittredge as evening came closer. Hunger was stirring.

Common sense dictated that he would take Will Jirsa first, the stronger one. The next time they stopped, he decided. He dragged his eyes away from the pulsing of the man's throat. Not while the van was moving. He needed time, at least three minutes to drain a grown man, more time to properly savor what

27

he took. Anticipation always made it better. He could wait. Maybe he'd take both of them, sate his blood-lust for once. The baby . . . Kittredge gave a reflexive shake of his head. No. Rarely in his existence had he sunk to that extremity.

Jirsa finally pulled in at a roadside store where a few cars were gathered. A man approached belliger-ently, but backed off when he made out Kittredge and the shotgun following the driver out of the van, nod-ded acceptance as the woman climbed down carrying the baby.

"There's not much left except water," he offered grudgingly.

"What I could use is gas," said Jirsa, his look going to the other cars.

The other man's eyes followed. "So could we all." He was not the storekeeper, then, Kittredge con-cluded, just another refugee-looter.

"I'll take water," Jirsa said. He looked from the store back to his van, distrustfully at the man in the parking lot.

"You mind waiting out here?" he asked Kittredge.

"Sure."

He leaned back against the side of the van, holding the shotgun loosely, watching the other man calculate his chances against the shotgun and dismiss them. Growing hunger made him hypersensitive. This one would do very well, as well as Jirsa. It was a good time. The parking lot was empty now. He started to set the shotgun down to get it out of his way.

The sound of a car made him pause. Headlights were visible on the road. In a minute, a car was slow-ing, turning into the parking lot, illuminating it.

Frustrated hunger made Kittredge snarl a curse aloud. The car braked to a stop, door swinging open, and a man jumped out, yelling, "Hey, what the fuck are you doing? Get out of here!"

In the headlights, the gun in his hand was visible, and the other refugee was suddenly looking to Kittredge for support.

"Hey, mister," he said placatingly, advancing toward the newcomer, "what's wrong?"

"You just get the hell out of my place, all of you! Goddamn looters!"

The store owner came on, waving the gun wildly. A few yards more and he would pass by Kittredge, still hidden by the side of the van.

He heard, "Now you just wait a minute—"

The gunshot cracked, loud. Blood erupted, spraying the air, fine droplets splattering Kittredge's face, his lips. His bloodlust flared, his lips drew back from his fangs, and the store owner, turning around, saw. Wide eyed, he swung the gun around. . . .

Kittredge's finger jerked involuntarily on the shotgun's trigger. The explosion rang in his ears. The store owner's face and chest were pulped. The atmosphere was saturated with blood while the two men, one still, one still twitching, lay on the pavement, their lifeblood draining uselessly away.

Kittredge threw the gun down, staring hate at the thing. It had still been in his hands, he had never meant to pull the trigger.

Human figures were running from the store now, shouting—*what happened, what was going on?* Kittredge was trembling, on the edge of frenzy. Bloodwashed vision recognized Will Jirsa running toward him: his prey!

But there were at least a dozen of them, more than he could take at once. Danger brought back a remnant of his control. He spun and fled into the night.

Briefly, they called after him. From his concealment in the trees behind the store Kittredge saw that

29

Jirsa had picked up the shotgun. The box of shells, the pack of food were still back in the van. Jirsa would be better off now without the stranger he had picked up. Kittredge watched while the man went back to loading his van with supplies from the store, now in common purpose with the rest of the looters.

The scent of the blood splattered over his face and clothes was tantalizing, feeding his hunger and need. He crept closer to the store, one with the shadows.

Jirsa had found a length of hose somewhere. With the shotgun propped up against the side of the store-keeper's car, he was draining the gas from its tank. The others seemed to be respecting his claim, keeping their distance, intent on their own business.

Kittredge struck him from behind, dragged him down as his fangs hit the throat. Jirsa struggled, lungs gasping for breath, heart laboring with the effort. The savor of his blood was dark and rich with rage. And that same peculiar bitterness . . . Suddenly, Kittredge's gut convulsed. He shoved Jirsa away from him, letting the man fall to the pavement as he retched, bringing up black-clotted gouts of blood—*contaminated!*

He fell to his knees, shuddering, as weak as his half-conscious victim. *Radiation disease!* After over a century of immortality, he had never considered whether thermonuclear radiation might be one exception to the general immunity of his kind.

Was he full of death even now? He shuddered again with a final spasm. No, the poison was expelled. He *knew* this, just as he had known in the beginning to dread the sunlight, to seek the safety of the dark.

From his knees, he looked up at the featureless black of the sky, at the smoke and dust thick enough to blot out the daytime sun. There was nothing to reveal that it was radioactive, toxic, deadly to humans and all other forms of life. Yet it was drifting down even now, poisoning their blood, the blood he needed to exist.

If the humans had exterminated their own kind, could his survive? Could he?

His laughter was bitter as he knelt in the parking lot next to the dying man. The Apocalypse was not over at all! It was only beginning.

# 1833

This existence might not have been so hard to endure if I had not first known life, if I had not retained its memories. It would have been better if I could have forgotten Eleanora, if I had never loved. But there had been flowers lying on the raw earth of my grave.

Her memory haunted the long sleeplessness of my days. Heedless of the risks, I knew only that I had to see her again. One night, disregarding hunger, I made my way back to the house where we had lived, climbed up and clung to the stonework outside her window. She was there, the young widow, now solitary in her marriage bed. I watched as she picked up one of the pillows and held it to her face, burying tears.

I could not restrain myself. I raised the window sash and dropped into the room. She looked up, gasping, and held out her arms to me.

She was still mine, even as I had become. I could come into her arms, night after night. There would be no fear with her, only pleasure.

I trembled with anticipation as she lifted her face to me. I lowered my mouth to the pale, veined marble of her throat and a single red drop welled out, so bright.

I took her life with such rapture!

And only afterward, such grief.

# Danby

## 1

Gene Solokov had been prepared — as much as any man could be prepared for the end of civilization. For over twenty years he had seen it coming, had tried to warn the rest of them. The minute he'd seen that flash of light to the east, he knew there was only one thing it could have been: Indianapolis exploding into a nuclear fireball.

His wife Vonnie had come running out of the house just a few minutes before it happened, yelling that there was a warning on the radio. Thank God, he'd been right there in the yard at the time, and he dragged her with him down to the shelter that had been waiting, ready, all that time until they finally needed it. He'd kept his shortwave set down here shielded from the electromagnetic pulse that had already put paid to the regular channels of communication. Now he switched on the set and started to scan the channels, hoping to pick up some information — anything. What was going on? Was it just Indianapolis — an isolated incident? Or was it the real thing: doomsday come at last?

Stored in the bunker beneath his house Solokov had everything he would need to survive even doomsday: canned and freeze-dried food, seed, tools, a radiation detector, drugs — never mind where he got those. Once the country went up in smoke, you wouldn't be able to take your prescription down to the Rexall on the corner.

He had another cache of supplies, too, that no one else knew about, not even Vonnie — what he called his fallback position, in case it came to the worst. Most important, he had the guns and ammunition to protect it all, to protect him and his own.

Vonnie. He looked up from the radio, saw her over there in the other corner, her face white, watching him. She whispered, "Gene?" and he was over there, holding her when she started to cry. "Laura, what about Laura? What's happened to them?"

A pang of grief and loss shot through Solokov's heart. Laura — their only child, the grandchildren. Laura had never said so, but he knew she thought he was crazy, saying they should have some kind of shelter in their house. If the bomb — or whatever it was — had hit Indianapolis directly, there was no use pretending she would have had a chance, even if she'd heard the warning in time.

And all he could do about it was shake his head and hold Vonnie while she cried.

They'd been married twenty-five years ago, before Solokov was sent over to Nam, and she'd been there waiting for him with Laura when they sent him back. And ever since. Now Vonnie was all there was left.

And as he held her, Gene Solokov looked around his shelter, at the supplies that could keep the two of them alive for years if it came to that, and he knew it would never work. Not for Vonnie, shut away all that time with no company but him.

But he had drawn up other plans, with no real hope of cooperation from his neighbors. For years he'd tried to encourage them to get ready for the inevitable. Oh, a couple of them had made some half-assed efforts, stocking a shelf in their basements with a few cans. But the rest would just shrug their shoulders and say, "So they nuke Washington, New York? How's that going to hurt us here in Danby?" Or simply, "Come on, Gene, it'll never happen!" Even his own brother-in-law had called him a right-wing survivalist nutcase.

Well, now it *had* happened. They'd nuked Indianapolis, and that *did* matter to Danby. Everyone in town must have seen the sky to the east lit up and *felt* the blast rattling the windows of their houses. It was too late now to say, "I should have got ready."

Across the room, a voice came through faintly on the radio. Solokov strained to listen.


The citizens of Danby, gathered in the auditorium of James Whitcomb Riley Consolidated Elementary School, looked at each other, at Gene Solokov, the square-built, solid, part-time sheriff's deputy who had told them all along that this was going to happen. Well, he'd been right about that, for sure. It made them willing at least to come here and listen to what he had to say.

Most of them, anyway. "You never gave up hope, did you, Gene?" Brian Mercier whispered bitterly as he came up to his brother-in-law. Solokov ignored the remark. Time was too short. And, like it or not, Vonnie's brother was the only doctor living here in Danby. That made him indispensible.

The news from the shortwave had confirmed Solokov's worst fears. None of these people here realized yet what they were facing. They'd go along trusting in the government and find out too late that the government couldn't do anything because there *was* no government any more, at least outside the county level. That they couldn't buy any more food at the IGA, because the IGA warehouse had gone up in the blast, and you could bet that whatever supplies they had in Lafayette or Terre Haute—if *they* hadn't been nuked, too—they were going to keep for themselves. And that pretty soon the people in Lafayette and Terre Haute and anyplace else you wanted to mention were going to run out of food and some of them were likely to end up *here* looking for it, and were not going to ask politely, either.

"Oh, come on. You're telling us folks are going to be showing up here with guns?"

"Damn right I am. Look, Chet, your place is about a mile outside of town. What are you going to do when they kick your door in? How are you going to hold them off, all by yourself, with just that old Winchester of yours? What do you think is going to happen to your wife and kids?"

Chet Scofield frowned. "So what are you planning to do? Shoot every stranger who comes into town?"

Solokov's grim expression was answer enough, but he made it explicit. "The ones who won't turn around and leave, I do."

"Now, you just hold it a minute, there, Gene." Hank Daschle, the police chief of Danby, stood up with his hand resting on the holstered gun at his waist. It was time to put a stop to this and assert his authority right now.

Solokov stared him down. "No, you hold it, Hank. You ask yourself, what else can we do if some gang comes roaring into town—take them down to Granger to the county jail? Wait for the judge and jury? Those days are gone. The only force we can count on to defend our homes and our lives is us!

"You just think about it, all of you. How many million people lived within twenty miles of Indianapolis? Most of them may be dead by now, but the ones who aren't, where do you think they're going to go? All right, so maybe most of them won't have guns. But they'll be sick, they may be carrying disease. Who's going to take care of them? Where can we put them — in your house, Hank? What are we going to *feed* them? Yeah, think about *that*. Think about what *we're* going to eat."

"That's flat-out murder," snapped Brian Mercier. "If we turn sick people away with no place else to go, they're going to die. I'm not going to have any part of it."

"Shit! You want to save lives, Doc, just drive east for about fifty miles. Just tell me, are you ready to take your family with you, Beth and the kids?" It was a bluff. Vonnie would never let him send Beth Mercier and her kids away. Hell, they'd probably end up in his own basement!

"Look, people *are* dead already, millions of them. You think Indianapolis was the only place that got it? And more of them are going to die, no matter what we do. The only question is, who's it going to be — them or us? Believe me, that's the *only* question. If we try to help everybody, we all die."

There was a shuffling of feet on the auditorium floor as people looked at each other. Then Jack Rodebaugh said, "All right, Gene, you sound like you think you have the answers. So tell us — what are we going to do about food?"

Solokov exhaled with relief. They were with him now. They were starting to understand how it would have to be if they were going to survive. He was not a man with illusions about human nature. He was grimly aware that, even with his weapons, he couldn't hold off a determined mass attack, whether the mob was strangers or his own starving neighbors, who all knew damn well about his stockpile of supplies. If they'd only listened in the first place . . . But the time to think about that was long gone now, and no use dwelling on it.

"First of all," he said, "we pool what we've got, all of us. No hoarding. Canned stuff, dry goods—that kind of thing is what we want. Everything left in the IGA—sorry, Thomas, but that's the way it's got to be.

"The thing is, we're lucky, luckier than a lot of places. We've got the canning plant. I figure, with everything including the cannery, we've got enough to last us all for months, a year maybe, if we have to cut things that tight. The bad news is, that might not be enough. Conditions could get hard. So the stock is going to have to go. We may need the feed for ourselves."

The expected protest: "We can't eat cattle feed!"

"You can eat corn. You can eat soybeans," Solokov insisted. "The time may come when you'll thank God to have that cattle feed. Now, the farms around here—I figure we've got altogether maybe a couple hundred thousand bushels still on hand, wouldn't you say, Chet?"

"Wait a minute! You're not going to slaughter *my* stock!" insisted a hog farmer.

"You want to wait till they start to glow in the dark? Shit, man, fallout's going to kill your stock anyway. Hogs wouldn't be fit to eat. And you won't be able to feed them, either. You go out there in the open, you'll just end up just as dead as they are."

Someone else started to say something, but Solokov cut her off. They'd sit around and argue forever if he let them. "Look," he insisted, "it's only a matter of hours before the fallout level starts to get dangerous. What you've got to understand is it wasn't just Indianapolis. From what I heard on the shortwave, this was a worldwide thing. The whole atmosphere's going to be radioactive. By the time the stuff gets here, it'll be too late unless we get organized now!"

The objections died out as the protesters began to realize that Solokov had the majority with him — you either went along or you were on your own, and don't bother changing your mind and asking for help later on. "We're not going to tolerate any free riders around here," he warned.

As the citizens filed out to get to work, Solokov caught up with his brother-in-law. "Look, Doc," he said. "I really want you in on this thing. I'm not exaggerating — things are going to be bad. We may not all make it, but we've got the best chance if we stick together. You being here, that'll make a difference. But, the thing is, I can't make exceptions. You let someone get away with taking advantage, the next thing, everyone's doing it. Your being Vonnie's brother, that would make it worse."

Brian Mercier balled up his fists inside his pockets. He had never gotten along too well with Gene. But, this was his home, his family. "I don't suppose Laura . . ."

Solokov shook his head. "Vonnie's taking it hard. It wouldn't be easy on her if I've got to shut you out. But I'd do it, Doc, if I had to."

"Yeah, I'll bet you would," said Mercier. Gene usually did mean what he said. It was either a good point or a bad one, depending on how you looked at it. "All

39

right. I don't like it, but you may be right."

Danby was a farm town. Its people were hard-working men and women who were used to getting things done. They had tractors, trucks, and heavy farming equipment. Not a few of them had worked in the building trades for a time when cash got tight on the farm. Soon people had to shout to make themselves heard over the roar of farm machinery on the streets, plowing up earth and piling it up against walls as a radiation barrier. In only a few hours, the population of fifteen hundred had been moved into shelters in the basements of the consolidated school, the Elks lodge, and the Methodist church.

Solokov had planned everything out in advance, just in case, made provisions for ventilation, sanitation, all the necessities. Everything had to be done outside while it was still safe, before the fallout came. Mechanics worked to set up generators to provide electricity in the shelters. Food was moved from the IGA, drugs from the Rexall, all of it distributed to the three shelters. Where it wasn't practical to move essential supplies out, like the canning plant, the grain elevator, or the gasoline tank at the Texaco station, the places were put under lock and key.

Solokov had a list of what was necessary and a fair estimate of what supplies were in town. Squads of teenagers in pickup trucks went from house to house, loading up with consumables, hauling the stuff out in bucket-brigade lines. It was all common property now, and nothing could be held back, not if you wanted into the shelters.

Of course, he was realistic. He knew people would try to try to keep back a few essentials for their own families. He doubted that it would do most of them all that much good if looters came around. The fact was, he was keeping back his own hidden emergency cache. It bothered him, making that decision after what he said about hoarders and making no exceptions, but in the end it came down to simple survival. Shit, if they'd all listened to him in the first place, the problem wouldn't have come up. His contribution was worth more than any ten of the rest of them, anyway, and they all knew it. Who else had a dosimeter, for God's sake? Or a pair of Uzi submachine guns?

When the radiation detector started to register the buildup of atmospheric fallout, people started to come into the shelters. Solokov had specified: bring your own mattresses and blankets. Everybody was allowed one suitcase, that was it.

Of course, he was ready for trouble. People tried to bring in more than their share. Mrs. Hadley tried to smuggle in her pet poodle, and it took her son Mike to drag her into the shelter when Jack Rodebaugh pulled the animal out from under her coat. Solokov was ruthless, ignored the tears and the hysterics. The shelters barely had room for what was necessary. In a month, she'd be ready to eat the goddamn dog.

But most people made no objections to Solokov's orders. By that time, they had all heard about what happened in front of the IGA.

It was just after things had gotten underway, while they were hauling the food out of the store to take to the shelters. That car came roaring into town right down the middle of the street—a big, dark green Mercedes. Solokov knew who it belonged to. There weren't too many cars like that one in Fulham County. The man was a big-city lawyer named Archer, had a fancy summer place over on Sugar Lake.

The guy jumped out, right in front of the store,

41

waving around his credit cards, started yelling, what the hell was going on, why wouldn't they let him inside, he had to get supplies to take back to his place. Solokov had gone up to the car, explained to him how the supplies were all being reserved for the community shelter. He knew that type. The guy would have loaded up half the damn store in his car and just driven off. To hell with the rest of them, with the people who really belong to the town, who'd lived here all their lives.

"You'll just have to find your supplies someplace else," Solokov told him.

But Archer was belligerent. "I'm not driving another half hour to the next town!" he said, and started to push his way through to the store. He grabbed hold of a carton that a couple of kids were loading up into a truck, and Solokov could see that things were starting to get out of hand. He raised up his shotgun and clicked off the safety.

The lawyer turned around and sneered, "You're not going to use that thing!"

But the lawyer was wrong.

Hank Daschle, the police chief, had come running up, his gun still snapped up inside its holster. Mouth hanging open, he stared at the dead man lying on the street, stared at Gene Solokov holding his shotgun.

"Well, that was the first one," Solokov said. Then, to the rest of them all standing around and gaping, "Come on, we don't have all day to get this done!"

And the loading went on, people stepping around the body until he had someone haul it back to the car.

That was when Gene Solokov had his single moment of regret about the shooting, when he looked into the car and saw Archer's kid sitting there, about sixteen years old, frozen scared and white-faced from the shock. The kid had seen the whole thing.

Solokov told him to get going, to drive home before it got dangerous to be outside.

But after that, no one made any trouble when he started to organize the town's defenses. At least now they understood how it was going to have to be. Archer wasn't going to be the last stranger to try to come into Danby and take over their supplies. And Solokov damn well meant to be ready for the next one.

## 2

They *had* hit Springfield. They — whoever they were. Most people assumed it was the Russians, but there was some doubt about that. The question was, these days, a matter fairly remote from more urgent concerns. But Springfield — if it was gone, Indianapolis probably was, too, and St. Louis.

Blaine Kittredge obtained this information in a transient shelter in the basement of a VFW hall about twenty miles south of Kankakee, Illinois. It was hard to conceal his disappointment. For most of his existence he had hunted the cities. Now that Nightfall had come, they would have been the perfect place for one of his kind. He had entertained the image of human thousands crowded into the subway tunnels designated as civil defense shelters in Chicago, every one of them a potential victim. Refugees and strangers everywhere, authority breaking down, random human violence: in such an environment his own depredations would have gone overlooked.

But the cities were gone.

"Go on," he told the gray-haired man sitting cross-legged on the basement floor. "Here." He took out a can of pineapple juice from the backpack near his knees and popped it open.

The human looked up, incredulous gratitude brightening his haggard face. People did not so freely give away canned food these days, not even for information. He took the can with a black-nailed hand, then upended the contents down his throat.

As he exhaled deeply, Kittredge leaned toward him and said again, "Go on. Tell me about Springfield."

Elsewhere in the shelter, eyes, dark with envy and hunger, watched avidly as the man put down the can. Kittredge ignored them for the moment.

"You have family in Springfield, is that it?" the man asked. "Sorry, I wouldn't hold out much hope. I mean . . . I wasn't in town myself, you understand. But I could see—I was close enough to see . . . the whole place. No one could have lived through that. Not if they were right in town."

Kittredge nodded. "What about other cities? Have you heard anything? What about St. Louis?"

The man shook his head. "People on the road said St. Louis was gone, too. It took me four days to get this far." He looked around the shelter, at the refugees crowded into their jealously staked-out corners, then back, longingly, at Kittredge's backpack, which he was carefully strapping shut again.

The juice had been wasted. Kittredge had caught the scent as the gray-haired man reached for the can: contaminated. He had been close enough to see Springfield blown up, close enough to receive a lethal dose of radiation. The basement was full of them, some already retching their lives away. The stench of their sickness soured the air in these crowded, poorly ventilated quarters. And they were lucky to be here.

Kittredge stood up, casting around for a healthy victim. He was in no hurry. It was still only the middle of the afternoon. He was careful to keep his face in the shadows. There was electricity here, still, and running water. Even flush toilets, which the refugees would heedlessly keep using until they overflowed. Best of all, for his purposes, the shelter was unpoliced. A lone man, obviously carrying food, without a gun, might have been at risk. But Kittredge had retrieved his shotgun, as well as the .38 Will Jirsa had taken from the storekeeper's body. The human predators could find easier victims.

One woman, standing up leaning against a wall, caught his eye. She licked her lips, smoothed down her clothing. Seeing his attention, she smiled invitingly, and Kittredge raised his eyebrows. She was slightly plump, with dark, curling hair and freshly applied makeup. How soon, he wondered, would such things as makeup disappear from the world?

Well aware of being watched, he made his way casually in her direction.

"You got more of those cans in there?" she asked him, clearly nervous, embarrassed by what she was doing.

"Maybe I do," he temporized.

"Well. Why don't we go someplace more private and take a look?"

Someplace more private was not easy to find in the conditions of the shelter. But by a tacit agreement among the refugees, the short hallway leading to the restrooms was kept clear. Kittredge took the woman to the dimly lit corner at the end of the hall and brought a hand up under her skirt, pulling her to him. Prostitutes of both sexes had frequently offered themselves as his victims during his existence. On the whole, he preferred the boys. Women, all too often, aroused unwelcome memories.

In a moment he had learned what he wanted to know. The scent was untainted by radiation.

46

"Hey!" she protested, "your hand's cold! How about the food first?"

"OK," he agreed, unstrapping the backpack and pulling out another can. "Here."

He opened it for her, stood close while she scooped out canned tuna with her fingers, licking every scrap and drop of oil, drawing out the eating as long as she could. Kittredge could afford to be patient. He would have preferred to wait until night, until his hunger had risen, but he decided not to let this opportunity go to waste.

Finally she let him take the empty can away and press her back up against the wall. "My name's Evelyn," she offered, an attempt to humanize the encounter a little. Kittredge silenced her. He never wanted to know their names. Roughly, he lifted her skirt and thrust his body against hers, counterfeiting as best he could the act his undead flesh could no longer perform. He lifted her up, forcing her head back, and his mouth went to her throat.

The gasp as he struck was choked off, and his body pressing hers against the wall kept her struggles to a minimum. He drained her slowly, without the intense rapture of bloodlust. It had been, after all, too soon. When he finally, sated, let her slide down the wall, she emitted a small moan.

Still alive! Startled, he looked at her again, bent down to find a weakening pulse. He had known it could happen. There was even the possibility of saving them, with hospitals and transfusions available. But there was no chance of that here and now. Nervously he looked behind him, knowing the humans would be watching the hall, torn between prurient curiosity and embarrassment. He could not let them see her lying on the floor, half-naked, blood welling slowly from her throat. For modesty's sake, he pulled her skirt down and dragged her into the darkest shadow of the corner.

Now his plans must be altered. He would have to leave the shelter. Everyone had seen the two of them go into the hallway together. The humans might not realize, might not be willing to accept this evidence of what he was, but even in the Nightfall world, killing was not yet so easily tolerated.

Picking up his backpack and shotgun from the floor beside his victim, he went without obvious haste across the basement, up the stairs to the door.

"Hey, you're not going back out there, are you?" someone called out to him. It sounded like the man from Springfield, still hoping for another handout. There were other shouts, that it was dangerous to open the door, but Kittredge made no reply.

There was no one in sight as he came out into the empty streets of the town. What was its name — Graysville, Grenville? It was hard to tell one of them from another. By the time he had passed beyond its limits he knew there would be no attempt at pursuit. One more refugee was dead, that was all. The humans had more pressing concerns. This was freedom! It was the way his existence was meant to be. For so long, the increasing complexity of the human world had thwarted, frustrated him, born to the ways of much simpler times. But Nightfall would cause the world to revert. No longer would he be forced to evade the probing of police detectives, forensic pathologists. No, the humans would be forced to survive on his terms, now.

Night came while he was still alone on the road, true night, the sky turning from twilight gray to utter black. After a while, it began, quietly, to rain. His clothes were soon uncomfortably soaked. He wished he had thought, back at the farmhouse where he

48

killed the looter in the cellar, to look for a raincoat. They were impossible to find these days, people thinking they could provide protection from fallout. There was much discussion in the shelters about fallout, more of it ignorance than not, but Kittredge had made himself listen. Whatever affected the humans also affected him.

He turned his face upward and let the rain fall onto it. He licked it from his lips. The rain was almost certainly radioactive, falling from those clouds, but he could taste only smoke, nothing of the bitterness that tainted the blood of the contaminated humans. On such evidence, he was assuming he was immune to the direct effects of the fallout. But envisioning the rainwater soaking the crops, running into the lakes and rivers, he thought that eventually he and the humans might come to the same end after all, by different routes.

He walked on. After a while, he began to leave footprints behind him in the snow.

Kittredge stopped to rest for a few hours around noon the next day, breaking into an empty hay barn and slowing his heartbeat, drifting with the movement of the earth. Emerging well before dusk, he could feel the first stirrings of hunger.

The sensation disturbed him. Despite the twilight covering the earth, he *knew* it was too early. He had disrupted the normal rhythms of his existence by taking that woman in the shelter yesterday afternoon. Evelyn.

But hunger made his senses more acute. He could detect the presence of humans sheltering below the house a few dozen yards away from the barn—like rabbits, he thought, warm in their burrow while the wolf prowls overhead. The scent of them was tantalizing.

Angrily, he left the barn and made for the road again, determined to assert his control over the needs that drove him. Too many others of his kind had been destroyed when they let their instinctive cravings overwhelm their will. Over the long years, his own mastery of himself had been hard won.

But the hunger did not abate, it throbbed through his veins as he walked, gradually making each heartbeat a recurring torment. The rain continued, too, a chill, soaking drizzle. The brief snowfall of the night before was already melted away, but this was hardly warmer. Kittredge did not feel the cold—the cold was a part of him—but his clammy clothes chafed his skin. The thought of being dry soon drew him almost as much as the hunger.

Another farmhouse came into sight up the road. He crossed the muddy fields, angling toward it. As he approached, his senses, sharp edged by now, caught the human scent again—they were here, waiting for him, vulnerable. . . .

No, not all humans were so vulnerable. He had seen enough killings already in the Nightfall world to remind him of that. He would have to be cautious. The humans in this house might have guns, might be prepared for intruders. But for human intruders. Not one of his kind.

As he expected, the doors were locked. But in the years of his existence Kittredge had acquired considerable skill as a housebreaker. Now he began to climb, using handholds impossible for a human, up the wall of the house to an upstairs bedroom window. He pushed the sash open and climbed through.

The clothes here did not fit as well as the ones he already had, but they were at least dry. He changed,

50

leaving the wet ones on the floor, and stuffed a few more dry things into his backpack. Next, he checked to see if the farmhouse still had electricity. It did not. He smiled grimly, making his upper lip draw back from his fangs. The idea of finding his victims in the dark appealed to his bloodlust.

His heartbeat measuring the seconds, he tried to make himself wait until full dark, but the hunger and the proximity of the humans were too compelling.

Near dusk, he went down the stairs and into the kitchen. There, sealed with duct tape, was the door leading down to the basement. But he was too wary to go down those stairs, not with humans who might be waiting at the bottom with guns. The invulnerability of his kind had its limits, and a shotgun at point-blank range could possibly exceed them. No, there were other ways.

He went to the back door of the house and kicked it open, a sudden crash in the kitchen's silence.

A stifled scream from below, then voices whispered to each other. One called out: *"Hey, who's up there?"*

Kittredge waited. They had given themselves away. He knew what would happen next.

Footsteps on the stairs, slow and cautious. One man only. The sharp scent of nervous sweat. The sound of duct tape being peeled away from painted wood. Kittredge was motionless, anticipation pulsing.

It happened as it had so often before: the man with his gun, not quick enough to see what was waiting behind the door. Kittredge was on him instantly, seizing the human in an unbreakable grip, carrying him up the stairs to the bedroom. There, his fangs plunged deep into the flesh, releasing the rich, clean blood. He fed avidly, relishing the savor of fear, as his hunger exploded into bloodlust, until the moment when the heartbeat faltered and ceased. Then, as always, he

51

must struggle for control against the bloodlust demanding *more!*

His vision cleared, and he listened to the voices calling to the man—women's voices. They had come up from the basement and run out into the yard through the back door he had left open. Now he waited to see if someone would come up the stairs, planning to retreat through the window if necessary. He wanted no more confrontations tonight.

He frowned, recalling that he had left the gun on the kitchen floor. An oversight. But after a while, he could hear them barricading themselves back inside the basement. A smile of satisfaction exposed his fangs. They might have fled, out into the radioactive twilight. Now they were his!

Throughout the day he waited in the bedroom, not quite daring to fall into rest and leave himself vulnerable, not in the same house with humans who had a gun. And so he avoided the temptation of the bed, pacing soundlessly across the floor of the darkened bedroom.

The body, cooling and stiffening, was a distasteful presence, a mockery of the living thing. A shallow pool of blood was clotting on the floor, as revolting to Kittredge as excrement to a human. The scent of death soon drove him into another bedroom. His thoughts made him restless. He had been wrong, thinking to search for his victims in the remaining cities. There was going to be a vast die-off of the human kind. Unlike the refugees from the devastated cities, the population of the country had not been exposed to the blast radiation. The farms, the small out-of-the-way towns—this was where he would find uncontaminated blood. There were at least two more of them down there. If they could stay safe in their shelters . . . How long would it take? Weeks? Months?

Longer? And how many would remain when it was finally over?

Hours had to pass until night would come again and his hunger come alive. The waiting was hard. Terror permeated the entire house, rousing his bloodlust. They had to know, somehow, that he was in the house with them. He could imagine them down in the basement, waiting for him, not knowing when, or how, or even what it was that would come upon them, holding the gun in readiness, not daring even to sleep. . . .

At last, when it was fully night, he crept through the bedroom window and down to the ground. Carefully, he dug away the dirt piled up against a basement window. Light shone through from the inside — they had a candle burning down there!

He paused to count his victims. An old woman and two children were sleeping on cots on the floor. The younger woman was in a chair facing the door leading up to the kitchen, head fallen forward, one hand clutching the gun. His victim.

Kittredge worked to open the window he had cleared. It swung inward, and he dropped soundlessly to the floor of the basement, quickly blew out the candle.

The woman started awake, opened her eyes to blackness. A scream stuck in her throat, choking her. The scent of her fear was as intense as he had ever experienced. He moved slowly toward her, knowing she could sense his approach through the dark, the nearness of him. Held in the motionless grip of terror, she waited, paralyzed, voiceless, and blind.

He trembled with an ecstatic thrill of anticipation. He bent down, feeling her shiver at the cold touch of his breath. He took her slowly, almost tenderly, savoring every pulse of her blood with such rapture. . . .

Abruptly, he drew away. Her head fell back — dark blood on white throat. As he held her, the heartbeat

53

ceased, and she sighed, dying. Eleanora—

*No!* Rapture turned to bitterness, he straightened, letting the body fall away from him, the limbs loose in death. He stared at the face, making himself see that this was not her. Why, after all these years, must he still remember? What good would it do him to grieve, when he could never undo what he had done?

He remembered, suddenly, Evelyn, the woman in the VFW hall. She had lived, if only briefly. She might have been saved. He looked down again at his dead victim and felt a sense of loss, as if something irreplaceable had been wasted. Her blood had been pure.

Uneasily, he glanced at the other sleeping figures. The woman must be eighty, at least. The children—he had always avoided taking the young, except as a last resort. But without their parents now, these two would never survive the Nightfall world. They and the old woman would give him three more nights before he would have to move on.

Kittredge went back out as he had come, through the window, carefully piling the dirt back against it to keep them safe from the radiation outside.

And then what? Another farmhouse? There had to be a better way. What if one day he came upon the last human alive on earth? And after he had killed him, what then?

It had been three weeks since Nightfall when Blaine Kittredge came upon the sign:

DANBY, IND
pop. 1,280

On such signs throughout the Midwest there had once been the assurance of welcome from civic organizations below the name of the town. No longer. Not here.

KEEP OUT
TRESPASSERS AND LOOTERS
WILL BE SHOT

A dead dog lay stiff legged in a ditch a few yards away from the sign. Fallout radiation. On the farms, animals lay dead and dying everywhere. He had seen them lying in heaps, shot by an owner who must have wished to spare them the suffering. But after three weeks of exposure, Kittredge still was suffering no ill effects. He supposed it had to be another immunity of his kind. But, he wondered, how many had been caught up in the conflagrations? There had never been many of the undead to begin with. Could he be the last?

As for the humans, every one he had encountered out in the open recently had been contaminated. Without shelter from the fallout, they were no better off than the dog had been. But the supplies in many of the public shelters were already running low, especially where they had opened their doors to the refugees. Danby, he could see, was no such place.

It was a charmless town. Route 59 ran through the center from north to south, with a single stoplight at the main intersection. But there were signs of a certain utilitarian prosperity in the white-painted towers of the canning plant on the east side of town, the grain elevators of the local co-op, the new bright-green painted combines displayed in front of the John Deere dealership.

A high-steepled white clapboard church provided a single counterpoint on the landscape. And beyond the buildings, the fields, their yellowed, frost-killed crops already nearly buried under the unseasonable snow, lay flat and unvarying beneath the gray sky.

The human scent was strong. Kittredge's senses focused on a large contemporary school building just a block down the street from the canning plant. Testing the threat of the sign, he walked past it and down the highway, Danby's main street. He had not gone more than a few yards when the shot rang out from the school, loud in the wintry silence of the street. It was a warning. Kittredge halted, put up his hands above his head, and started to back away slowly toward the town limits.

He was intrigued. A place this well defended deserved investigation. He would come back tonight, less openly.

Now, though, he cut across the open fields to the south, heading away from the town. He soon discovered that the nearby farmhouses were deserted, stripped of valuables—almost as if looters had torn some of them apart in a futile search for food. But no living humans.

Then, as dusk approached, Kittredge caught a faint sound breaking through the Nightfall stillness. He held his breath and listened. It was a car engine. Someone was either foolish or very desperate, risking exposure. Inviting contamination.

But he was curious. The engine sound came from a belt of woods about three miles south of Danby. He continued across the fields and into the nearly total darkness of the trees. As he grew close the sound abruptly cut off, but he had the scent now, and he followed it eagerly.

The car, a dark green Mercedes, had slewed off the snow-covered drive and into the trees where the ground sloped sharply down to the blackness of a lake. He could see where the snow and dirt had been churned up in a futile attempt to get it back onto the drive. His eyes followed the tire marks back into the woods, where he could make out the shape of a house built into the side of the hill.

It was an impressive, contemporary structure—not the grace and elegance of Kittredge's own time, but with low, sweeping lines. The entire west front, looking out over the lake below, was glass. It must have afforded a spectacular view across the water in better times, before Nightfall.

But Kittredge's attention was already on the garage. Inside the open door he could see a figure moving in the dim, wavering glow of a flashlight. The slam of a car door, the harsh, futile noise of a starter grinding, a muffled curse—"God *damn* it!"

A woman's voice, on the edge of hysterical tears. She flung the car door open, stepped out, was halfway to the open garage door when the flashlight beam caught the figure of Kittredge outlined there.

Her mouth opened to scream, and in that single arrested instant he saw her face clearly. The wide gray eyes, the oval shape of the face, the soft blond hair were . . .

Another instant revealed the differences. Eleanora's mouth had been fuller, softer. But his arms were already held out in a gesture that he meant her no harm, and the scream came out as a sharp gasp instead.

"Miss, don't be afraid," he said softly, resisting the strong wave of fear-scent. "I heard your car, I thought someone might need some help."

He could sense her terror abate slightly as he carefully set down the shotgun against the door frame and started to take off his pack. But her eyes darted back and to the side, searching for escape or possibly a weapon. The flashlight beam wavered, then shone full into Kittredge's face, dazzling his eyes momentarily.

But he moved more quickly than she could have believed, had taken the light from her hand before she had a chance to make a move of resistance. She stumbled backward into the car, radiating panic, but Kittredge had been close enough to be certain that her blood was uncontaminated. Her terror was compelling. Her Eleanora-eyes were huge with it.

He stepped back away from her, aiming the beam at the hood of the car. "Do you want to show me what the trouble is?"

There was no sound in the garage but her breathing. Finally she swallowed. "It . . . won't start. I think the battery's dead."

Kittredge was not certain if this was something that could be fixed or not. There had been cars for over half of his existence, but mechanical things were alien to him. Except for locks —

"The Mercedes," she was saying, "outside. If we could just get it back on the road . . ."

It was better now, her fear was receding. "But where are you going to go?" he asked. "I just came past the town up there, and somebody fired a shot at me."

To his surprise, her composure broke utterly into a wave of hate and grief. "They killed my husband!" Suddenly he was a fellow victim of the town. "When the warning came on the radio, and we knew what had happened, he drove into town for supplies. We'd only just opened up the house for the summer, and there was hardly any food. But the . . . people there — they wouldn't even let him into the store! They told him our money wasn't good anymore, that the food was for the locals, not outsiders.

"And then they shot him!

"Rick — my stepson — brought the car back and told me what happened. We've been down in the basement since then, but we can't just stay here and starve!"

"But aren't you worried about the fallout?"

"Of *course* I'm worried about the fallout! But there's no water in the house! We haven't had any food for three days! I just don't know what else to do!"

She broke down sobbing, her face buried in her hands, shoulders shaking. Her distrust was gone now, helplessness drawing her to him as to someone who could help, a man who could take care of her. Kittredge encouraged it. "That's terrible, I know.

But I'm afraid that kind of thing is happening everywhere now. A lady like yourself, alone . . ."

"But what can I *do?* I have a little girl!"

"I might be able to help you a little." Hope shone in her eyes like a sudden beam of light. "I have a few cans here in my pack. Not much," he added.

Her face hardened slightly as she considered the probable cost of his help, but his eyes were fixed on the pulse throbbing visibly beneath the white skin of her throat.

*The blood crimson on her alabaster throat.*

That ancient guilt and grief, so long buried. Like Kittredge himself, it could never quite die.

He tore his eyes away. He *had* to succeed this time, not leave her lying wasted like the others, her untainted blood pooling on the floor. It could be done, he *knew* it could be done. The woman Evelyn was proof. And this one, so much like Eleanora . . .

But his bloodlust each time had been stronger than his will. The hot, rich intoxication of their blood pressing against his fangs, pulsing, spurting — he could not make himself stop until they were drained.

It was early yet, he thought. His hunger was still dormant. And her fear had been stilled. But he worried that it would not be enough, that he would lose this one too, killing the untainted humans one by one until there were none left.

"I . . . would be very grateful," she said finally, resigned against her will to taking the way out that had come to offer itself. "If you would care to come into the house?"

He could wait no longer. As she moved to step past him, he took her by the wrist. She struggled briefly, but he had her by then, was pulling her

60

down to the floor.

"Don't fight it," he whispered. "And don't be afraid. It isn't what you think, but it will be very, very dangerous if you're afraid."

Slowly, cautiously, he pulled up the sleeve of her coat and brought her wrist to his mouth. This time, if he avoided the throat, if his control were strong enough . . .

Slowly, so carefully, his fangs bore down, bursting through skin, blood welling up. Then it was spurting—hot and sweet, pure. His grip tightened against her struggles. The taste of her terror was rapture, rising up . . .

*No!* With an effort of will, shuddering with frustrated bloodlust, he pulled her wrist away before the pulse could weaken. Her head was fallen back against the tire of the car, eyes closed. But she was still alive.

Blood seeped from her wrist. Kittredge went to his pack and with unsteady hands took out a shirt, tore it, and wrapped the punctures, applying pressure until the bleeding slowed. He did not quite dare to look at her face.

He had done it! Suddenly grief surged up, overwhelming his brief moment of elation. *Oh, Eleanora!* Why now, a century and a half too late?

Conscience, an implied promise, made him leave the food from the backpack there next to her. Let her eat and get back her strength. He bent down, whispered quietly, "I'll see you again."


With no need to take a victim in Danby, Kittredge had the whole night to explore the town. This was his own element, the true dark, the earth's shroud of deadly smoke blotting out the moon and

61

the stars.

He passed silent, empty houses. The human scent came from ahead, from the center of the town. There was one shelter in the school, two others, one in the basement of the high-steepled church. They all appeared sealed off from the hazard of the outside. *Someone* here knew what he was doing and meant for them to survive.

But there had been at least one sentry. Guarding—what? What was there to guard in the Nightfall world? The obvious answer, the canning plant, just one block from the school shelter where the shot had come from, its doors locked and windows boarded over. Cans. Canned food.

He broke in by way of the roof, through the ventilation ducts. The interior of the plant echoed, even to his cautious footsteps. The machinery stood like robot sentries guarding the emptiness. Was everything gone? Had it all been taken to the shelters already?

No, why bother to guard the place if it were empty? He found a locked door at the rear of the plant, got it open without having to force it—locks were a thing he had learned early in his existence, in a challenge to the belief that one of his kind could enter a house or room only if invited. Like many other such beliefs, it was not true, and until the advent of electronic security systems he had prided himself on the fact that no door had been able to keep him from a victim.

The door opened onto a loading dock. Cartons were stacked eight feet high, solid walls of cartons. A few of them lay torn open on the cement floor, some cans strewn here and there, overlooked.

Danby, obviously, was not going to be running out of food any time in the near future. If, he reminded himself, they could keep the looters away. He considered the image of them safe in their shelters, well fed, uncontaminated, waiting for the fall-out to end so they could emerge to take up their lives.

Danby was what he had been looking for. Kittredge left the canning plant with no sign of his entrance to learn more about this place. The largest shelter was in the school building. He approached it, his senses alert, remembering the shot fired from this place. In the stillness of the night a motor thrummed steadily—a generator. They might have everything down there, electricity, light, water, heat.

He scouted the building until he found a way in through an upstairs rear window. Scent led him through hallways branching like tunnels to the guard post in an unlighted classroom at the opposite end of the building, facing the road and the canning plant. Two men sat at a sandbagged, tape-sealed window, holding rifles. Kittredge stood in the doorway behind them, invisible in the dark. Beyond them, through the slot of window, the night was deep black. Any light, even a match, would show up like a signal flare.

The sentries, it was soon clear, were not entirely happy with their post.

"Shit!" one of them muttered, his voice echoing in the dark, "There's nobody gonna be out there! Why are we risking our asses up here?"

"Packard caught some looter this afternoon, trying to sneak into town," said the other. "There could be more of them out there."

The first sentry shook his head. "Then they're crazier than we are! The radiation level's still climbing. We need all the protection we can get, downstairs, where it's safe."

"Yeah, well, you go tell Solokov that."

"Look, I admit he was right—about nearly everything. But he's carrying this security shit too far!"

The other shrugged. He, at least, was not going to complain to Solokov.

Kittredge repeated the name to himself. *Solokov*—the human in charge. He watched the two sentries, their backs to him, vulnerable. He could take them without too much trouble, even with their guns, but only if he killed one first. And after that the others would be alerted to what was hunting them.

There should be a better way. He remembered the woman at the lake house. There was a better way. His hunger was sated until tomorrow, at any rate.

He was heading back down the hall the way he had come in when he heard voices. Light spilled up a staircase. Kittredge instantly hid himself inside a doorway, tried not to breathe as two men with a kerosene lamp came down the hall and went into the guardroom. They were the relief sentries, and after a few moments the other two came out and started back down the stairs to the shelter. *Always two together,* Kittredge noted.

He followed them. There was someone waiting inside the door to the basement, expecting their return. Once the sentries had gone in, the door was firmly closed and sealed. He heard the click of a lock.

Whoever Solokov was, he was carrying his "security shit" rather too far for Kittredge's convenience. He went back upstairs to leave the school the way he had entered. Possibly the security would be less strict inside one of the other shelters. He had no more luck at the Elks lodge, but the Methodist church was an old wooden structure, promising. He bent his head back to look up at the steeple. *Tomorrow night,* he told himself.

He had other business to finish while it was still fully night.

He went back down the highway to the drive that led into the woods above the lake. The woman had not been alone. There was a stepson, she had said, and another child. And he had given them food.

He passed a mailbox at the head of the drive. The name on it was Archer.

As he came up the drive, Kittredge saw the house again, comparing it to the shelters in Danby. To the east, it was built into the hill, affording half of the basement good protection from fallout, but on the west side a row of low windows faced the lake below the upper story balcony. Kittredge frowned. He knew enough to be sure that such exposure was a radiation hazard, and he meant for the Archers' blood to remain pure.

With no electricity, the expensive security system was useless. He entered the house, walked through the rooms observing the taste of the furnishings. He noticed a faint ghost of light coming from beneath the door that must lead to the lower level, and he frowned again. The door was unsealed. Then he considered himself, the contamination he would be carrying down there on his clothes.

He retreated back outside, stripped off the things he had been wearing outside for weeks. Then he went down the path to the lake and plunged in. Coming to the surface, he gasped in shock. Even for him, the water was cold, close to the freezing point — in July!

Back inside the house, he dressed in clean clothes from his pack. The lake water itself was contaminated, he realized, but he felt better now that the grime of the last weeks had been washed off. He had not wanted to face her looking disreputable, like a tramp. He hesitated, feeling absurdly, foolishly nervous, and almost looked around the house for a mirror.

His entrance into the unsealed basement was soundless. She was sitting in an armchair, wrapped in a blanket, with her feet drawn up under herself, staring into a guttering candle flame. A kitchen knife lay on the table in front of her. She looked pale, bruised, and thin.

Kittredge did not want to startle her into panic. Quietly, he stepped into view.

Her head jerked up. She snatched up the knife and held it in front of her defensively.

"No," he said, "I didn't come for that now." He stepped closer to take the knife from her, but she surprised him, slashing at his arm. He seized her wrists harder than he had meant to, holding them in a punishing grip until the knife fell to the floor. But the carelessness had been his. If she had spilled his blood, he might not have been able to maintain control. Ruefully, he glanced at the torn sleeve of his clean shirt. It had been that close.

And now he was starting to feel her fear. He said tightly, "I would like you please to control yourself and not be afraid. I haven't come here to harm you."

This was not beginning auspiciously. She watched him, hostile and terrified, as he let go and moved around to the other side of the table, putting distance and a barrier between them.

"Earlier this evening," he said, "you told me that you didn't know how to choose between the fallout and staying down here to starve to death. Radiation is invisible, you can't feel it killing you. But I've

66

seen people who were dying that way. It isn't a pleasant sight. Starvation is easier. You're lucky. You haven't been exposed yet to enough to make you sick."

Her heartbeat was slowing gradually, the adrenaline-rich panic surge diminishing. "How could you know that?" she whispered.

He took a breath, easing his own tension. "You know how. If you were contaminated, your blood would have been . . . distasteful."

She shrank back from him, eyes wide with horror across the table in the dying candlelight, and hugged her bandaged wrist to her chest. "No."

"Yes. I am what you think. We do exist. But not everything you may have heard about us is true. As you can see, you're still alive."

"Am I?" She was staring, horrified, at her wrist, only now beginning to believe, to realize what she might become.

Kittredge sighed. "Yes, you're alive. And most probably you won't . . . change, either." It had been a long time since he had had to make this explanation. "There's nothing supernatural about this condition. We don't really know the exact cause. Obviously, it's something passed through the bloodstream—a virus, I suppose. But most humans have a natural immunity. They simply die, nothing more. I was one of the exceptions."

He could not tell her the whole truth—that he had never before managed to avoid killing his victim, that he really did not know what might happen if she lacked the immunity. As far as he knew, the metamorphosis only occurred after death, but he had no guarantee of that. He knew of no precedents.

But there were never guarantees. How many

nights had he waited beside Eleanora's grave, with what measure of hope and dread? Perhaps it was best that nothing had ever emerged from the earth where she lay, but Kittredge would never know.

With a shake of his head, he brought himself back to the present. She was still watching him, quieter now.

"What do you want, then?"

"You. Not now—later. And the others."

"No!" She struggled to free her legs from the blanket.

"Sit down," he said, softly, with a hint of menace. "Do you think you could keep me out?"

At that moment, the candle finally went out, and unrelieved black filled the space between them. She gasped, a half scream.

"It's all right," he said. "I'm not coming any closer. You can hear my voice, you can tell where I am."

"Just listen to me. You're just about out of candles, aren't you? And we already know you're out of food. Except for what I gave you. And I can bring you more. Enough to keep you all alive.

"You see," he went on, his voice still quiet, "before I came here, you had the choice between fallout and starvation. But now that I've found you, I'm not going to let either of those things happen. You can cooperate and live, or you can die quickly, my way. All of you, one by one. You can't run away from me, you can't hide. I can tell you from my own experience, it isn't so bad—not as hard a way to die as the other two choices you had. But I don't want that. It would be a waste."

"Why?" she sobbed. "Why me?"

He shook his head in the darkness, unseen. No, he would not tell her that.

68

Finally the sobs diminished. "What do you mean . . . cooperate?"

"Not to fight me. Not to resist. That's all, really. You know what it's like. You're still alive. The fear is the worst part."

She shuddered. "And if I do . . . what you want?"

"Then you live. I'll bring you food, enough for all of you. When the fallout is over, I'll be gone."

"For how long?"

"As long as necessary."

"And if you—"

*"Lorraine?"*

Kittredge had already seen him come into the main room of the basement. He was about sixteen years old, nearly six feet tall and still growing, a face that had not quite completed forming the square jaw and chin he would have as a man—if he lived. Rick, the stepson who had witnessed his father's murder?

The boy called out again as he groped his way through the dark, "Lorraine, are you awake? Are you talking to someone?"

Kittredge was at her side, hand on her shoulder, ordering in a whisper, "Tell him. Now."

She shrank away from his touch but said, "I'm here. Yes, this is . . . the man who gave me the food."

So she—Lorraine—had not told him about the attack. Kittredge went closer to the boy, put a hand briefly on his shoulder. It was shrugged off, angrily, apprehensively. The blood was not tainted.

Kittredge bent down to Lorraine, whispered, "Make sure he knows, before tomorrow night. Make sure he's ready."

He left them without a sound, so they could not

be sure, in the dark, that he was really gone.

Dawn was coming. He wanted rest. The thought of the soft leather seat of the car in the garage — a station wagon — was inviting. He was walking around the house to the garage when the sight of glass caught his eye. Those basement windows, the western exposure of four feet above ground level. He paused, looking at them, seeing how easily the radiation could pass through the glass, contaminating everyone inside.

The one obvious solution . . .

Irritably, Kittredge stamped into the garage to see if he could find some kind of shovel around the place.

Rest would have to wait.

# 4

Kittredge came out of as deep a rest as he had ever known. It was no more than an hour before sunset, but his hunger was already compelling. He was dismayed. Would he have the control to keep from killing Rick Archer? What if he couldn't do it again? All his plans, all that *work* . . .

He left the garage and went around the corner to look at the west side of the house, the windows now blanketed safely in earth. He wiped his hands on his jeans. The skin of his palms still felt tender. There would have been blisters if he were still alive. He had forgotten how much plain, unremitting labor life involved.

He tightened his hands, pressing his nails into his palms. He would *not* fail. He would not waste this effort.

But then he had better do it quickly, before his hunger grew. He tested the door to the basement. It was unlocked. Good. They hadn't tried to lock him out. He hoped it meant they wouldn't resist.

They were waiting for him, the woman and boy together in the dark. He could see their faces turn to the stairs as they heard the basement door opening. Then the weak yellow beam of Lorraine

71

Archer's flashlight struck him, and he stood for a moment letting them see his face, what he was.

Rick Archer's eyes were terror-wide.

In life, Blaine Kittredge had been vain in his appearance. It was one of the curses upon his existence that he was unable to see exactly how the metamorphosis had altered him. His hands, all those parts of him he could see, were substantially the same. He suspected that he had not aged since the night he had died, at twenty-eight. But what of his face? He knew, from the reactions of others, that he could pass for human in dim light, at a distance. Eleanora, when he had come in through her window that last night, had recognized him immediately. *I do* not *look entirely monstrous.* He willed himself to believe that it was so.

As if to deny it, the boy's fists tightened at his sides. Fear-scent radiated from him. So she had told him.

Kittredge came the rest of the way down the stairs. Then, unexpectedly, Lorraine Archer darted the flashlight at the earth-covered windows. "You did that, didn't you?" she accused him. "Blocked out all the light."

He was taken aback. "Of course," he retorted sharply. "If light can get in, so can radiation."

"Oh."

It hadn't even occurred to her. All that work.

"But we can't live in the dark!"

Kittredge knew that others were surviving in far worse circumstances, in dirt-floored cellars a fraction the size of this spacious lower level, in overcrowded shelters filled with the stench of human wastes, of the dying. He sighed. "All right. I'll try to find more candles for you. Or batteries. Afterwards."

She nodded nervously, her eyes moving to the boy standing next to her.

Kittredge came closer, hunger throbbing, and reached out for him. The boy jerked his arm away. The rush of terror made bloodlust surge through Kittredge's system, crimsoning his vision.

"Don't be *afraid*," he said tightly. "Look." He grabbed Lorraine's arm, ripped off the bandage to show him her wrist. *"She* did it."

It was the right approach. Rick set his teeth, and defiance overrode his fear. Kittredge pulled him away, through the door to a room that turned out to be an empty wine cellar.

"Sit down," he ordered. "Lean back against the wall."

"No," Rick protested, finding his voice at last. "This isn't real. You're some kind of a queer, aren't you, some kind of pervert?"

"Would you rather I was? No, this is real. And it can kill you, if you can't get a hold on yourself."

"But —"

"I know what I told Lorraine. But you've got to cooperate. Relax as much as you can. Don't fight. It doesn't really hurt all that much. And I mean it, try not to be afraid."

Kittredge damned himself for a hypocrite, because the boy was doing at least as well as he was. But he could hardly explain that the real risk was from his own shaky self-control. He made himself wait while Rick finally shut his eyes and exhaled. Kittredge watched him for a moment, to master the hunger. Could he really do this again?

He reached for a wrist, feeling the boy's muscles tense at his touch. The flesh was blood-hot, pulsing with life, damp with sweat. He could wait no longer. Slowly, he bit down.

Minutes later, he forced his head back, gasping as he struggled to subdue the bloodlust. He wanted more, wanted the ecstasy of the kill.

Rick moaned weakly. Kittredge did not have to check his pulse to know he was still alive. It had been easier this time, after all, to stop. His first success had taught him. He did not *need* the rapture of draining a victim to his death. It was something, like the frenzy, that he could overcome.

With the bloodlust fading, hunger appeased, he turned his attention back to Rick. "It's finished. You did all right." The boy turned his face away. Never mind, it would go easier the next time. He would know what to expect. They both would.

But—he looked more closely. Rick's face was as white as his own. He was shivering. How soon, how often could he stand this?

Kittredge picked him up, ignoring his protest, carried him out into the main room of the basement, and put him down on the couch. The dim light of the flashlight focused on the burden in his arms, and Lorraine Archer inhaled sharply.

"He's alive," Kittredge told her. "Why don't you get the first-aid kit? And a blanket."

As she wrapped the slowly seeping punctures, he added, "He ought to have something to eat. And liquids."

"There's no water," she said flatly.

"What?"

She turned on him, her face sharpened by tension. "We need water. At first, we filled the bathtub and saved as much as we could, but it's gone now. The pump doesn't work. If you want him to have liquids, you're going to have to do something about it."

Defensively, he said, "There should have been something in the pack. Soup or something." He couldn't remember. "I'll try to find water. Is there anything else?" He had, he reminded himself, made this bargain.

"You said you'd get candles. And batteries, some kind of light. We've got no heat and there's no way to cook down here."

Kittredge looked at Rick Archer shivering on the couch. "All right," he agreed. "I'll see what I can do."

He found his backpack again and got ready to leave. It was close to full darkness outside, and the air held the threat of snow. This could cause difficulties if he were going to be breaking into Danby's supplies, but he supposed there was nothing he could do about it. He grinned suddenly. If all the legends about his kind were true, he could turn himself into a bat and avoid leaving footprints altogether.

But since he could not, he had better get in and out of town before the snow started. On the way, he considered his current set of difficulties. Candles—by now, the whole world was probably running out of candles. Light, then—light and heat. And clean water. He knew that the water from the lake would be contaminated. But what about the groundwater? Lorraine had talked about a pump.

In his lifetime, things had been done differently.

75

But even then Kittredge had not understood such matters well. He had been a gentleman, not a mechanic. Perhaps, he began to admit to himself, he had promised Lorraine Archer more than he would be able to provide.

Food, at any rate, he could obtain. Once again he broke into the canning plant, and tearing open one of the cartons in a back row where they would not notice it right away, stuffed the cans into his pack.

Light, water—those were greater difficulties. A cursory check of the empty houses made it clear that such necessities must have been taken into the shelters. The Methodist church, then, would be his next stop.

Snowflakes stung his face as he left the cannery, but the way it was blowing, it might cover any tracks. He wondered just how cold it was, how much worse it could get.

He had only just gotten to the church when floodlights burst into life behind him. Then he heard the shots. He tensed, ready for flight, but then he detected blood-scent on the air, from the direction of the canning plant. So Solokov's sentries had finally spotted a looter!

Drawn by the scent, Kittredge approached cautiously, around the side of the building out of sight of the guard post, unlit by the floodlights.

A man was on the ground, crawling, dragging one leg behind him. When he saw Kittredge standing above him, he cursed though clenched teeth, "You bastard!" and fumbled for the gun he was still carrying.

Kittredge snatched it out of his hand. "Take it

easy!" he whispered. "It wasn't me—I just heard the shots!"

Then he looked up with the alertness of a being who has been hunted often enough in the past. Human voices, shouting. They were coming! The human heard them too. He glanced at Kittredge with a look of hopeless appeal.

And Kittredge looked quickly from his face to the spreading stain on the man's leg, the scent of blood—untainted! He did not have much time. He decided suddenly.

"We have to get you out of here," he told the injured man, lifting him up and slinging his body over one shoulder. There was a clear trail of blood in the snow from the front door of the cannery to the spreading stain on the snow.

Hoping now that the sharp wind would blow away any footprints, Kittredge ran to outdistance any immediate pursuit. He finally stopped at the relative shelter of an open, abandoned garage near the outskirts of Danby and lay his burden down on the floor. "Let me see that leg," he said, ripping open the man's pants. The man was wearing a waterproof rainsuit as protection against fallout. A rifle bullet had gone through the leg just below the knee. Nothing necessarily fatal. The bleeding had already slowed. The man would probably live. Kittredge felt sharp disappointment. Bloodlust urged at him. His hunger had already been satisfied, he made himself remember.

"The leg's broken," he announced.

"Bastards," the man groaned.

"What happened?"

"Danby . . . they got the canning plant locked

up! Tried to get in . . . somebody starts shooting."

"Didn't you see their sign?"

"Produce in that plant doesn't belong just to Danby. They don't have the right to keep it all for themselves!"

"Look," Kittredge said, "obviously we can't get you a doctor in Danby."

The man shook his head. "Didn't come here by myself. A bunch of us . . . from Green Springs. Got a truck parked just south of town here. Just . . . get me there."

But Kittredge had other plans. "I've got a place just down the road," he said. "I can take you there for right now, get that leg fixed up."

He was a big, heavyset man, and it cut off his objections when Kittredge, easily fifty pounds lighter, lifted him back up and started to carry him the three miles to the lake house.

"Who is he?" Lorraine Archer asked when she saw what he was carrying down into the basement. The man was unconscious.

"I don't know his name. They shot him in town—just like they did your husband. It looks like he was trying to get Danby to share their supplies with the rest of Fulham County."

"But what are you doing with him *here?*"

Kittredge gave her a hard look. "You know."

Rick was no longer on the couch, and he put the man down there. "Go get your first-aid kit."

A flashlight beam wavered behind him. "Here." Rick thrust the kit at him and watched with a hostile intensity while Kittredge did what he could to clean and set the leg.

Kittredge looked up when he was finished.

78

"What's the matter? What did you think I was going to do?"

The look on Rick's face—and Lorraine's—now they couldn't meet his eyes. They were keeping something from him. But he already knew what it must be—Lorraine had told him herself, in the garage. A child, a little girl.

He stiffened, backed away from the stale blood-stench of the injured man, and cast around the basement like a bloodhound, searching out the scent. There!

When he had almost reached the other door Lorraine suddenly cried out and rushed at him, but he grasped her arm with one hand as he tried the knob. The door was locked, from the inside. Kittredge frowned, glaring at Lorraine as she twisted in his hold, moaning, "No!" Then he splintered the door with a single kick.

There were two of them, crouched under the laundry sinks. The boy was three or four years younger than Rick, the girl around four years old. Suddenly he let go of Lorraine, who rushed forward to the girl, falling to her knees, pulling the child into her arms.

Kittredge knew he could not take blood from a child that small without killing her. He would save this one, just in case. As for the other, the boy . . .

He looked down at Lorraine, then back at Rick, frozen in the doorway of the laundry room. "Him," he said, "tomorrow night. The other one is too small."

Lorraine sobbed in relief, still holding her daughter, but Kittredge reached down and pulled her up to her feet. "It's about time we got something straight. All of us."

He led Lorraine, with Rick following, back into the main room of the basement. The younger boy, after a moment, came after them.

"All right. Outside this basement, the fallout would be enough to kill you in a few days. And there are men with guns who might do it faster. Then there's me, down here. I don't want to kill you. I want you all alive, and you know the reason.

"Now, maybe you're thinking that man over there can help you get rid of me, get out of here. Let me remind you, he's got a broken leg and he's not going anywhere for a while. And I don't sleep. I can see in the dark. And," he sketched a cross on his chest with a finger, "that won't work, either, in case you've got ideas along those lines.

*"You can't hide things from me.* So, whether you like it or not, we have an arrangement. And I think it will be to everyone's benefit if we all carried on that way. All right?" He fixed Rick with a stare that made him nod.

"Good. Now I may be bringing more people down here. The reason should be obvious, if you think about it. The three of you — four, now — won't be enough. You wouldn't want me to have to resort to other sources. Would you?" This time he was looking at Lorraine Archer, who knew what other source he meant. She clasped the child closely. She had never looked less like his Eleanora.

"All right. So you'll take care of this man while I'm gone. Don't let him bleed to death. I'll be back."

Four of them, he was thinking. Lorraine, Rick, the other boy, and the man, when he was strong enough. Maybe three or four more—once a week for each of them. It might work. But more lives meant more mouths to feed. Kittredge sighed as he left the house. He had left the backpack with the food all the way back in Danby.

# 1833

Few of my kind come into existence, and even fewer survive the blood-soaked frenzy of their first night.

As that first sunrise approached, I was drawn again to my own grave. Some primal instinct was urging me to claw my way back down into the sheltering darkness of the earth. And yet, despite the baptism of blood with which I had entered into my new existence, I was still a being of reason. Wondering, I traced the cross carved into my own gravestone with a finger and felt no pain.

But I knew that come daylight, when the sexton saw the disturbance of my grave, he would think of desecration, of grave robbers. My rest would be disturbed, my flesh exposed to the searing touch of the sun.

Desperate with the coming of day, I fled to the closest sanctuary I could find, to a crypt within the church itself, beneath the stones of the floor. There, in the company of fleshless bones, I passed my first day of rest in self-loathing, attempting to understand what I had become.

One hope I clung to: that I was not a creature utterly unholy. Damned, yes, for what I had done. But I lay within the church itself, I had endured the touch of the cross. In those first days, with habits of life so recent, such thoughts still had meaning for me.

Yet my nature overwhelmed whatever compunctions remained to me. Night came again, and with it the hunger for blood. It drove me to kill yet again, the ecstasy of bloodlust overcoming my own horror at what I was doing, until at last I killed the only one among the living who still might have claimed me. From that time, I sought to sunder myself from humanity.

I embraced the dark wholeheartedly. In those early days my existence was a fugitive thing. I avoided churchyards, with all their associations, and found my resting place in cellars, deep in a played-out mine, within a cave. There I rested during the days, with my heartbeat slowed to the measure of the earth's movement.

Since the first I had obeyed my instincts and sought to shelter myself from the sun. But there came a day when I was to learn just how vulnerable I was. I was hiding within a root cellar I had thought long abandoned. Voices came to me from outside — children at play — but I accounted them no threat. Then one of them found the place and lifted up the door. A shaft of sunlight struck me.

Never in life had I felt an agony so intense. But I was fortunate. At the sound of my scream, whoever had lifted the door dropped it back and fled in panic, leaving me in the darkness with my anguish.

Humans have dealt me many injuries since that day, to their regret, but for a century I bore the scar from that one alone.

# Shelter

## 1

It had been enough trouble stealing the generator in the first place. Carrying it through the darkened church, all the way up to the top of the steeple and down the outside of the building. Once, he had nearly dropped it. And now none of them knew how to hook it up.

Kittredge had drafted Rick to help with the job in the hopeful assumption that he would know something about these matters. Now Rick was snapping at his brother, "Dammit, hold the flashlight steady, Danny!"

The basement smelled of ozone and gasoline fumes. Rick sucked at a blister on one of his knuckles. He looked up at Kittredge standing uselessly next to the generator. "I thought you were in charge around here. Why don't you fix the damn thing?"

"Because when I was born," he snarled back, "the damn thing hadn't even been invented yet!"

From the couch where he was lying with his leg stretched out, Paul Krusack laughed weakly, painfully. "That's good. That's just great!"

Kittredge shot a glare at him. Krusack was pallid, his eyes looked bruised. After the blood loss of his gunshot wound, the amount Kittredge had taken last night was almost too much. Even so, the man had fought him, so hard that his blood had been harsh and acerbic with hate.

The reason went beyond the blood-taking. Krusack might possibly have admitted to owing him that much for saving his life in Danby. Once, maybe. But taking him, holding him here like this . . .

Kittredge frowned. His other donors had agreed, under duress, to this arrangement. Krusack could turn out to be dangerous. It was just as well, perhaps, to keep him weak.

Lorraine had been listening. "You know how to hook that up, don't you?" she accused Krusack.

"So what if I do? I can hardly get up and go over there to work on it, can I?"

"No, but you could tell them what to do."

"Maybe I could, lady. But why should I? You want electricity, you go figure it out for yourself."

"We *need* that generator!" she said through clenched teeth. "We need light, water, heat." She was looking pointedly at the blanket that covered him, one of her own.

"No, *you* need it. I only need one thing—to get out of this place. If you want to stay in here with the vampire, that's your business."

At the sound of that word, Kittredge clamped his mouth tight. Krusack could not possibly know how much he hated it, yet he used it with as much deliberate malice as if he did. But Lorraine was equal to the big farmer.

"Fine," she said, "we'll just get in my car and drive over to Green Springs. I'm sure your friends there will take us in and feed us. Just the way *we're* feeding you now. Taking care of you. Keeping you alive."

Kittredge saw him wince. He decided to leave for a while and let her work on Krusack in his absence. Lorraine Archer was formidable opposition. Even if she was right, and the generator turned out to be the solution to all their problems, Kittredge could still not understand how she would persuade him.

The reminder about the cars worried him, even though he had already siphoned the gas from the tanks to run the generator. But if Krusack could fix that, he might be able to get one of the cars started. He got the hood open on the station wagon and randomly started to detach leads that ran from one incomprehensible part to another. It was snowing again. He didn't think either car would be able to make it through the growing drifts, but it was better to make certain.

He was putting too much effort into this. Now he had Krusack to take care of, and there still weren't enough of them. It would have to be Lorraine's turn tonight again. After only four days. Too soon, if he were going to keep this up. Then Rick, Danny, and Krusack again. No, none of them could survive it at that rate.

He had to find more donors, uncontaminated. Danby—but Danby was his last resort. No, the ones he wanted now were the ones like Lorraine, running short of food in their shelters, the ones who would be forced to venture out into the contaminated atmosphere before they starved to death. Kittredge understood human nature well enough to know which choice they would make if caught between the immediate pain of hunger and the invisible fallout. It would take hours, perhaps even days, for the radiation to accumulate in their tissues, but then they would be useless to him.

He considered Green Springs—Paul Krusack's home. Lorraine's taunt had been accurate. A town running short of food would not welcome four more refugees to share their diminishing stores. But it might furnish more donors. Or the farms lying between the two towns might be even better sources.

Kittredge threw some of the parts he had removed from the car far out into the snow-covered yard where Krusack would never find them. He stared at his filthy, grease-covered hands, then wiped them on his jeans—his outside clothes. From his life, he had retained a preference for fastidious personal habits. He had not expected to be able to maintain them in the Nightfall world, but neither had he expected to be carting filthy electrical generators around, or dismantling cars. He wanted a hot bath, he wanted clean clothes, and not these damnable jeans.

All futile. He went out into the snow-covered landscape, finding it peaceful after the contentious atmosphere of the basement. The deep twilit gray sky spread low over the countryside. This was the second day in a row he had had no rest.

He went south, skirting the edge of the lake, in the direction of Green Springs. As he passed a farmyard he could detect the scent of death. Farm stock, either slaughtered or radiation-killed. The same scent, more faintly, had been in the woods.

The wildlife was dead or dying, too. But even on the farms the odor of decay was faint. The cold had preserved the carcasses from it, and now they were only mounds under the snow. Once spring came, though, the stench from so much death would be unimaginable—if spring ever did come again. It was hard even for Kittredge to remember that this was supposed to be the height of summer.

But the scent of human death was unmistakable to one of his kind. Kittredge paused. This was a farmhouse like any other, an isolated place, the kind he would have chosen to look for victims. Had someone else had the same thought?

The scent led him to a low, snow-covered tumulus in the farmyard, not far from the house. Kittredge brushed away the snow and exposed staring eyes, frozen, sunk slightly in their sockets. The blood spattered onto the face was dried and stale, dark like the bullet hole below in the man's chest. There were two other mounds a few yards away.

But there were still living humans here. Their scent came from the farmhouse. Whoever was inside must be considered dangerous, whether they were the residents or the intruders.

The gunshot wounds looked to be from a handgun, he judged, a .38 like the one of Paul Krusack's that he was carrying now. Kittredge suddenly felt uneasy thinking of Krusack, of guns. He still had the shotgun he had taken from the looter near Chicago and the gun he had found on Will Jirsa's body, which must have come from the dead storekeeper. They were hidden now in the garage—hidden safely, he had thought. But maybe it would be best to check when he got back. As soon as he got back.

Handguns, though, usually meant looters from the city. The local farmers preferred shotguns, hunting guns. He brushed snow from another of the mounds, uncovered the face of a woman, middle aged, naked. Then part of the rest of her body. It was clear to him now what must have happened, though he had little interest in the details. But none of the bodies carried the distinctive taint of radiation poisoning. He cursed quietly in irritation at the murderous ways of humans.

Kneeling in the snow beside the woman's body, he stared at the silent, dark farmhouse. Unwillingly, he thought again of Paul Krusack, who planned to kill him. But Krusack was not without justification. Humans killed his kind and he killed them. Kittredge brushed more snow from the woman's body. But whoever did *this* — he could not possibly bring such a killer back to the lake house and leave him there with Lorraine and four-year-old Julie Archer.

A shiver of bloodlust went through him at the thought of killing again, the ecstatic moment when the heartbeat flutters to a halt. He wondered how many there were in there, whether their blood was tainted. At the least, even if it was only one, it would spare his others for another night.

He came up to the house cautiously, aware that he might be facing no easy victim. His hand, for an instant, went to his own gun. If there were too many of them, perhaps, just to even the odds . . .

No. The very thought grated against his instincts. To kill like a human, to waste the blood — no. They would be *his*.

Under the snow, the basement windows had been covered with dirt. Kittredge walked around the house, considering how he would enter. In the back there was one basement window exposed. He knelt, looked through into an old unused coal cellar. The wood of the frame was so old and gouged at the bottom of the sill that he could easily slip his fingers inside and undo the latch. The window swung open, and he went through, dropped soundlessly onto the floor.

He faced a door leading into the rest of the basement. Then he looked around behind him, where a faint, dim light came in through the window. Kittredge looked around the cellar, found some old pieces of drywall stacked against one wall. He propped one up against the window to cut off the light. Then, from the darkness, he approached the door.

The stench almost drove him back. Vomit, human waste, stale secretions . . . Swallowing hard, he endured it as he eased the door open far enough to see what was beyond. He was glad he had blocked off the window. There was no light in the basement, and he would have been visibly outlined in the doorway. Even now he tensed, prepared to draw back. But soon he could see there was no need.

One figure about five feet from the door was sprawled out on a fouled mattress. The scent was palpable even from that distance, repulsively tainted. The man was already half-dead from radiation poisoning. Beyond him were others, but Kittredge already knew they would be in the same condition, rotting while still alive.

91

He started to ease the door shut—no, wait. Over there, in the corner. He started in sudden shock. Her eyes were open and staring—directly into his own. It was a girl, almost naked, despite the cold. She was curled into a fetal position, unmoving, only the eyes seeming alive. A madwoman's eyes.

The entire story was in them: how the killers had come to the farm looking for shelter from the radiation that had already poisoned them, killed the older couple outside and whoever lay under the third mound of snow—her parents, perhaps, and a brother. But they had saved the girl for themselves, and in doing so, saved her for him.

Kittredge slipped through the door. It was uncanny, the way she seemed to be watching him in the total darkness. Could human eyes adapt so to the dark? He had to be careful, approaching her. The mad were unpredictable. He did not want her to scream at his touch and alert the others, for despite their condition, they were still armed.

He stopped. It would be simplest to kill them, but the thought of touching them revolted him. Then he remembered his gun.

He hesitated, recalling his resolution of less than an hour ago. Then the basement rang with the sound of the shots. It was deafening in the enclosed space. The girl had begun a thin, high-pitched screaming. Kittredge went up and took one of her hands. Yes. Her blood was untainted.

She was trying to shrink away from him. He lifted her and carried her up the basement stairs. She would need clothes before he tried to take her back to the lake house.

Observed more closely, her condition was appalling—filthy, bruised, half-starved. Abuse and shock must have driven her mad. Her staring eyes were focused not on him but on her own interior horrors, and the scent was arousing his bloodlust.

He wrapped her in blankets first to keep her warm, then took her wrist in one hand and brought it to his mouth. She never flinched, not even when his fangs pierced her skin. The first taste of her blood almost overwhelmed him. Dark, dark horror, nightmare-rich. She was wholly, entirely consumed by it, oblivious to what was happening to her now.

Gasping, Kittredge pulled away. What rapture there would be if all the world were mad!

When he was fully in control of himself again, he found her clothes and got her into them, wrapping her up as completely as he could against the exposure to the cold and radiation of the outside. He would not for the world have such blood tainted.

He halted abruptly as he came near the lake house with the slight weight of the girl in his arms. Something—what?—was different. He thought immediately of Paul Krusack. Anxious, he went around to the garage. The car was still there. And the guns.

Then he recognized the sound—the generator was running. They had electricity. Krusack had done it after all.

Light came from the basement as he opened the door. After so long in the dark, it hurt his eyes and made him blink. Lorraine stood up nervously as he came down the stairs and looked around for a place to put his burden.

Then she saw the condition of what he carried and her expression turned to loathing and contempt.

"Just a minute," he said hastily. "I didn't do this."

"Oh, no?" She snatched at the girl's wrist, held it up in accusation, the marks of his fangs plainly visible in the light.

"That's not the trouble with her," he insisted.

"Then what is? Oh, put her down, for God's sake."

Krusack was trying weakly to lever himself up from the couch without jarring his broken leg, but Kittredge lowered the girl into a chair, where she curled up into herself the way she had done in the basement of her own house. "For one thing," he said stiffly, "she was raped."

"So?" Lorraine accused.

Then Krusack understood. "Ha!" he said under his breath. Outwardly, Kittredge ignored him, though a pulse of red appeared at the edge of his vision.

"She'll need to be cleaned up," he told Lorraine. "I take it that the pump is working now?"

She nodded her head, approaching the task with distaste. "You two go into the back," she told Rick and Danny, who were drawing closer and staring wide eyed.

"Fine," said Kittredge, holding himself under control. "I'm glad to see that everything is in order. I won't be needing anything more from the rest of you tonight."

He left the basement immediately. He suddenly could not tolerate their presence, their constant

94

sidewise looks at him, Krusack's sneering. He would have given a great deal not to have had Krusack learn of that particular failing of his kind. He had once, after all, been a man.

He sank into an expensive leather chair in front of the cold, empty fireplace. Oh, he was weary! Tomorrow, he was going to have to get some rest. But for now, he had another living mouth to feed, and the generator would be needing gas, and he still had to find a safer hiding place for the guns. . . .

## 2

"*What?*"

Gene Solokov stared at the CB in frank disbelief at what he was hearing. "You're sure about that?"

"What do you mean, am I sure about that?" Hank Daschle had been—still was, in fact, dammit, he kept telling himself—chief of police in Danby, and he damn well knew if something like the auxiliary generator was stolen or not. "I looked myself," he insisted. "Nobody saw a thing, but the damn thing's not here anymore!"

Solokov finally switched off the CB set. Unless they could find the missing generator—not too likely, he had to admit, there was nothing they could do about the theft. It had just been a backup for the one at the Methodist church. But—shit!—somebody breaks in right under their noses and walks out with something that size! Maybe this would put the fear of God into the idiots who were supposed to be keeping watch.

Solokov was coldly angry by now. Someone was making a fool of him. No, they'd made a fool of Hank Daschle, who was supposed to be in charge over at the church shelter. Let them try something like that over *here,* he thought grimly. In the main shelter, here in the school, *he* was in undisputed command.

*Who was it?* An outsider, breaking in? Or one of their own? But where could he have put the thing, then? Who could hide something the size of the generator with conditions as crowded as they were? People were doing a little pilfering, maybe, but this was something else.

Solokov frowned. There had been reports these last couple of days. He'd discounted most of them. Things missing—batteries, stuff like that. Over at the church, mostly.

But even over here, some of the sentries on watch were saying they had a funny feeling lately, like someone was watching them. A kind of cold feeling down the backs of their necks. Solokov snorted at the notion. They were afraid of the dark, that's what they were! If they spent less time looking around to see if someone was sneaking up behind them, maybe they could see what was going on right in front of their faces!

He leaned back in his chair and gnawed the remains of a thumbnail, considering the situation. This thing could be just what he needed to shake things up. Too many people still thought security was some kind of joke. Shelter from the fallout, sure, they could see the need for that. (Because they could see the daily readings from the radiation detector, was why they could see it, he grumbled to himself.) And food rationing, that made sense, especially to the idiots who hadn't made any provisions—they'd be starving by now if it weren't for him. Now they were living off their neighbors' bounty. But security?

Even after they'd run off or shot two or three dozen intruders already, they still balked at the necessary measures. Last night, the generator. Before that, someone trying to break into the canning plant—and he hadn't been alone, either. Solokov didn't like it at all, that somebody was out there in the dark, somebody who could just disappear without a sound, almost without leaving a footprint. But there *had* been a few faint footprints that other night at the canning plant.

The church, that was where most of those crazy reports were coming from. Security over there was full of holes. Solokov looked at his watch. It was almost noon, just about time for a shift change. Maybe he should pay Hank Daschle a visit.

He wrapped himself up in his rainsuit, with the makeshift helmet and the filter for his breathing. Vonnie wouldn't like it when she heard he'd gone out again, but—face it—they weren't going to be having any more kids. Men only, was his rule about going into the open, and men who had already had two or three kids, at least. He didn't want them coming out of this with their hands full of some kind of mutant monsters.

Ann Scofield was the door guard. *Damn!* She was sure to tell Vonnie. "Going outside," he said brusquely, and watched as she logged him out. "Over to the church."

Hank Daschle wasn't particularly happy to see him. "You should have called over to say you were coming," he complained.

"Sorry," said Solokov. He knew how Hank still

resented his authority, the fact that he wasn't elected or anything, just took over, put himself in control. But the police chief had lost his real opportunity to take charge the day Solokov had shot the lawyer in front of the IGA and Daschle stood by without doing anything about it.

And besides, as they both knew, Daschle didn't know half of what Solokov did about most of the problems facing them now.

The fact was, Solokov had deliberately come over here to the church without informing Daschle in order to test his security. Now he almost wished he could have found more to complain of. The church just wasn't as securable a building as the school or even the Elks lodge, that was a fact, but the place was sealed up about as tight as it could be. He'd checked around the whole perimeter and been challenged by sentries twice, found all the entrances sealed off. It was all in order, as far as he could tell.

Of course, maybe things had tightened up around here right after the generator was stolen. If so, he hoped they stayed this way.

"Anyway, security looks good," he commended Daschle. "You've still got no idea how the guy got in?"

Daschle shook his head. "Come on. I'll show you."

"You're sure this happened at *night?* And no one saw any kind of light around here?"

"Nope. And I'll tell you something else. Most of the weird stuff people say has been happening—it's been at night."

They were looking at the working generator now.

"It was standing right here," Daschle said, pointing to the spot.

Solokov glanced around. "Were there any footprints or anything?" Daschle was the cop. Solokov was perfectly happy to concede when someone else knew what he was doing.

The cop shook his head again. "Nope. Ron walks in here first thing this morning, it was gone, that's all. He's working on another backup right now."

*First thing this morning?* "You didn't say anything about it till now?"

"This shelter is my responsibility," Daschle said defensively. Solokov let it go. The loss wasn't a real disaster. Any halfway competent mechanic could assemble a small electrical generator if he had the right parts—even a lawnmower engine would do. No, what bothered him was how the guy had gotten in—and out again—with no one spotting him.

"Look," he said to Hank Daschle, "It had to be somebody from outside, right? I mean, nobody down here has it stuffed under their mattress or anything?"

"I don't know," said the police chief. "What if it's somebody sneaking stuff out? Stashing it somewhere outside where he could pick it up later, then coming back in?"

Solokov considered the possibility. He had to admit—it made sense. Better sense than some guy walking through walls in the dark. "Could be," he said thoughtfully. What if Chet Scofield, say, was sneaking out with stuff while his wife was on duty at the front door? Improbable, sure, and stupid, too. But possible. Suddenly, "a little pilfering" wasn't a minor issue any more.

"Damn!" he growled. "All right, why don't we start right here? We check everybody, see if anybody has something he shouldn't have. The generator isn't the only thing missing around here, is it?"

"No, but won't this tip off whoever it is? I mean, you don't really expect to find the generator?"

Solokov thought for a moment. "No, but we might turn up something smaller. And we can get the people here watching everybody else. I just don't like thinking it was one of our own people who's doing this."

The police chief shrugged. "I guess in the end I'm the only guy I can really trust."

"It's a hell of a thing. But then, look why we're in this mess to begin with."

They finally called in a dozen of their most reliable men, checked them out first, then let them in on the plan. It was a thorough, methodical search. The team went through the gear of every one of the five hundred individuals in the shelter, one by one. They were all gathered into the nave of the church and no one was allowed to leave until it was over.

They bitched, all right. No one liked people pawing through his things. But Solokov managed to divert most of the resentment. "Don't blame us. Think of the rotten bastard who's been stealing from every one of you in here! Well, by God, we're going to find him!"

The search seemed like it would take forever. It was already night when a voice was heard, "Hey! Look at this, Hank, Gene!"

People moved closer, murmuring ominously, as Jack Rodebaugh held up a can of corned beef. They'd all been crowded in here for four weeks, sleeping on the floor with no privacy, kids screaming all over the place, waiting in line for half an hour just to be able to go to the bathroom, and no chance in all that time to have a shower or get a decent meal. They'd had to leave most of their things back at home, and God only knew if they'd be there once this was all over, and now they had to stand here and be searched like criminals, all on account of one rotten bastard.

Earl Thomas cringed into himself. "Hey, all right," he protested, "so I kept out a little for myself! I'll bet I'm not the only one who did the same thing!"

Rodebaugh interrupted him by pulling Thomas's suitcase out from under the church pew and upending it. About twenty cans of tuna and processed chicken fell clattering onto the wooden floor of the church nave. Shrieking, a couple of kids chased after the cans, gathering them up.

"Oh, you did a little hoarding, is that it?" Solokov accused. "Or maybe you just broke in and helped yourself from the storeroom?"

Thomas blanched and started to babble his innocence, that he'd only taken a few cans from the store shelves while they were packing it all up to go to the shelters. In point of fact, Solokov privately figured he was most likely telling the truth. Earl Thomas was the assistant manager of the IGA, and no one knew for a fact that there was tuna missing from the Methodist church storeroom—it had been days before anyone got around to doing inventory.

There was no evidence whatsoever to link him to the theft of the generator.

None of that mattered. Thomas had been caught hoarding, in public. The mood in the church was hostile. Here was a chance to really crack down, let people know that hoarding and theft weren't going to be tolerated. And fortunately the store clerk had no close relatives here in town.

"Shut up, Thomas," Solokov ordered. "We've got no *proof* you took those cans from the storeroom. Or anything else that's missing," he added, damningly. "But you *were* hoarding. Does anyone doubt it?" he asked, raising his voice and looking around the crowd.

"Hell, no!" came the answer in a dozen different voices.

"All right, that's it, then." Watching Hank Daschle out of the corner of one eye, Solokov slowly pulled out his .45. Just as the police chief started to open his mouth to protest, Solokov said, "Right now, take your stuff and get out of here. There's no place in here for damn thieves."

He turned around to face the now-silent crowd. "That goes for all of the rest of you, too. And anyone caught taking stuff from the storeroom won't get off so easy as he is." He slapped the butt of the gun in emphasis.

Earl Thomas, staring at it, didn't dare to protest his sentence. He had been there to see Solokov gun down that man from the lake house right outside his store. Jack Rodebaugh shoved his suitcase, lighter now without the cans, into his arms, and other hands picked up the rest of his things, his blanket, shoved them on top of the case.

Awkwardly, Thomas followed Hank Daschle as he made a path through the crowd toward the shelter exit. Several times he was shoved, hard, making him stumble.

"No," he begged weakly as they unsealed the door and opened it onto the lightless night. "No, please, God, I'm sorry, I never took anything, I swear it—"

A final shove sent him backward into the snow. The door slammed shut behind him. Alone now, with no one to see or hear, Thomas let the tears slide freely down his face. They hadn't even let him have a light!

He groped for his things and got up out of the snow, started to trudge, burdened, away from the church. He knew he had to go somewhere, find some kind of shelter—alone, in the dark, in the cold. His own place was over in the trailer park—about as safe from the fallout as standing out in the open. Sure as hell they wouldn't let him in at the school or over to the Elks, Solokov would make sure of that, God *damn* the merciless bastard! And what was he going to eat? He knew he wasn't the only one who'd kept back a little for himself. It had all come from his store, anyway. Damn, it wasn't fair!

Suddenly, Thomas shivered. It was as if the night were solid and man-shaped in front of him, though he actually couldn't *see* anything at all. Then he yelped aloud as a voice came out of the darkness, almost on top of him.

*"What's the matter, did they kick you out of the shelter?"*

The sudden racing of his heartbeat slowed as he

104

realized that the sound of the voice was sympathetic! Eagerly, with growing relief and hope, he began to babble the story of his unjust expulsion, accused of a theft he had never committed.

The voice sounded amused as it said, "Then it looks like you'll be needing a place to stay."

# 3

Lorraine Archer, then Rick, Danny, Paul Krusack, the nameless girl from the farmhouse, and now Earl Thomas. Six of them, possibly enough for Kittredge's needs. Except that the girl had been starved for weeks and even now it was hard to get her to eat. Lorraine, annoyed and disgusted, had resorted to spooning mashed canned peas into her mouth. The girl swallowed them vacantly and opened her mouth for more, but couldn't be persuaded to feed herself.

"Look at her!" Lorraine demanded. "If you don't watch her, she sits there till she wets her pants! And I suppose you expect *me* to clean her up!"

Kittredge shrugged. At least she no longer considered him responsible for the girl's condition. "It's just shock. Maybe after a while she'll come out of it." In fact, he doubted this. For his purpose, it was all one and the same whether the girl regained her mental faculties or not, but her blood, though madness-rich, was still starved of nutrients. It had not done her condition any good to lose what he had taken, and another time might be too much.

Lorraine glared at him. Kittredge noticed that she had started biting her once-polished fingernails. She saw him looking at them and balled up her fist defensively.

Kittredge sighed inwardly. If he had been a living man, he knew he would have been attracted physically to Lorraine Archer, even as she looked now, with her blond hair stringy and unwashed, pulled back away from the fine bones of her face. He could *see* what was there, but there were places within him that were dead, incapable of responding. If she had been Eleanora, come to life again, he feared it would have been the same. Yet there was that faint ghost of a resemblance that kept returning his eyes to her.

Lorraine was biting her nails. There were lines visible at the corners of her mouth. It would have been her turn again. Twice now, she had waited, anticipating the ordeal, nerves drawing more and more tight as night came on. Twice, she had been spared, first by Krusack's arrival, then the girl's. But each new donor meant more complications, more humans crowded into the basement, less privacy.

Now Earl Thomas. The former assistant store manager was stowing his possessions into the corner he was allotted, responding with an ingratiating smile every time someone looked in his direction. Kittredge was pleased with Thomas as an addition to his donors. He should be no trouble, at least. He wasn't hurt and he certainly wasn't starving, not with the fat rolling over the waistband of his pants.

The man still did not know. He had been almost incoherent with relief and gratitude when Kittredge brought him to the lake house and he saw the light, the running water, the food. Such good fortune was not to be questioned. People didn't *do* this kind of thing these days, they didn't open their doors and let in strangers to share their shelters.

Kittredge wondered if he had realized that the light was produced by the stolen generator which had caused all the trouble in the church shelter, that the food had come from the same storeroom he had been accused of pilfering.

A faint grin of anticipation twitched the corner of Kittredge's mouth as he recalled the panic that flared when he had touched the man in the dark. Tomorrow night, Earl Thomas would find out the price of his generosity.

Rick Archer walked into the room, rubbing his eyes. He had been asleep after the long day's work of setting up the generator and getting the pump running again. Now he blinked in surprise at seeing Kittredge returned so soon to the house, then noticed Earl Thomas, who stood and nervously introduced himself.

"Um, Mr. Kittredge has invited me to stay with you generous people. I had no place to go. . . ."

His explanation broke off as Kittredge said, "They kicked him out of a shelter in Danby— hoarding or stealing food or something."

Rick glared hate at Thomas. "They killed my father in Danby. They shot him down in the middle of the street."

The grocery store manager's face flushed red, his mouth dropped open in recognition. "Oh . . . I

. . . that was a terrible thing. I saw it all. Gene Solokov, that's who it was. One of those survivalists. Now he's turned into a dictator over there. They all take his orders. I never stole their food, I swear it! He was going to shoot me, too. He had the gun right in his hand!"

Rick turned away from the man, frowning, then stepped back to Kittredge and asked in a low voice, "He doesn't know, does he?"

"Not yet. Do you want to tell him?"

Rick looked uncertain. "It sounds crazy. He might not even believe me."

Kittredge shrugged his indifference.

"Anyway, what if he does? What if he takes off?"

"Then I find him. Tell him that."

Rick bit his lower lip. "It's not right," he muttered angrily.

Kittredge took another look at Rick. *Right?* Right and wrong were distinctions he had abandoned along with his humanity. But he still recalled the Stoic philosophy of Epictetus, who had been a slave in ancient Rome: *if you consider only what is truly in your own power, then no one will ever compel you, no one will restrict you.*

None of them were locked in. In the end, their own decision was what kept them here, not any force of his. He wondered if Rick understood this. If any philosophy was apt for these Nightfall times, it would be the Stoics, he thought.

"I don't think it would make much of a difference in his case," he told Rick. "Tell him if you want to. I can't stop you from talking."

Then he recalled the one of his donors who was

109

in fact being held against his will, the one whose hate was the deepest. Why hadn't Krusack warned Earl Thomas? He had never kept his mouth shut before.

The big farmer had been moved from the couch to the mattress that had been Danny's. Kittredge walked over to look at him. He frowned. The man's face was flushed, he was moving restlessly.

Kittredge looked up. "Rick, come over here."

"What?"

"Touch him. Does he feel hot?"

Rick felt the man's forehead. "God, yes!"

Kittredge pulled off the blanket and unwrapped the bandage from the broken leg. Matter had seeped through the cloth. The wound was swollen and angry red. He hissed air in through his teeth. "Infected!"

Krusack moaned at his touch. ". . . fuckin' hands off . . . ," he mumbled.

Kittredge lifted his head and saw Lorraine Archer looking on. "Look at this!" he demanded.

She winced at the sight of the leg but said, "So, am I supposed to be nurse to everyone you decide to drag into this house? Now I've got *her* on my hands, too, you know!"

Kittredge frowned again. In his lifetime, a wound like this would have meant gangrene, amputation, probable death. Those things didn't happen anymore. Or, they hadn't used to. But this was the Nightfall world now.

*Antibiotics,* he thought. Lorraine had by now brought over the first-aid kit and was starting to wipe the wound with hydrogen peroxide, the best thing they had. At contact with the purulent mat-

110

ter, the antiseptic foamed.

He walked away. Infected blood was tolerable at best. He could take Krusack out of turn, tomorrow night. That would put an end to it—a merciful end, if the infection was going to get worse. And Krusack was trouble. Would be more trouble if the leg ever healed.

But there were the others. They would know what he had done. What had he just told himself a few minutes ago—*no one can compel you, no one can restrict you?* It was true. He could kill them, but it was their choice to submit to it. And it was a great deal more convenient for him if they would submit. What if they did resist—would he break all of their legs? Chain them to the walls?

They would have antibiotics in Danby. He had to go back anyway, now that there were more of them needing food.

"You're going out there again, like that? Don't you know there's fallout?" Thomas asked him. Kittredge turned back to Rick. *Maybe you'd better tell him,* said his look.

He always tried to come into Danby by a different route. This time he circled around through the trees, by way of the creek that led into Sugar Lake, before cutting across a snow-covered cornfield. The silence in the woods was disturbing. It made the scent of death seem all-pervasive. He glanced up. The branches of the trees were nearly bare by now, as if it were truly winter.

From the edge of town he could see the Methodist church steeple, an obvious lookout post, if

111

the observer would not have been exposed to the full effect of the fallout. Kittredge looked carefully, but there was no watcher visible in the steeple.

Still, something was wrong. It was not instinct warning him, but the experience of over a century and a half. From Earl Thomas, he knew that the humans had discovered his thefts. They would know that the store clerk had not taken the generator. They would have a trap set for the real thief. They would be waiting for him to come back to the church. The one named Solokov, who was so concerned about security—he would be waiting.

Of course, the humans of Danby did not know the nature of the thief they were expecting to trap, but experience had taught Kittredge not to be overconfident.

At any rate, most of the drugs were in the school building, not the church. Earl Thomas had volunteered this information after looking at Krusack's swollen leg. The school was where the doctor was, he had added.

"You'd expect them to treat him after they shot him in the first place?" Kittredge asked scornfully.

"He might. Doc Mercier's one of the few decent human beings in this damned town."

"This man *needs* a doctor," Lorraine had argued.

Kittredge had shaken his head, refusing. Krusack would not leave the lake house alive to expose his hiding place.

So it would be the school, he supposed now. The shelter where security was tightest. The doors were all locked and guarded, and there were sentries on the upper floor looking down into the streets. Those measures did not pose major problems for him. It was simple enough to get into the building. The hard part would be getting into the basement itself. Kittredge prowled around the perimeter of the school. There was a loading door in the back going down to the basement level, but it was buried under several feet of insulating earth. Digging it away would let them know how he had gotten in. He would try another way.

His fingers clinging to the brickwork, Kittredge climbed to the upper floor of the school, to a different window than the one he had used before, just in case they had discovered signs of the break-in.

From his last visit to the school, he knew that the door down to the basement was at the bottom of a staircase, locked and guarded. The lock was no obstacle, but the guard could be. This time, his search was more thorough. There were no ventilating ducts that he could pass through. Finally he found a possibility—another staircase in the rear of the building. The door at the bottom was locked like the one in front. It was sealed, too, with some kind of caulking. But was it guarded like the other?

For a long time, he listened, one ear pressed against the door. On the other side were the sounds of hundreds of humans, most of them sleeping. But were they all? Was one of them even now watching the other side of this door?

The risk was too great. But Kittredge paused. If the door was caulked shut, that must mean it was not intended to be used, would not be guarded.

113

At last he began, very carefully, to pry the caulking from the door frame. When it was finally removed he went to work on the lock.

Soon there was a satisfying click. He waited a few moments, in case someone might have heard. He was pleased with his skill, especially after the debacle this morning with the generator. It was not, he thought defensively, that he was totally inept in these matters. It was simply that he had never had occasion in his existence to learn about such things as generators and cars. What use would they have been to him? His mastery of locks had been quite a different matter.

He slowly turned the doorknob and pulled. The door moved. With so many humans in such a confined space, they would never have done something so risky as nail shut one of the only two remaining exits from the shelter. Light escaped through the crack. Kittredge blinked. In human terms, the light was quite dim, appropriate for the human sleep-cycle. Yet he would not have the advantage of the total dark. Once his vision adjusted, he searched through the crack in the door but could see no one watching it, no humans awake nearby.

Cautiously, he pulled it open far enough to slip through, then shut it behind him, hoping that no one would see how he had disturbed the seal.

He walked as much in the shadows as he could, unchallenged as he passed the sleeping humans. Doubtless they thought he was just another one of their number, on an errand to the bathroom or a sentry returning to his sleep. He walked down halls, past rooms, most of them crowded with humanity like all the transient shelters he had seen in

114

the weeks after Nightfall. The odor of them over-whelmed his senses.

His time was limited. At any minute, he might be spotted as a stranger in the shelter. He kept going through the halls. The place he was search-ing for, the storeroom for the food and the drugs, would be locked, very possibly guarded. Yes, espe-cially after today's incident with Earl Thomas at the other shelter. The humans could not trust one another.

*There!* Kittredge turned his face away and walked casually in another direction from the man standing in front of a door. A guard—this had to be the storeroom! But how to get inside? He cursed under his breath. With so many of them around he could not take this one man. He thought of Earl Thomas again. Of the stolen gen-erator.

Slowly, a grin spread across his face, exposing the tips of his fangs. He fought it down.

The sound led him directly to the building's gen-erator. It was a more substantial model than the backup he had stolen from the church, and he ex-amined it thoroughly, wishing he had seen how the one at the house had finally worked. He did not want to simply shut the thing off. He needed more time than that.

He quickly pulled connections and snapped wires. As the engine shut off, the lights flickered and died, the ventilator fans whirled into silence.

*Hey!* came the first shouts from outside the gen-erator room as Kittredge slipped into the conceal-ing dark. More cries followed as the sleepers were roused to discover themselves without light. The

115

degree of confusion was not quite what he had hoped for. The shelter residents were used to crises by this time. Voices were raised almost at once, trying to calm the others, telling everyone to stay in their places until the power was restored. Here and there the beam of a flashlight cut through the dark.

The storeroom guard, though glancing around nervously, had remained at his post, and he was one of those with flashlights. He almost caught sight of Kittredge in time to recognize his face as a stranger's. But not quite.

Kittredge lowered the unconscious sentry to the floor, then hesitated. The blood-heat, the steady pulse of the heartbeat under his hands, the whole shelter full of the scent of humans close to panic . . .

Breathing hard, he let one finger brush against the man's throat. Bloodlust, coming to life, urged at him.

*"Erlanger! Shit! Where is he? Anybody seen Dan Erlanger?"*

Kittredge moved quickly. A single strike at the storeroom door sent it flying open, and he dragged the unconscious man inside before he wedged it shut again. He cursed himself for the instant's loss of control. He could not afford such lapses. He had almost let himself be caught out there.

He glanced at the sentry again and reminded himself that he had already fed tonight, that he had no time to waste.

He pulled his backpack out from under his jacket and started to ransack the stores, stuffing

116

things inside without too much regard for what he was taking. There wasn't the time for that. Within two minutes he had filled the pack.

Then he frowned, eyes searching around the room, at the shelves, the stacks on the floor. No drugs. Where *were* they?

The man on the floor stirred slightly. Kittredge glanced at the door—no light shone through. The generator was not yet back in operation. He still might have time. Reaching down, he lifted the sentry to his feet and shook him to consciousness. The man groaned weakly, then gasped as he felt the chill of Kittredge's hand holding him.

"The drugs," Kittredge hissed urgently, "where are they?"

The human looked at the darkness that had hold of him and shivered. Something cold and menacing had grasped him. His fear—Kittredge shuddered as his vision turned red, compelling . . .

*No.* He knew that the man was sensing his bloodlust, just as he could sense the human's terror. He took his hand away, brought out the .38, and pressed it against the sentry's head. Terror diminished, its savor dimmed as the man recognized a merely mortal threat.

"The drugs," Kittredge demanded again.

"Solokov keeps them locked up," the man said, eager to cooperate, to keep that dread chill from touching him again. "His office."

"Where?"

"The . . . janitor's closet."

He would never find it in time, not by himself. "All right, you come with me, show me the way," said Kittredge, grabbing his arm.

117

The man cringed at his touch, and Kittredge let go. He opened the door and used the reassuring gun to prod his captive through.

"It's dark!"

"Never mind, you know the way. Just give me directions—left or right?"

The door to the office, the janitor's closet, was locked. No time—again he broke the door open, dragged the sentry inside. "Where?" he demanded.

"The file cabinet."

Metal grated as Kittredge ripped a locked file drawer open. Ammunition. He cursed in a whisper, opened another drawer. There—drugs! This time he had to be sure he had what he needed. He searched through the drawer until he found a name he could recognize as an antibiotic—amoxicillin—and filled his pockets with it and other medical supplies he thought they might need at the lake house, wishing again he knew more about this kind of thing.

Suddenly, the lights went on.

Kittredge froze momentarily, in the act of shoving a foil pack labeled CODEINE into his jacket. Then a slight movement caught his eye—the sentry, eyes wide, staring at him, edging toward the door.

*What does he see when he looks at me?*

Kittredge snatched up the gun he had laid on top of the file cabinet, and the man's motion halted, his eyes moving to the .38.

Kittredge thought with desperate urgency—he had to get out of here. He might be trapped already. There was no hope, not with the lights on again, of getting out without being spotted. They would be searching for an intruder the minute they saw the broken door to the storeroom.

He reached out to grab the sentry again. With one hand around the man's throat and the other holding the gun to his head, Kittredge moved them both out into the hallway. He kept his back to the walls, dragging the sentry along with him on his way to the front door, the closest exit.

The crowd of humans in the basement backed away from him and his hostage. Someone cried out—perhaps the sentry's wife or mother. Kittredge ignored the sound, kept moving.

Then a man pushed through the others, and stood directly in Kittredge's way. He was not a particularly large man, but the solid mass of him gave an impression of size. The gun in his hand was steady, and his dark brown eyes met Kittredge's with unflinching hostility. There was no fear.

Kittredge stopped. The man was not going to move out of his way. This was an experience unique in his existence, that a human could face him like this and not feel even the slightest shiver of fear. A crimson film began to spread across his vision, but, still, the human's eyes did not turn away.

Fear—the sentry's terror was enough. Holding the man, Kittredge felt that he was on the edge of a killing frenzy. And he must not give in to it. Behind the one man stood others, at least a dozen of them with guns. But the danger came from the one he was facing. This, he knew, was the one named Solokov.

He stepped sidewise past the man, pulling his hostage with him. Now he was at the door. Its guard was there, and he could see her hand shaking with the weight of the gun she was holding on him. They thought they had him trapped, that the only question was whether they were willing to exchange the hostage's life for his.

It would be Solokov's decision. But as Kittredge backed up closer to the door guard he could see a change in the expression on the human leader's face. He glanced at the woman, back to Solokov, and he realized suddenly that he had a hostage here who was far more valuable to him than the sentry. He started to turn in her direction, but then he hesitated, stopped by the look in Solokov's eyes.

*Touch her,* it said, *and you die. No matter what it takes, you won't get out of this place alive.*

He froze, then told himself that another hostage was not necessary. He tightened his grip around the terror-stricken sentry's throat. After a moment, Solokov made a gesture, and the woman quickly but unsteadily went to put her key into the lock of the door.

Almost dizzy with relief, Kittredge pulled his hostage through and up the stairs. There was no one on the ground floor who was willing to give him trouble. The guards there moved away from the front door and let him through to the outside.

Kittredge took a deep breath of the chill air to clear his head. Then he led his captive, hugging the wall to avoid the floodlights, around the corner of the school. The man was sobbing by now, a low, choking sound. Kittredge bent down to him, then paused. His bloodlust was gone. Kittredge considered for a moment taking the man with him back to the lake house, but reason intervened, warning him of a dozen ways that doing so would be a serious mistake. So would staying here any longer.

He took away his arm and let the human fall forward onto the damp gray snow. By the time Dan Erlanger could lift up his head again, Kittredge had disappeared into the dark.

*Stupid, stupid!* Kittredge berated himself. He had stopped in the woods to let his frustration ventilate itself. This expedition had been a complete disaster! This whole impossible scheme!

For all of his existence he had relied on stealth, on concealment. He was not supernatural. There were limits to his abilities, limits he had carefully observed, up to this time. Now, what had he done? Five hundred humans must have seen his face in there! The sentry, at least, knew what he was. He had left that door into the basement unsealed—he would never be able to use it again.

And for what? The food? He dug a hand into a pocket and came out with a handful of drug packets. No, for *this,* because Thomas had said the drugs were kept in the school shelter. Almost, he threw the the packets into the snow. But finally, reluctantly, he stuffed them back into his jacket. No use wasting them. The harm was already done. For Paul Krusack's sake.

It would have been better to let him die.

But there was more. There was worse. Kittredge forced himself to face the fact, for he had never fled from self-knowledge, no matter what it revealed. He had met a human's eyes and turned away. *Solokov.* He whispered the name aloud, like a curse. Solokov had faced him without fear, and he had backed away. From a human. He had not even been able to take the terrorized sentry afterward. This knowledge of his weakness shook him.

Lorraine came to meet Kittredge when he finally got back to the lake house. "He's worse."

"Here," he snarled, making her flinch as he dug medicines out of his pockets and threw them at her, onto the floor. Earl Thomas was shrinking back into his corner. Kittredge sensed his awakening fear. So they had told him.

*Tonight!* his look promised the store clerk.

"Jeez! Lookit his *eyes!*"

As Rick frantically jerked his brother into silence, Kittredge realized that he had to get out of the basement, away from the fear-scent, before he broke into a frenzy and savaged them all. The bloodlust that had been subdued by Solokov's wordless threat seemed poised to erupt once again. It was unnatural for one of his kind to exist like this!

Kittredge leaned against a tree outside and stared into the slowly lightening east. Dawn. Time to shelter from the sun. Time to rest. He considered how long it had been since he had any rest. In the last two days he had made three—no, four trips into Danby, brought back the generator, brought back the girl from the farmhouse eight miles away . . .

No wonder he was weary!

He stumbled into the garage and lay down on the soft leather seat of the station wagon. A nagging reminder came to his mind that the generator would soon be running out of gas. He ignored it. The humans could sit in the dark.

He shut his eyes. But he was unable to banish the image: brown eyes, meeting his without fear. Solokov. It was over an hour before his heartbeat began to slow.

# 4

A sound roused his attention. Kittredge's heartbeat quickened, throwing off the lethargy of rest. *What is it now?*

It was just past noon. He got to his feet, alert now, relieved that he could feel no hunger stirring yet, no bloodlust. Perhaps all he had needed was rest.

The sound came again, a pounding. As if someone was—banging on the door?

Kittredge jumped out of the car and looked outside toward the house. It was true. Two humans, a man and a woman, were standing in front of the door, and the man was raising his hand to pound on it again. Incredible. Thoughts of spiders and flies came unbidden into his mind.

He was just about to call out to the people when the door opened. He could make out Lorraine Archer standing inside. Furious with her, he shouted out loud, "What are you doing out of the shelter?"

The refugees turned to the sound of his voice as he came up to the door. Their faces, dark, with the broad cheekbones of their Aztec blood, were nervous and apologetic, but desperate above all.

"Don't you have any sense?" Kittredge demanded of Lorraine, ignoring them. "Do you want to end up like *her,* opening the door to anyone who comes along?"

Lorraine's face tightened a little at the mention of the girl from the farmhouse, but there was no hesitation in her voice. "I thought *you* were supposed to be around here, making sure nothing like that happens."

"Please," the man at the door broke in, "we mean no harm. We only came to ask for someplace to stay. We do not want to beg. We will work, anything, just if we can have shelter. My wife, you see, the baby, her milk . . ."

Kittredge looked again at the woman, wrapped up in layers of clothes under a large man's raincoat that came close to dragging on the ground. Yes, underneath it all she was holding something. He had heard, somewhere, that radiation finds its way most readily into milk and bone. And certainly, for an infant in these Nightfall times, its mother's milk was the only food available.

"You say you'll work for your keep?" Lorraine was asking. "Cleaning, any work?"

"Yes, yes," the man said eagerly. His wife, her face lighting with hope, nodded. "You see," he explained, "we were working on a farm west of Granger. The family, they let us stay with them when the bombs came. But now there is no more food, and they told us, they were sorry, but we had to go. We look for someone who will take us in, but they all drive us away. Some say they will shoot. I tell them about the baby, but they do not care.

"And here, all the houses are empty but there is no food. If we stay inside we will starve, but they say the poison is still outside, all around us. . . ."

"Yes, well I think there's no reason you can't stay here," Lorraine told him, "as long as you're willing to work. There's a lot to do. Two sick people to take care of."

"Yes, anything," the refugees both insisted.

"Wait a minute," Kittredge protested.

"Why? Isn't that what you wanted? More of us?"

Kittredge ran a hand back through his hair. He had not planned on keeping more humans. They would mean he would have to bring back more food, just when things were more difficult in Danby. But it was true, if Krusack and the girl both died . . .

"You say you were in a shelter?" he asked the man.

"Yes, until yesterday morning, when they say we have to go. We were walking all day, outside. My wife, if the poison gets into her milk . . ."

"Let me," Kittredge said, reaching out his hand, "let me see for a minute."

The man pulled back as he took hold of his wrist, but his story must have been true. There was no taint of the poison.

"All right," he agreed. "We'd better all go inside."

"I'm Joe Flores," the man said, "and my wife is Connie. I promise you, we are no trouble. You don't regret this."

Kittredge took them to the bathroom, where they could wash down before he would let them into the shelter. "We should have some clean clothes some-

126

where, too. The ones you're wearing will be contaminated."

He left them inside the bathroom while he went to tell Lorraine to find them something to wear. She looked particularly satisfied.

He frowned at her. "I don't understand," he said. "You've complained every time I brought people back here."

"Well, at least these two will work for their keep, which is a lot more than you can say about the ones you dragged in. And it's better, isn't it, for everyone if there are more of us?"

The newcomers would postpone her own next turn for two more nights, after Earl Thomas. And now there was also someone to take the girl off her hands.

He shrugged. "You find room for them, then." At least Joe and Connie Flores looked like the type that wouldn't be trouble. Their baby would make sure of that, the same way he had ensured Lorraine's cooperation. She was always careful to keep her daughter Julie out of his sight, but the threat of what he might do to her was enough.

When the Flores couple came out of the bathroom, awkward in the borrowed clothes but much better off for being clean, Kittredge took them down to the basement where the others were waiting. Lorraine led Connie to the corner where the girl sat with her arms wrapped around her knees, staring into the darkness that was all her mind would see. "You'll be taking care of her now."

Connie exclaimed in horrified sympathy as Lorraine explained, "Looters killed her family and raped her. She just . . . sits like that."

"And this man?" Connie asked, looking at the mattress where Paul Krusack was lying.

"The vigilantes in Danby shot him. His leg is broken and the wound is infected. You do understand, don't you, how to take care of an injury like that?"

"Christ, Lorraine, what'd you do, go out and hire a maid?" asked Rick. His stepmother gave him a venomous look and went on as if he hadn't spoken.

Rick turned away and went to where Kittredge was standing next to Joe Flores. "Did you tell him yet? Or is that my job again?" Flores looked nervously from one to the other of them as Rick demanded, "Well, did he happen to mention the real reason he let you stay here?"

Now Earl Thomas was listening too, as Rick went on relentlessly, "Our good friend Mr. Blaine Kittredge here happens to be a vampire. He drinks blood, sucks it right out of your veins. We all take turns supplying him, one of us every night. *That's* why he let you in, no matter what other story he told you."

Kittredge stood rigid through Rick's merciless revelation. Joe Flores was slowly crossing himself. Across the room, Connie's hand had grasped the crucifix around her neck. Unlike many others, they believed.

He nodded once, very stiffly, as Flores asked, staring at him, "What the boy says, it is not true, it cannot be true?"

Flores backed a step away, toward his wife and child. "But then, you are all . . ."

"No," Rick admitted. "He doesn't kill anyone, he

just . . . does what I said." He held out his own wrist for proof, but Flores's eyes were still fixed on Kittredge, on his face. He clutched his own wrist, where the cold touch of that being had rested for a moment. *"El Diablo!"* he whispered.

There was an urge to kill in Kittredge, not in bloodlust, but cold anger. "No," he snapped, and reached for Flores as the man drew back. There was a scream from Connie. Kittredge fought down his reaction to the terror-scent and pulled out the crucifix that he had known would be inside Flores's shirt. He held it up, pulling the man closer to him until their faces almost met.

"Look," he said. "I can touch this." Slowly, he brought the metal up and touched it to his lips, exposing the tips of his fangs slightly as he kissed the crucifix. Then he dropped it abruptly, letting Flores stagger back. "You see? No burns, no blisters — I didn't go up in smoke. Neither will you."

Once again the presence of humans was suddenly unendurable. He went out into the welcoming gloom of the Nightfall day, the air, like his own flesh, cold. For a while, he watched the door of the house, waiting to see Joe and Connie Flores leave with their baby, willing to brave the radiation rather than endure his own, unholy touch. They would not find anyone else who would take them in, he knew that. Within a couple of days, the radiation would have contaminated them thoroughly and they would be no more good to him.

Deliberately, he let the bloodlust rise. The crosses at their throats would not save them. Perhaps, he thought cruelly, he would take them both, the one while the other watched and realized their hope of escape had been totally futile.

But the door remained closed. No one emerged. Gradually, Kittredge realized that he had been right in the first place, that they would accept any conditions, even his, in exchange for shelter.

That made eight of them, then, assuming the girl stayed alive. And Krusack. Krusack probably would live, at least, now that he had his antibiotics. In another week, he would be ready again. Earl Thomas would be tonight. Eight of them, then, plus the baby and Julie Archer.

Ten humans. In a day or so, they would be needing more food. The generator was still short of gasoline. How many of them, he wondered, would sell their souls for his own, damned, despised invulnerability? Would he, in their circumstances, choose to be what he was now?

Kittredge opened the door of the Mercedes and stretched out on the soft leather seat to wait until night. He had never been given such a choice. Nor was it in his power to extend it to the others. They belonged to him now, and he would deal with the consequences if they occurred.

# 1833

For the first months of my existence, I was no more than a fugitive, hiding wherever I could find safety from the sun, emerging during the brief hours of the summer night to take whatever victim I could find before dawn sent me searching again for shelter. It was my near destruction at the hands of a heedless child which taught me that this existence would be my permanent condition, that I must make more secure arrangements for my rest.

I was by then far from my former home and associations, and I finally located a man who agreed to rent me the cellar of a building he owned in a part of the city frequented by criminals and other unsavory elements of society. His name was Taylor, a man whom disease had left twisted and dwarfed, and I believe he was a dealer in stolen goods. Doubtless he thought I was in similar circumstances. He made no comment when I sealed shut the windows and secured the door from the inside with an iron bar. There, at last, I could rest in peace.

With my new vault, my existence became easier with the nights beginning to lengthen into autumn. At that season the hunting was easy among the transient criminal population. I did have to meet with Taylor upon occasion to pay my rent with money taken from the pockets of my victims, but he did not find it unusual that I preferred to conduct my business during the hours of night. Others of his associates did the same.

Taylor was the one human I must not harm as long as I needed the refuge of his cellar. Necessarily, he knew my face, but he had only seen it in the shadows, and I was by then using a name other than my own and had no fear of recognition in this city where I had never lived.

Taylor kept his own rooms in partial darkness—I think that many of his various acquaintances preferred to keep their identities disguised. One time, when I had settled my account and felt comfortable enough that I had accepted his invitation to a glass of wine—which I left untouched—I observed a chessboard on a table in the corner of the room. He noticed my interest and asked if I would care for a game.

We would play by the light of a single candle upon the table, and it surprised me at first that an individual of Taylor's station in life could so have mastered the game. I think that he had always had difficulty in finding someone equal to his skill. Soon I began to discover him waiting for me on the staircase when I returned from my nightly hunt, and often I would find myself considering the hours left until dawn, whether there would be enough time for us to have our game.

I finally allowed myself to believe that our sessions might continue even if Taylor should discover what I was, that my nature would make no difference between us.

Yet the end was inevitable. Winter was hard on the city's poor, and I had been forced to roam farther in search of victims. Late that night, too close to dawn for my peace of mind, the man I had finally chosen clutched at his chest, his heart failing even before my fangs could pierce his flesh. Sunrise was coming, and I would be forced to return to my cellar with hunger raging unappeased.

Taylor must have been waiting for my return. At the sound of my footsteps upon the stairs, he stepped out into the hallway, holding out the two pawns, the black and the white, one in each hand for me to select.

It was well over a century before I would touch the pieces of the game again.

# Hunger

## 1

Memory of the red-eyed face of death that had stared at Greg Reichler for an instant in the Wallace farmhouse had faded during the long weeks in the Duchons' basement. More recent horrors filled his mind these days, and that vision only surfaced sometimes in his nightmares. But he had other reasons for not going back to the ghosts and the emptiness of his own home.

Sure, the supplies from the Wallace place would have lasted him longer if he weren't over here, sharing them with Al Duchon and his family. But he knew by now that he never would have stayed alive on his own long enough for it make a difference.

Reichler had figured right from the first that it was the food in the pickup that decided Al Duchon to let him come inside with the rest of them. It didn't bother him all that much. What mattered right now was that they had four armed men in here—Al, Jake, Matt, and himself.

The firing stopped. The air smelled like one of the days when he and Dad had been out duck hunting—that same sharp gunpowder smell. It filled the house. Reichler peered through the slot in the boarded-up window and saw nothing moving out there, only a heap of rags lying in the snow.

He had been on watch this time, had seen them coming, five or six limping, raggedy scarecrows. Looters. Reichler had gotten over hating them by now. Lots of times, they'd take off if you just fired a couple of shots. This bunch didn't. They had guns. Al, Jake, and Matt came running up from the basement, took their places—with the four of them, they had all directions pretty well covered—and started firing. By the time the looters figured out they'd taken on more than they could handle, it was too late. Reichler wouldn't have minded letting them get away, but Al said no, that you never knew they might not come back to try again, at night, maybe.

Reichler stood up. Al came in from the kitchen, Jake from the dining room. "You all right, Matt?" Al called out, anxious.

"Yeah, Dad. Just got a splinter." Matt came in, blood running from a cut in his scalp.

Al frowned. "Better get your mother to take a look at that."

The other three looked at each other. Reichler shrugged. "I'll do it."

"We'll cover you," said Al. He went to the front door, pulled away the insulation that sealed it.

Reichler set his teeth, walked outside. The snow was deeper than the last time, dark, dirty gray snow that reminded him of the piles the snowplows made in the city, black with the exhaust from all the cars. He stepped out into it, not much reassured that Al Duchon was watching from the window he had occupied during the firefight. If one of

135

the looters was still alive, there was no way Al was going to get him before it was too late.

He had volunteered, partly so as not to give Al a chance to say, "Why don't you go out there again, Greg?" He figured they all considered him the expendable one—hell, he guessed it was true!

He reached the heap of rags he had been able to see from the window slot and prodded it with his foot. The shot had hit in the gut. The face—Reichler stared at the evidence of radiation damage, the ulcers visible on the face and the scalp, where the hair had fallen out. The looter had been half-dead before the shot even hit him. He shuddered, looked around him at the dark gray sky, the dirty snow. What was *in* it?

Reichler bent down and picked up the looter's gun. Then the part he hated—he looked for spare ammunition. He didn't like to touch them, as if it was catching, somehow. But there was no question that they couldn't afford to leave the guns and stuff lying out here. He went on to check the other bodies. It was funny, he thought—he didn't even much notice anymore if they were black or white.

When he had finished with the bodies, he came back into the house, and Jake helped him take the guns. Reichler looked down at his boots, at the snow he was tracking into the house. He went back outside and stomped, hard. Then they started to seal up the doors and windows again. Until the next time.

"Hell of a lot they'd have found if they did get in here," Jake muttered as he helped Reichler carry the guns down the basement stairs.

Reichler nodded glumly. It was true. They were

running short on food. Even the supplies from the Wallace basement were nearly gone by now.

What had happened to the Wallaces? he wondered. Were they right, getting out while they had the chance? It was easy to tell yourself that when you had nothing to do but sit down in the basement and remember, and think about your mistakes. But if the Wallaces ever did come back, they'd find some gang had taken over their place and wrecked it. Reichler didn't worry anymore that Al might find out where he had gotten all that food in his pickup. He figured Al would just hope he hadn't left any for the looters.

He sat down on his mattress next to Matt and leaned back against the basement wall. Now that the crisis was over, he felt kind of weak and dizzy. It was hunger, he figured. They were cutting the rations shorter all the time. His joints kind of ached. But he wasn't the only one. Martha Duchon complained sometimes about the closed-up air down here, and the kerosene fumes from the stove giving her headaches. Fumes wouldn't be a problem much longer—the kerosene was almost gone. It made Reichler wonder what they were going to do for light.

"You OK?" he asked Matt.

The younger Duchon son touched the bandage on his head. "Yeah, sure. Just a splinter, like I said."

Jake came to sit next to them. Jake had been just home from college for the summer when the attack came. Reichler was ten years older. He had never been to college. He had been married with kids of his own and farming in partnership with his dad, getting ready some day to take over the place on his own. Now all it looked like they could look forward to was starving to death down here.

It was Jake who brought the subject up, now when Al was upstairs taking the lookout duty. "What are we going to do when we get that hungry?"

Reichler shook his head, remembering the scrawny, starveling bodies of the looters outside. "At least we're safe down here, from the fallout. I don't want to end up like them out there, that's for sure."

"I'd rather take my chances than starve to death," Matt insisted.

"Look," said Jake, "Fallout—radiation—it doesn't last forever. It's been almost two months! The worst of it has got to be over by now. It might be safe out there. And we sure can't stay down here like this forever. This close to Chicago, it stands to reason things are better someplace else."

"Yeah, but can you be sure?" argued Reichler. "What about those looters outside—have you seen what they look like, rotting away while they're still breathing?"

"Well, that's what I mean," said Jake. "That kind of damage takes a long time to show up. It doesn't mean we'd end up like that if we went outside *now*."

Reichler shook his head. Maybe Jake was right—he'd been to college, after all. But he sure would rather starve than die like those men had outside.

"So," said Matt, "have you talked to Dad?"

Jake nodded glumly. "He won't go. Not with Mom and the girls."

Guilt, never far from Reichler, made him remember again—Frieda, Mom, the kids. Left alone, undefended. Al Duchon still had his family while he had nothing left. The world outside was no place for a woman, not with gangs of men roaming around and no law anywhere. Al had two teenage daughters. He was trapped here, in his own basement.

Reichler knew that Al was a decent man. He had let a neighbor into his shelter, and he wouldn't kick him out now that the food was starting to run short. But he wouldn't hold him here, either.

What if he and Dad had never gone to the Wallace place? What if they had driven the looters away that day? How long could they have survived on the food they had? What would they have done when it ran out?

But they were dead, all of them. He had nothing left, nothing to hold him here.

And what if Jake was right?

# 2

After a few weeks, existence in the basement of the house on Sugar Lake had become routine. For Blaine Kittredge, at least, there was still the regular necessity of excursions into Danby for raids on the canning plant or the gasoline tank. A few times he had broken into the church again, and the Elks lodge, but never the school. Not since that night.

There wasn't so much to find anymore. The days of canned delicacies like salmon were over forever.

For the humans, shelter existence was crowding and short rations and plain, unremitting boredom. Tempers were short. "Is this the best you can do?" Lorraine demanded, faced with another load of canned peas. Julie refused to touch them. Kittredge considered telling her to let the brat starve if she wouldn't eat, that she was no use to him anyway. It was incredible to him these days how he could have ever thought she resembled his Eleanora.

Human emotions still disturbed him too easily. They blamed him for everything, but he had done his best. He had even brought back a few loads of books from the Danby library. Solokov, for all his security precautions, had neglected this resource. Kittredge had wandered through the empty, dusty stacks, glad when he discovered an ancient copy of Marcus Aurelius's *Meditations*. The Stoics again. The old books, the classics he had read in his life, still had the power to move him. He could have been a scholar, then. He could have done so much more than he had, if he had known his time would be so short.

In a neglected-looking cabinet in the library, he had discovered a chess set. Pensively, he slid open the lid and looked at the pieces, black and white. Not knowing why, he had included it with the books. But Rick Archer was the only one of the humans who knew how to play the game at all. For want of a partner, Rick was trying to teach his brother the moves.

Lorraine, discontented, was putting away the supplies. She had turned the nursing chores over to Connie Flores. The antibiotics from the school had conquered the infection in Paul Krusack's leg, and it was slowly mending now. *Krusack*. There was another problem. Whenever Kittredge looked up in Krusack's direction, he could see the big farmer watching him with dark, hostile eyes. The rest of them, at least to some degree, had come to accept the arrangement. They at least had food and shelter.

But not Krusack. It would be a problem soon, what to do with him. Already he was starting to limp around the basement on a crutch he had made from the remains of one of Lorraine's Shaker chairs. The man was a kind of craftsman, it seemed. But it was clear that he was just waiting until he could walk again, all the miles through the snow to Green Springs.

Kittredge knew he could not allow it. This place must remain a secret. And he had seen that look in Krusack's eyes before this—humans would never allow one of his kind to remain undestroyed. They would come from Green Springs with guns and with fire.

But it was equally dangerous to keep the man here. Kittredge had already, for caution's sake, found a better hiding place for the guns, and he no longer took his rest in the garage. As soon as Krusack could walk . . .

There was only one solution. *To kill again* . . . Kittredge meant to take advantage of the opportunity. He would sometimes allow his bloodlust to rise a little in anticipation of that hunt. Let Krusack go. Let him think he had a chance to get away—a half hour's head start through the woods. *Just wait,* he silently told the grim, brooding farmer, and there must have been some hint of his intentions on his face, because Krusack turned his eyes away, and the air suddenly held a trace of fear. Krusack was waiting, and making plans. They both were.

He could sense the relief in all the humans as he left the basement. Relief and a measure of envy, as well, for the immunity that allowed him the freedom to come and go.

Now, without his presence, they would talk freely. Kittredge could have laughed at their simplicity. They never realized how acute his hearing was, or how silent his footsteps. From the solitary comfort of Lorraine Archer's crewelpoint armchair, he listened to their voices as they plotted once again what they would do with him.

142

"I think he cannot be killed." (Joe Flores — it was most convenient for him to believe he was helpless in the face of the supernatural, so he could not be expected to resist.)

"Bullshit! Don't hand me any of that superstitious crap! If you had any balls, any *co-jon-es*, you wouldn't just sit there and let him get away with this! That was your wife he had in there tonight!" (There was the sound of furniture crashing, and curses in two languages. It was Krusack, of course, trying to goad the others into trying something. It was more than once that Kittredge had to pull Flores away from him. He wondered now if Rick and Thomas could manage to hold him back.)

"I suppose *you* would do something?" (Rick Archer, out of breath. He took Krusack's remarks almost as badly as Flores did, but never quite dared before now to assert himself against a man his father's age.)

"If we all got together, we could jump him. There's four men down here! Whatever he is, there's only one of him!" (Four men — one of them crippled and one just sixteen.)

"And what if it doesn't work, huh? What's he going to do then?"

"Yeah. It's not really so bad . . ."

"Shut up, Danny!"

"What's the matter, kid? If you don't like your little brother hanging around with the vampire, why don't you do something about it? None of the rest of us would be down here if you people hadn't made your little deal in the first place."

"We should wait. The sun's got to come back some time." (Earl Thomas.)

"You believe that about the sun?"

"Well, something's got to be able to kill him." (Rick.) "What about a stake though his heart?"

"Yeah! Like Dracula!" (Twelve-year-old Danny, producing repulsive sound effects to punctuate his remarks.)

"Goddammit, Danny, I said *shut up!*"

Kittredge almost laughed aloud. *Oh, yes, Rick, now you're getting the right idea. But how are you planning to accomplish it? Excuse me, Mr. Kittredge, but would you mind lying still while I pound on this stake?*

He let them go on for a while longer, but they failed, as usual, to come up with a concrete plan. He had little to worry about, for the moment. He got up from the armchair and got ready to go back outside, leaving them alone to quarrel with each other.

He paused when he was still a half mile distant from Danby. The town squatted there in the middle of the level sameness of the fields—what had once been some of the richest farmland in the world. His town, his survivors. Gene Solokov's town. Since that night in the school basement, Solokov had been determined to destroy him.

Kittredge did admit to himself that some of the traps had been clever, as if Solokov had once been involved in jungle warfare. But they were traps for a human, as if Solokov had never looked into his eyes that night. Or had the man simply denied what his eyes had plainly told him, as humans so often did, unable to let themselves believe?

Kittredge knew his own abilities and their limits. It would be almost impossible for a human to take him, unawares, in the dark. He could sense their presence, the traps they had set were visible to his eyes. What could destroy him was his own carelessness, overestimating his invulnerability.

So if he foraged occasionally outside the town, in the unguarded farmhouses, it was not for fear of Gene Solokov, he would tell himself. There were still resources to be discovered there — not food, of course. But the lake house by now had a supply of several hundred light bulbs, for example, that he had unscrewed from their receptacles in buildings throughout the county. How long before human civilization would be ready to produce more of them?

And he was not alone. Not all of Solokov's traps went unsprung. There were more looters and foragers around these days, daring the fallout in the open.

Kittredge paused again outside a house near the outskirts of the town, alerted by human scent. Whoever it was had not been careless. There was no light, no visible sign of their presence in the house. Refugees who did not learn such lessons would not survive.

Kittredge entered the house by picking the back door lock, expecting correctly that he would find them in an upstairs bedroom, asleep. The darkness in the house was so deep that the LED display on one sleeper's wristwatch seemed to illuminate the entire room. There were two of them in the first bed, a man and a woman, both still dressed in dirty, worn outdoor clothes, only their boots removed. Kittredge caught the scent of old, spilled blood. He wondered whose — their own or their victims'? And—he came closer, bent over them—the taint of radiation disease, faint, but intensely repellent to him.

He straightened, not really disappointed, for contamination was what he had expected. These two looked like they had been too long in the open. They were both thin and dirty, and each had a gun lying at hand next to the bed, and a pack.

In the Nightfall world, it would be hard to stay alive without shedding blood. He wondered again, where would these two go? How many would they kill to survive until the death already working in them took its course?

He thought of the three men he had shot in the farmhouse where he found the nameless girl. The contaminated eliminating the uncontaminated. His hand went to the .38 he always carried now when he went out. It would not be a waste. It was their living, consuming, that was the waste. Then he shook his head—these two were not in his way. And, besides, the shots might alert the sentries in Danby.

Kittredge went from one side of the bed to the other and took the packs. Their lives were useless to him, but their supplies were not.

There were three others in other bedrooms of the house, all contaminated to some degree, and he took their packs as well, indifferent to where the supplies might have originally come from. There was all together enough food to make this night's excursion a success. He would not have to go into Danby.

Halfway back to the lake house, it occurred to him that he might have strangled the looters silently or broken their necks. He paused. No, it was not worthwhile going back. Let them live as long as they could manage. He had left them their guns, after all.

They had not expected him to come back to the lake house after so short a time. Except for the nameless girl's continual whimpering, the basement was quiet. Paul Krusack sat in his chair whittling a piece of wood to a point at one end, but Kittredge ignored him. Rick was sitting at the chessboard with his brother. He raised his eyes and glared as Kittredge came in.

Lorraine took a brief look through the packs and held out a crumpled plastic bag with—he did not recognize what was in it.

"You expect us to eat *this?*" she demanded, with a look of distaste on her face. "There are *worms* crawling around in here!"

"Think of it as protein," he snapped defensively. Nothing was ever right. "If you'd seen where I got this, you might have some idea how lucky you are down here."

"Lucky," muttered Krusack. He took a vicious gouge with his knife at the stake.

Lorraine's lips tightened, and she went back to the closet where she kept the supplies locked up. The girl, probably, would end up eating whatever was in that bag.

"Shit!" came a soft-voiced curse from the table where Rick and Danny were sitting. The younger boy was scowling resentfully at his brother, who looked down as he saw Kittredge glance their way.

147

He stood up and walked over to stand next to the table. His eyes were on the chessboard. It had been so many years. Danny had the white pieces.

"You might try moving your rook out," he advised. The boy looked up at him for an instant, then back at the board. He reached to move the piece.

Rick's face tightened. He took one of Danny's pawns with his bishop, knocking the piece so hard it fell off the board—a useless move.

Kittredge turned around and went to the corner where he sat sometimes. He picked up his copy of the *Meditations*. But after a few moments he looked up to see Danny standing in front of him nervously with a pair of pawns in his hands, white and black. "Rick didn't want to play any more."

Kittredge hesitated, then pointed, not touching, to one of Danny's fists. It opened. The black pawn.

The boy only knew the most basic moves. It would take a while before Kittredge could teach him to play a real game. It astonished him how, after so many years, he could remember every move, every gambit, as if the last century and a half had never intervened.

"Isn't it kind of weird, for . . . you know, you to play chess?"

"I used to play—a long time ago."

"Oh yeah? *How* long ago? I mean, I heard you tell Rick they didn't even have electricity back then."

"I was born in 1804."

"No shit!" He could see Danny mentally calculating the years. He brought his bishop down and put

148

the boy's king in check. "That's what happens when you don't pay attention to the game."

They played for a while in silence, with Danny concentrating on the board. Kittredge could feel Rick's eyes on his back. *1804,* he was thinking. *Almost two hundred years.*

"Can we play another game?" Danny asked.

Suddenly Rick was there, dragging the younger boy away, his chair clattering on the floor. He glared at Kittredge. "You leave my brother alone!

"You think you can keep us locked up down here forever, is that it? Well, how come you can go outside all this time when we can't? How do we know there really is fallout out there any more?"

Kittredge turned on him, "You want to go out there? Fine. Go ahead, then! Leave. Find your own food! Maybe you'd like to be the one to go into Danby every night?"

It was a challenge he had made several times before. But this time Rick did not back off. "All right. I will."

"Rick, no!" Lorraine cried, alarmed. Even Paul Krusack looked like he was going to say something to stop him.

But Rick started toward the basement stairs, saying, "No, the bloodsucking vampire just thinks I don't have the guts to do it!"

Kittredge had taken enough. In a rage, not of bloodlust but of something approaching cold human anger, he seized Rick by the arm, pulled him up the stairs. Frightened now, Rick tried to resist, but Kittredge's grip was unbreakable. He dragged him through the door, slammed it shut, then shoved him up against it. The impact was audible throughout the house.

Kittredge could see Rick's breath as a white mist in the chill dark of the deserted hall. His own breathing, cold against the boy's face, was invisible.

"You want to die? Is that it? Well, I can oblige you with no trouble," he snarled. His voice was feral, unhuman, lips drawn fully back from his fangs. But there was no bloodlust. His vision was clear, his hands steady as he held Rick pressed back against the door.

"You use *that word*—do you think you know what it means just because you've lost a little blood? Go on, have a good look! Just how many people do you think have seen this face and lived? What makes you think you can stand there in front of me and *dare* me to kill you?"

Rick was choking audibly, and Kittredge eased his grip on his neck, took a step backward. Slowly, Rick reached up to rub his bruised throat as Kittredge said, "So, what is it? You've been listening to Krusack? He doesn't want to be here. He thinks you've made a deal with the devil, just to survive. He wants to kill me, doesn't he? Well, just tell me—has *he* tried it yet? Or is it all just talk?"

The harsh sound of Rick's breathing was his only response. And the tantalizing scent of his fear.

"Let me tell you this," Kittredge went on. "Krusack may not live very much longer. Do you want to join him? Is that what you want? Maybe I should have killed you that first time, and Lorraine and Danny and your sister, too. *That's* the only choice you have, all of you! You don't like our deal? You want me to go down there and put an end to it right now?

"How many times do I have to tell you I'm trying *not* to kill you? Why do you have to keep making it so hard!"

*I didn't mean to say that!* But Kittredge could see Rick's eyes widen in sudden understanding. He leaned forward so that their faces almost touched and Rick had to hold himself rigid not to flinch away. His voice was a low, chill whisper. "Do you understand what I'm telling you? I *want* to kill. I *enjoy* it. It's *hard* to stop."

Rick stood there, pinned helpless against the door, and he could feel how close his death was. With every pulse of fear from his heart Kittredge could sense his own responding bloodlust. But then he thrust himself back.

There was utter stillness for a moment, and finally Rick was the first to exhale. He still could not speak.

It was Kittredge who did that, surprising himself with the steadiness of his voice. "Go back down the stairs. I'm going to go get some rest."

# 3

Greg Reichler stood aside a little, shifting his gun from one hand to the other, as Martha Duchon held onto her sons. He wished this were over with. Fifteen-year-old Lori Duchon was crying, too—she didn't want to stay behind.

"Come on, Mother," Al said finally, pulling Martha back. "They've got to get going now that it's light." He gave Jake and Matt each a hard hug, looked at Greg Reichler, gave him one, too. "Take care," he told them.

There was not much more any of them could say, pretending the three of them were going to be back in just a couple of days with food and news of a safe place to stay, somewhere the bombs hadn't hit. Al had finally admitted they couldn't all stay here like this much longer, with the food running out, but he refused to take his wife and daughters out on the roads, with so many bands of looters running loose, not even knowing where they were going.

They were taking their guns, and most of the ammunition they had left. There was no food to spare. They would have to find that on the road, any way they could.

Snow had blown up onto the porch. They had to shove hard to get the door open. The gray drifts covered everything, as far as they could see, even the bodies of the looters that lay unburied somewhere out in the yard. Earth and sky, it was all the same, gray, lifeless, the color of death. Resolutely, he made himself not think about that, about the death that could be seeping into his bones right now—in the snow, in the air he was breathing.

"Shit!" Matt whispered, coming out behind Reichler. His breath hung white in the air in front of his face. "It's cold!"

Jake pushed past them, the drifts up to his knees as he stepped off the porch. Reichler shrugged the slight weight of the pack on his shoulders and followed. If they were going, then there was no use putting it off.

They had all three been brought up on a farm, were used to working and hunting outside in the cold. But this was different. There was not going to be a warm house to come back to at the end of the day.

Reichler paused a minute as he caught a look at the drifts where Al Duchon's soybean crop had been up, the acres of pale green rows, just two months ago. Sixty days, the best part of a growing season. Now the furrows weren't even visible. And his own crop . . . His own farm, his land, everything they had—what was it worth now?

Jake was standing by the wrecked, looted shell of Reichler's pickup, the only vehicle left on the place. Looters had gotten the rest. Reichler shrugged, kicked at the snow. "We'd never have gotten through, anyway. Not this snow. Even if we could find gas."

"So where do we go?" asked Matt.

Reichler's own farm was just up the road, but he didn't want to go past there again, didn't want to see what was left of it. Obviously, they couldn't go anywhere in the direction of the ruins of Chicago. "Down I-57," he suggested. "South. Maybe we could make it as far as Kankakee by the time it gets too dark to go on."

The other two followed him. Passing by the places where their neighbors had lived, they found the Noyes farm burned out, the Gilchrists' empty and abandoned. When they came close to the Michelic place, shots warned them off.

Reichler called out, "Hey, Stan—Stan Michelic! Don't shoot! It's me, Greg Reichler, with the Duchon boys. You know us!" But the only answer they got was another shot that kicked up a spray of snow at Reichler's feet. He figured either Michelic didn't want them to come up to the house—or that wasn't Michelic in there shooting at them.

He looked at Jake, Jake looked back at him. Either way, maybe it was best to move on.

It was slow, hard, cold going, slogging through the knee-high drifts. After a few hours Reichler could no longer feel his own feet, the muscles of his thighs hurt. The whole country was a wasteland. As they went south down I-57, every farm, every house had been looted and picked over, leaving nothing. Reichler wondered uneasily what the silent gray snowdrifts were hiding.

The light faded. At the next house, where they thought they might spend the night, the family lay slaughtered on the floor inside, the bodies stiff and

154

kept from rotting by the cold, the faces distorted and inhuman. Reichler refused to stay inside, and the other two didn't much argue with him. They slept in the barn instead, no colder, breaking open one of the big wheels of hay stored there and digging themselves inside, as close as possible for each others' warmth.

In the morning, they picked through some piles of spilled chicken feed, chewing the hard cracked grain. There was nothing else. The whole place had been ransacked.

"We got to get off the expressway," Reichler insisted. "Everybody from Chicago, they must of come this way."

Jake shook his head. "This is the quickest way to get to where we're going. We can't be too much more than ten miles or so from Kankakee. The sooner we get there, the sooner we can get back to the farm."

"But think about what we've seen around here! Just how many looters from Chicago came down this road, heading straight for the same place as we are! What makes you think there'll be anything left in Kankakee—or they'd let us have any if there was?"

"So, where *do* we want to go?"

"Away from the main road, places they haven't been. West of here's Joliet—that'd be just as bad, maybe even worse."

"What about someplace like Lafayette?" Matt suggested. He was supposed to have started college at Purdue this fall, where Jake would have been a senior. "That's far enough away, don't you think?"

"Lafayette! That's at least a hundred miles away!

155

Do you have any idea how long that would take? Mom and Dad and the girls could be dead by the time we got back!"

They could be dead even now, Reichler thought and did not say out loud. He was glad, *glad* it wasn't his own family back there waiting for them. It made things easier to decide.

He stood up, brushing off clinging hay. This wasn't his idea in the first place, leaving the shelter, but they were out now. The damage, whatever it was, was already done. "Jake," he said, "you can always go back if you want to."

"Maybe I could tell Dad how it is out here, get him to come with us."

"I donno. Seems to me that if Al wanted to, he would of done it in the first place. But you can try if you want. What about you, Matt?"

"What if he still won't go? Then what? Come on, Jake. Three of us together, we've got a better chance."

"Chance for what?" Jake asked bitterly. But he got to his feet and put on his pack, agreeing without words.

Reichler nodded. "If we can make ten miles a day, we should be to Lafayette in ten days, right? That's not so bad."


You could make out where the roads were from the fences. Reichler remembered how I-57 always had to be closed every time there was a blizzard, the way the wind blew the snow across the road. Now there were snowdrifts piling up behind the fences, and the three of them trudged along hoping

156

the buried roads were leading them in the right direction. With no sun, few landmarks, it was hard to tell sometimes where they were going. East and south, they hoped.

The shot came without warning from the direction of a house at the top of the hill. Reichler gripped his gun and stood looking around for a sign of who was shooting —

Another shot sent him to his knees, looking for cover.

"Stay *down,* fools!" came a loud whisper.

Reichler swiveled his head, searching for the voice. What the hell was going on? Someone was shooting — at them? Why? But — another one and then the impact of a slug just a few yards behind him. They sure were! He hugged the ground, crawling forward into a ditch beside the road, and lay there, not daring to lift his head. *Christ, we didn't do anything!*

The firing seemed to have stopped. Whoever was out there, they were probably saving their ammunition. But who was it had told them to stay down? Reichler lifted his head an inch or two and called out in a whisper, "Hey, where are you? What's going on?"

No answer for a moment. Then, "What you got for brains, just walking down the road like that, not looking out where you going? You want to get yourself killed?"

Shock froze Reichler as he recognized the sound of a black voice. Then he reached for the gun he had dropped into the snow.

"What, you gonna shoot me now?"

Reichler's hand stopped. He remembered, whatever he was, this was the man who'd warned them. "Not unless I have to," he finally answered.

After a minute, a figure appeared over the top of a snow mound to his left, opposite where the voice had come from. He was wearing a worn-out military camouflage jacket and boots, but Reichler couldn't help tensing as he saw what he knew he was going to, the color of the man's skin.

He made himself say, "Thanks for the warning. What the hell's going on?"

Jake Duchon crawled up, Matt behind him. The black stranger was looking from one to the other like he was trying to decide something, like he wasn't all too happy with what he saw. "You dudes know how to *use* those things?" he asked them finally. "You out of ammunition or something?"

"Yeah, we can use these things," Reichler said defensively. Who was this black guy, anyway, to be asking him that? If he'd been one of the looters who tried to break into the Duchon house, then he'd know whether they could use their guns or not. "I'd just like to know what's going on, first, before I start shooting."

"Good way to end up dead," said the stranger, making Reichler flush with anger. But then he added, "Look, how bad would you all like some chicken?"

"What?"

"Chicken—are you shitting us?" asked Matt.

"No shit, man. This is for real. There's an old dude over in that house, and he's got real live chickens!"

Jake was shaking his head and Reichler silently agreed—No, it didn't matter how hungry they

158

were—they weren't going to join this black guy trying to steal from some poor old man. They were both thinking of Al Duchon in there, alone, holding out against thieves and looters. It made Reichler feel sick; no wonder the man was shooting at them!

Maybe, he thought, if they took care of this guy for him, he might be grateful.

Just then another slug came flying over their heads—and it wasn't from the direction of the house. "Motherfuckers!" cursed the black guy, low.

Now Reichler was entirely confused. He raised his head higher to take a good look at his surroundings. The old farmhouse, paint flaking off the narrow window frames, stood at the end of a driveway winding up the hill. A hedge bordered the drive, which must have been where the black guy was hiding before they came along.

Just then, a movement must have caught the guy's eye, because he suddenly fired off a couple of shots in the direction of a grain bin to the left of the house. Reichler could hear the sheet metal ring with the impact.

"Watch out, Leon!" the guy yelled out. "Three of them over there," he explained, ducking down to avoid the return fire. "There's plenty of chicken for everybody, but, no, they don't see it that way. Have to have it all. Jimmy found this place first. Be damned if those mothers are gonna get a piece of it now, not unless they kill me, too."

It was only then that Reichler saw a pair of boots sticking out from behind the hedge a few dozen yards up the hill, and a red stain in the snow. "You mean those three guys up there killed this Jimmy and now they're shooting at us?"

"Yeah. Me and Leon got them pinned down so they can't get to the house. Of course, neither can we. But I figure, with five of us, we could get up there and get around them."

Reichler looked over at the Duchons again. "Well, I don't know . . ."

"If those other guys are going to get the chickens anyway, it might as well be us as them," said Matt. "It's not like we'd hurt the old guy."

"No need for that," the black guy agreed. "He hasn't even got a gun, as far as I can tell. Here, my name's Travis Butler."

Reichler wasn't sure about this, wasn't sure at all. "Jake?"

"If it's that old guy you're worried about," said Butler, "then you wouldn't want to let those mothers get their hands on him."

"I suppose," said Jake, unwillingly.

"Good," said Butler. "Now, here's what we gotta do. Leon and me got them pinned down over there near the barn. They have to cross the yard to get to the house. So now, if two of you can cover us from down here, we can go up behind the hedge, around the house, and get behind those fuckers. That's the way we learned to do it when I was in the U.S. Marines."

Reichler cautiously surveyed the situation again. Butler seemed to have it figured out. If he really *had* been in the Marines, maybe this was all right.

"Well, come on," Butler said. "Shit, you want those chickens or don't you?"

*This is crazy,* Reichler thought as he crawled on his belly through the snow after Butler, cradling his

160

gun in his arms the way the ex-Marine was doing, but more clumsily. Butler sure *looked* like he'd been in the Marines. But risking his life for a few damned chickens?

Better than eating chicken feed, the hollow place in his gut answered. Behind them, the sound of gunshots came from Matt and Jake's position at the bottom of the road. Reichler wondered if the Duchons were maybe using up too much of their ammunition. He just hoped the other side was running out even faster.

They were coming up to the body sprawled in the snow behind the hedge. Next to it crouched a skinny, shivering black kid with one gun in his hands, another propped next to him. The extra gun must have belonged to the corpse. Reichler glanced at the back of a blond boy's head, the hair stiff with drying blood. Jimmy. The looters back at the Duchon house—they would have had names, too.

"Leon, this is Reichler. Him and his friends are gonna lend us some firepower," Butler explained.

The skinny kid nodded.

Reichler peered out through the hedge and saw that they were directly opposite the barn where the three men were supposed to be hiding. Immediately, fire tore through the bare branches, and Butler shoved his head down. He was glad to hear the sound of Jack and Matt's guns from down by the road.

Butler fired back toward the barn. Then he turned around to Reichler and said, "You two stay here, keep firing, keep 'em pinned down. I'm gonna try to get up to the house."

Reichler nodded. The shots had made him realize

there was only one way out of this thing now—to take out those men behind the barn.

It took five, maybe ten minutes for Butler to crawl behind the hedge up to the house. Reichler fired nervously in the direction of the enemy, afraid that he and Leon could end up being the ones pinned down here if the ex-Marine didn't make it.

As he watched, one figure ran out from behind the barn, heading toward the grain bin a few yards closer to the house. Reichler realized he was trying to outflank Butler, and he fired, saw the man fall to the ground, twisting as he lay there. Reichler watched him writhe, sickened, hands clenched tight around his rifle. *Die, why don't you?* he urged his victim. He wouldn't have let an animal suffer like that. Why didn't his friends come out and get him? But Reichler knew why, and at last the man was still, dead or not.

A few minutes later, a volley of shots came from behind the house; then silence.

Reichler glanced at the kid named Leon. "You think he got them?"

"I donno!"

The kid's eyes were white and wild with terror. Reichler patted him on the shoulder reassuringly. "I bet he's all right. He was in the Marines, wasn't he?"

But Leon was too scared to answer. Just then, Butler stepped out slowly from around the back of the house, and Leon jumped up before Reichler could stop him. But there was no more shooting. He stood up himself and called out, "You OK?"

Butler waved and went down to the barn to check out the bodies of the men they'd killed.

162

Reichler turned around. "Hey!" he called out, "Matt? Jake? We got 'em!"

Where were they?

Slowly, a single figure stood up from the ditch beside the road. It was Matt. He wasn't holding his gun.

Reichler's heart suddenly lurched. *Jake?* He ran back to the road, stopped when he saw Matt's stricken face, then looked down to where Jake Duchon lay face down in the reddened snow. He bent to turn him over, but Matt grabbed his arm. "No, don't." His voice was a hoarse whisper.

Reichler let himself be pulled back up, but he had already seen the pulped, bloody brain matter splattered onto the snow. "God, Jake!" he gasped.

"That's too bad," he heard, and spun around to see Travis Butler standing a few feet away. "You gonna come get those chickens or not?"

Sudden rage distorted Reichler's face. He clenched his fists. Jake was lying here dead, and all this black bastard could think of was *chickens?*

"Hey, man," said Butler, raising one hand to ward off Reichler's threatened attack, "he *paid* for them, didn't he? You may as well get your share — it won't do him no good if you don't."

Reichler looked at Matt, whose tears were running down his face into his stubble of beard. He dropped his hands. Butler was right, nothing would help Jake now. Or the blond kid named Jimmy, either, he remembered.

He led Matt, stumbling, up the hill to the farmhouse. Getting in was a simple matter of kicking the door down. Butler was right, the old man inside had no gun, just a kitchen cleaver he was wav-

163

ing at them, so scared he was shaking. Butler just went up and took it away from him.

The chickens were in the basement, about a dozen of them running loose down there. The place was cleaner than Reichler would have thought—chicken shit and feathers all swept away. There were bags of chicken feed up against one wall.

The old man was crying by now, saying how they couldn't kill the chickens, that they were egg layers, his breeding stock. Sure enough, one of them was a rooster. Reichler was thinking that he wished he'd thought of something like this. The old man must have been living on the eggs for weeks now. He even had a generator and lights so the hens would keep laying. Only what he didn't have was a gun to keep somebody else from taking it all away from him.

Except, Reichler realized, a gun might just have gotten him killed.

Butler had caught one of the chickens. Ignoring the old guy, he brought it back up from the basement and picked up the cleaver from the floor. He pinned the flapping, squawking bird down on the kitchen table. The old guy came up the stairs and ran at him, and Butler knocked him back down to the floor with the flat of the cleaver.

"You look here, old man. There's been five men died over these chickens already. You want, we can make it six."

Angrily, he brought the cleaver down on the struggling bird's neck. As it lay there on the table, its legs kicking in the death reflex, he started to rummage in the kitchen cupboards.

164

He looked back at Reichler. "Why don't you skin that thing or something? And get him to shut up, will you?"

"Here," said Reichler, taking over, "I'll do it." He could cook, anyway.

He shoved the old man back down into the basement before he put a pot of water to boil over the wood-burning stove. It was true, he thought as he worked. Five men dead over these chickens, not just Jake.

Butler and the kid Leon almost looked like they might bolt down the guts, raw, as they watched Reichler clean the hen. In a little while the aroma of simmering broth was filling the kitchen. Butler grabbed one piece out before it was more than half cooked, ate it standing there over the pot, juices running down his arm.

"Oh, Jesus," he said, chewing, his eyes closed. Leon ate like a starved cat, choking down his meat, pieces almost too big for him to get into his mouth.

Reichler, nearly as hungry, didn't wait any longer to snatch up a piece of his own. In a matter of minutes, all four of them, even Matt, had torn the flesh from the carcass with their teeth, were sighing in satisfaction, stomachs tight and aching, uncomfortably full.

When they were done, they let the old man out of his basement and offered him some of the scraps. He refused, though, shaking his head, tears running down his face.

"Like we was eating his damn kids," Butler mumbled.

"Listen," said Reichler, "this is a pretty good

setup he's got here. It wouldn't be a bad idea to save the rooster and a couple of the hens. Breeding stock could be important one day."

"You shitting me? We leave any of these birds, the next time somebody comes along, they gonna kill them and him, too, more'n likely."

Reichler shook his head. Butler obviously wasn't a farmer, he couldn't understand. But the trouble was, he knew the Marine was right. "Someplace else, things've gotta be better," he said, looking at Matt Duchon, who was sitting away from them, staring into the dark. Leon was already asleep.

"Ha!" Butler laughed bitterly. "Someplace else is just like this, man, except where it's worse. Where *you* been? Don't you know anything? Listen, the nukes hit *everyplace*, you hear? Whole damn USA's gone up in smoke, maybe the whole damn world."

"You know that, for a fact?"

"It's what people say, here and there. I been around."

Reichler was thinking. "We were headed down to Lafayette, Indiana. You know anything about things down there?"

Butler shook his head.

"That's where Purdue is. Jake . . . used to go to college there." Reichler paused awkwardly. "What I mean is, you just lost your one partner, we lost Matt's brother. Four of us might have a better chance of making it."

"No, man," said the Marine grimly. "I'm staying clear of places like that—cities."

Travis Butler's memories were dark. Cities. Like Joliet, he was thinking. Joliet, the day of the disaster. Thousands, maybe as many as a million people had coming pouring into Joliet that first night—more people than even lived there, people from around Chicago, mostly, people screaming, people burned and sick, people trying to get into some kind of shelter.

They had a couple companies of the National Guard and the Joliet police to keep order. But the prisoners rioted at Stateville, set the place on fire. There was no one to stop them. Most of the guards there had already taken off. The few who were left just opened fire when the cons rushed the walls, but upwards of five thousand of them got clear.

The National Guard blockaded Route 53 north of town, which was already choked impassable with refugees. That was when Butler started to find out what it was like when you were a black man in Joliet and you didn't have a local address—every motherfucker with a gun or a badge automatically assumed he was one of the convicts escaped from the pen. Orders were, shoot on sight.

He hid in whatever shelter he could find, while the people died, while the food ran out, while they started to kill each other over it. And there *were* dudes out of Stateville, gang members, behind a lot of that, and more. A couple of times Butler tangled with some of *those*. After the first time, he had a gun. Second time, he figured he'd had enough. If the cops didn't get you, the gangs would, or the next dude who saw you with a can of dog food hidden under your coat.

Butler got out of Joliet along with a couple of kids named Leon Pike and Jimmy, who might have been in the joint himself.

Butler didn't know if a place like Lafayette would be any better than Joliet, but he didn't care to find out. He was doing all right the way he was. But this white guy Reichler was right, though, that four of them would have a better chance surviving—especially now that Jimmy was dead.

"You want to stay away from those cities," he said. "Lots of places, they won't even let you inside. Too crowded, not enough food, no sanitation—they got diseases all over the place. Cops'll shoot if they even see you with a gun."

"But where can we *go?*" asked Matt.

"We can stay here," said Butler, as if the answer weren't obvious. "Till the chickens are gone, anyway. Then on to the next place. Believe me, there's no place else *to* go."

Matt and Greg Reichler looked at each other for a long time. Finally Reichler nodded, swallowing something bitter inside himself. Neither he nor Matt mentioned going back to the Duchon farm.

# 4

Gene Solokov paused one more time to frown down at the five bodies lying in a row on the street in front of the canning plant and the school. He paced up the row, back again, turning the heads carefully with the toe of his boot. Five raiders, three men and two women, this time. But none of them was the bastard he was really looking for — that thin blond guy who'd broken in, who'd threatened *Vonnie*.

As long as he lived, Solokov would never forget that face. Sharp, arrogant — there was something about him, something that wanted to make your guts turn to ice when you looked at him, into his eyes. Those eyes — in the light of the shelter they'd looked almost red, uncanny. But, maybe he was some kind of albino or something. His skin was almost as pale as the belly of a dead fish. Except the hair hadn't been white.

It didn't make any difference. Not after seeing the way the bastard had looked at Vonnie, standing between him and the door. Solokov broke out into a cold sweat every time he thought about it, every time he remembered those eyes fixed on his wife. Or standing there in the middle of the shelter, holding a gun to Dan Erlanger's head and daring—just daring him to try to stop him.

Solokov shuddered involuntarily. Dan Erlanger had been half out of his mind ever since, refusing to go out in the dark, babbling about how the guy was *cold,* how he'd *breathed* on him and his breath was cold. Solokov hadn't seen anything like it since Nam.

But none of these five was the right one, just ordinary looters caught trying to break into the canning plant during the day. The one he was after came at night, like he could see in the dark. And he was still out there, somewhere. Solokov *knew* it, and one day soon he was going to get the bastard. He would never feel safe until he did.

Brian Mercier came outside from the school. "So, what do you want, Gene? You know I've got two gunshots to look after inside."

"Yeah, how're they doing, Doc?"

"I think they'll both pull through."

Solokov nodded. Two of his men wounded. None killed. All five of the raiders dead. It could have been worse.

"What I'd like you to do," he said, "is look at these five here and see if you can find any sign of radiation disease."

"Oh, no trouble! I'll just take some tissue samples and send them down to the lab. Have the results for you right away.

"Oh, all right," the doctor growled after a minute when Solokov failed to react to his sarcasm. "Can you at least get me some more light out here?"

With a lantern next to the first corpse, Mercier

pulled on a pair of gloves and knelt down. "Damn, I always hated pathology," he mumbled to himself as he opened the mouths of the dead, pulled away their clothes, palpated their too-yielding flesh. At least they weren't stiff yet.

Finally he got up from his knees.

"Well?" asked Solokov.

Mercier shrugged. "It's hard to tell. I can't exactly ask them how they've been feeling lately now, can I?"

"What do you *think?*"

"That one has some swelling in the lymph nodes. The others—a few lesions, maybe. But it could be anything—it could be scurvy, for godssakes!"

He'd already figured out what his brother-in-law had in mind. "You're thinking of letting them out of the shelters, aren't you?"

"Radiation levels have been dropping. I wouldn't say things are safe out here yet for kids and pregnant women—"

"Neither would I."

"But maybe there wouldn't be too much exposure to send men out on patrols for a few hours a couple times a week. I mean, *these* bastards were running around outside and they hadn't dropped dead yet." He prodded a corpse with his foot.

"It's the long-term effects we have to worry about," explained Mercier. "No, they wouldn't drop dead, but ten, twenty years from now they could end up with cancer."

"Look, Doc, none of us may even be alive ten years from now if we can't protect ourselves from these raids. *That's* what I'm worried about now."

Mercier shrugged. "You're running this show,

Gene. You asked me for my professional judgement, and you got it. If there isn't anything else, I've got two men downstairs who might not be alive tomorrow if I don't get back to them."

"Um, Doc," Solokov said as he was starting to leave. "I'd appreciate it if you didn't mention any of this when you go back down. Until I've figured out what to do."

"Sure, Gene. Anything you say," his brother-in-law agreed cynically.

Solokov looked down at the corpses again after he was gone. How long had they been outside without protection? How sick had they been—were they sick at all?

*Damn,* it made him mad to think of these bastards sneaking around, breaking into the town while they were all holed up down in the basements, stealing them all blind. The sentries couldn't cover the whole town. How many of them were there? And the one who wasn't here, the face he had wanted to see lying here with the rest of them—where was he now?

Solokov forced his mind back to other matters. He was going to have to decide soon about opening the shelters. The trouble was, once they thought they were safe from the fallout, people would start wanting to go back to their houses, where they'd be sitting ducks for any killers who came along. What would he do with Vonnie, take her back to their own place?

Of course, a few more raids like this one might make them see sense.

"OK!" he yelled, waving to the men waiting inside the school doorway. They filed out, and Solokov picked up the legs of one corpse, to drag it off to the pit at the edge of town.

Soon, he hoped, he'd be dragging that red-eyed bastard to the same place. Especially once they could get some regular patrols going around, search all the buildings. *I'll get you then,* Solokov promised his enemy.

## 1833

I have always found it a paradox, that by nature we are territorial beings, but human enmity has forced us to become fugitives who must never settle for too long in one place. I think that it must have been otherwise once, before the dawn of history. Even human legends often tie us to the soil of our own graves. And I know of no other explanation for the instinctive hostility with which we react to the presence, the very scent of another of our own kind.

I never encountered the one who killed me. I never discovered what became of him. I did learn much later that soon after my death there was a fire in one of the old houses on the riverside, and that charred human bones were found among the ashes. They might have been the remains of my killer and his victims. But investigation revealed only that the house had been leased to an old gentleman who was rarely seen, either by day or by night. I was unable to learn more details of his affairs.

I have often wondered how it would be to meet that one again. I would know him. Even after the passage of centuries, I would know him.

# Winter

## 1

"Checkmate."

"Shit!" Danny Archer glared ruefully at the chessboard. "I thought I was gonna get you that time for sure!"

Kittredge let his mouth twitch slightly in a grin. "You will, one day. You can get your brother already, can't you?"

"Yeah, I guess. We got time for another game?"

Outside, the sun would have already gone below the horizon. Kittredge's hunger, now that the game was over, sent him a warning spasm. "No, I think it's too late."

Danny's face fell. It was his turn tonight. They had both avoided thinking of that, during the game. Now Kittredge stood up. "Come on."

The shelter in the lake house had been quieter since the night Rick and Kittredge had confronted one another in the hallway upstairs. Kittredge played either Rick or Danny in a chess game at least once a day now and was thinking about bringing a new load of books from the Danby library.

But now he took Danny with him into the wine cellar, a room no one ever entered except for this purpose, despite the number of people crowded into the basement. Danny sat down on the cushion there, looking pale, but the fear-scent was faint. He was used to this, no matter how much he wished they didn't have to do it.

"Which arm?" Kittredge asked him.

Danny held out the left. Kittredge nodded, knelt down, and took hold of the wrist. The bruises from last time hadn't quite faded yet. They were an ugly yellow-green. He bit down with as little force as he could, but he could still tell from the boy's intake of breath that it hurt.

With Danny, he had to be as careful as he could. The boy was his smallest donor, except for the mad girl, and he could not afford to lose too much blood. This time, when he stopped, Danny was still leaning up against him with his eyes closed.

"Are you all right?"

The eyes fluttered open. "Yeah, I guess. Just a little tired." He shivered. "Cold."

"I'm sorry if I hurt you."

"Yeah, well I guess you got to, don't you?"

"I've got to." His hand hovered a moment above the boy's hair. He had to do it. But maybe he could leave Danny off the rotation the next time, until he got his strength back. Just once or twice.

Kittredge dropped his hand and helped the boy up, reminded himself to make sure Lorraine gave him extra to eat.

As they left the wine cellar, Paul Krusack glared at him. Krusack was starting to get around the Archers' basement fairly well on his crutch. *Soon,* Kittredge thought, watching him. When it was Krusack's turn, the big farmer watched Kittredge take his blood, unflinching, with the contempt of a man

176

forced to witness some foul perversion. It was visible in his eyes: *You can't kill me. You need me for this. A lot more than I need you.*

Kittredge could have shown him, the way he had shown Rick, what fear really was, but by now he was content to wait. Soon Krusack would be able to run, to make his bid for escape. The thought of that hunt, bringing him down, the scent of his fear, the kill—Kittredge wanted it so much it almost frightened him.

Soon, too, the population of Danby would be accessible. The radiation level was dropping. Already there were men outside patrolling the streets. Soon he wouldn't need Krusack any more, nor any of the rest of them. He would have over a thousand donors in Danby.

The patrols tempted him already. Sometimes, as a pair of armed men passed by a place where he was hiding, Kittredge found it hard to restrain himself. But he did not want to reveal what he was before the population left the shelters. No more than he wanted his potential victims out unprotected in the open while the atmosphere was still contaminated.

The looters were proof of that danger. Two days after he had taken the packs from the five of them sleeping in their borrowed beds, he recognized their bodies in the pit near the edge of town. There were over a dozen in there by now, their stiffly frozen limbs protruding from the snow that buried them. One of the signs—TRESPASSERS AND LOOTERS WILL BE SHOT—was planted in front of the pit. The signs at the town limits of Danby were sometimes found torn down and broken. Always, they were replaced.

As Kittredge stood in front of the pit, he wondered if at the very bottom was the decomposed body of the man who had once owned the lake house, Raymond Archer. There were times when he thought Lorraine almost blamed her dead husband for what had happened to his family, for abandoning them. He had never seriously considered whether to kill Lorraine when he left the lake house. Perhaps he, too, was unfair, blaming her for not being Eleanora.

The sun was getting high behind the pall of clouds. He returned to his current resting place in the lake house garage.

Hours later his hearing caught the sound of snow crunching under human feet, voices whispering. The scent of the strangers stimulated his heartbeat, and he came fully alert. Quickly, silently, he retrieved the guns from their hiding place and slipped out into the woods to intercept the intruders.

There were at least a half dozen of them—cold, filthy, hungry, and armed—tramping through the leafless woods toward the lake house. Their kind would be looking for an isolated place, an easier target than Danby. Perhaps they had seen the corpse pit in town, or the patrols had driven them off. He planned to convince them to look elsewhere. Afterward, he would follow, to see if any of them might be uncontaminated.

He fired a single shot in the air. "That's far enough," he called out. "This place is already taken. Turn around and get out while you still can."

He could hear them whispering together, wondering how many of them there were in the house, how well armed. He thought they were just about ready to turn away when the door of the house slammed open and Paul Krusack came limping out, faster than Kittredge would have credited, followed by Rick, Joe Flores, and even Earl Thomas. All of them visibly unarmed, framed in the pale yellow rectangle of the doorway. Kittredge bared his fangs in vexation and cursed—the idiots had run up without closing the basement door behind them!

Not much light, but it was like setting off a signal flare in the deep gray twilight of the Nightfall woods—here was electricity! Light and the promise of warmth and food and comfort wiped out any intention of retreat in the looters' minds. Kittredge saw a flash from one of their guns, and splinters flew from the wood of the house.

"Shut the damn *door!*" Kittredge shouted out loud in exasperation. The idiots were making themselves a perfect target standing there in the doorway. He began to shoot in the direction of the looters, drawing their fire away from the house, but toward himself. Blood-scent erupted into the air, and he knew he must have hit one of them. Frustrated, he hissed again, cursing the waste. He fired again, hating the gun, this situation he had put himself into.

"Kittredge, for God's sake, at least give us a gun!"

Blaine Kittredge was tempted to laugh out loud. Krusack, begging him for help? But the men in front of the house were pinned down there, defenseless. Kittredge looked distrustfully at the guns he was not using. One of them was Krusack's own. Trust him with it? At least he probably knew how to use the thing. *Better than I can,* Kittredge had to admit.

He started to strip off one of the gun belts—Krusack's weapon and ammunition. He never knew if the movement exposed him or if one of the raiders had simply gotten off a lucky shot.

The impact of the rifle bullet sent him staggering back against a tree.

Now the blood-scent in the air was his own. The heat of pain, spreading slowly, like lava . . . *gut-shot! Not the heart!*

Kittredge's heartbeat began to race as his system went into hyperproduction, each pulse an agony of ravenous need. His hands tightened around the shape of a gun. He stared down at it. *What am I doing with this?* He dropped it and pushed himself off the tree, taking in great gulps of air. There was human blood-scent. Fear-scent. His blood-tinged vision focused on four human shapes staring at him in horror from beside the house. He started toward them—

Then a shot came from the woods, splintering the bark of the tree beside his head, and he spun reflexively in that direction, mindless now in a frenzy of pain and need.

The speed of his attack took the raiders by surprise. Before they could react, he was on them, fangs ripping deep into a throat, blood-rushing ecstasy flooding through him, obliterating all other sensation, all thought. He was entirely in the grip of the frenzy, and it had been so long. . . .

The impact of another bullet barely slowed him now as he seized another human, tore into his flesh—

*No!* The taste of tainted blood shocked him back to reality. He shoved the man away from him, to the ground where he lay looking up with wide eyes filled with horror and recognition, mouth working soundlessly as the bitter, poisoned blood pumped out from the wounds on his throat.

Kittredge staggered backward, looked down at himself. He was drenched in his own blood, did not know how many times he had been shot during the frenzied attack. He had not even felt the later bullets. Dimly, he knew how close he had come to destruction, if one of the bullets had hit his heart. But his senses were fixed on another of the raiders ahead of him in the woods, fleeing in terror of this thing that gunshots could not stop. His prey. It must not escape.

He came back to full consciousness more than an hour later, somewhere in a snow-covered field away from the lake. It was fully night. A man's body lay at his feet. He could not remember just how many there had been. Two, though, had been contaminated—he had still possessed enough control, even in the grip of the frenzy, that he had not taken that blood.

He felt wonderful. Completely healed, slightly sluggish with satiation. To kill again, to drain his victim's blood and feel the heartbeat die, to feel the coursing of rapture through his system—after so long!

Perhaps he did not need his donors anymore. The raiders—except for two of them, the blood had been untainted. He thought of the sentries in Danby patrolling out in the open, and glanced instinctively up at the sky. It was mid-September, almost the equinox. Over three months since Nightfall. If the fallout was coming to an end, perhaps it was finally time to hunt again.

Not to kill, though. Not until he could be sure how many viable humans there would be for the future. The thing he had done today could not be repeated.

Kittredge was not sure if he should feel relieved. He looked back down to the ground, to the corpse. It was strange to realize that this one would not be standing up again, clutching a bandage to his wrist, glaring weakly at him with resentful eyes. He shook his head, imagining Rick Archer lying there lifeless in the snow. The thought was strangely disturbing. He did not want to see Rick dead. Or Danny.

Suddenly he recalled, dreamlike, the red-tinged image of four humans crouched down next to the lake house, and he realized he did not know how many he had killed, or who they were, only that their blood had been untainted. Was it possible that in the frenzy he had killed one of his own donors? Rick had been out there!

Alarmed, he started to hurry through the snow back to the house. In the woods he encountered two more bodies, strangers. None of them contaminated. *Waste,* he thought, and wondered if the tainted ones were still alive somewhere.

The house looked different, somehow. He rubbed a hand over the scarred wood near the door. There were no bodies, no bloodstains.

He went inside. Rick came running up from the basement, and he inhaled sharply at the sight of Kittredge. "We all thought . . . ," he stammered. "We *saw* you . . ."

"It takes more than a bullet hole to stop me," Kittredge told him, not sorry to have the humans think him invulnerable. "What's going on around

182

here?"

"Krusack . . . left. He took a couple of guns and most of the drugs with him."

*Krusack!* For a moment, Kittredge almost ran out the door after him. Then he stopped himself. He had had enough hunting for one day. Enough killing. And Krusack thought he had been killed. Let him go back to Green Springs, then. Perhaps, one day, he would find him there. Paul Krusack, he thought, would survive until then.

Rick said, "Lorraine was pissed."

Kittredge frowned, confused for an instant. Then, "She wanted him to take her along?"

Rick nodded.

Kittredge could hardly blame Krusack. "What about the others?"

Rick shook his head. "Thomas is gone. And Joe Flores said it must be safe to be outside by now, so they left, too."

"He may be right."

"What do you mean?"

Just then they heard a woman's voice calling up from the basement. "Rick, is that you? Who's up there?"

"He's . . . he's back."

The rapid sound of footsteps on the stairs. Lorraine Archer burst into the room and stopped suddenly, a hand going to her mouth as she stifled a gasp of horror and disgust.

Kittredge knew how he must look, filthy, covered with drying blood, his own and the humans'. But he did not care anymore if the sight of him repelled her. She was not Eleanora.

*"Holy shit!"* Danny had followed Lorraine up the stairs and was staring at Kittredge. "They said you

were dead!" he breathed in awe.

*Oh, were you sorry, Danny?* Kittredge did not voice that question aloud. Why should they regret being free of him at last?

"They're gone!" Lorraine started to say. "They took everything with them. That farmer—"

"He's leaving, too," Rick said suddenly. "Aren't you?"

Kittredge nodded. He saw relief and consternation in Lorraine's face, confused. "But . . . what about *us?*"

He shrugged. "You're on your own. It should be safe to go outside to look for food now."

"So the deal's off?" Rick demanded. "You just go, and leave us here alone?"

Kittredge was amused. Suddenly he hadn't been keeping them prisoner. Now he was abandoning them!

"That's right," he said. "I kept my side of the bargain. You're all still alive, aren't you?"

"So—what'd you come back for, then?" Rick asked bitterly.

*To see if I'd killed you by mistake!* Kittredge almost snapped. But, why else had he, then? He didn't need them anymore. "I have some things here I wanted to pick up before I left, clean clothes, a gun."

"You can't just walk out on us!" Lorraine shrilled.

Kittredge ignored her and started to go to the garage where he still kept his things. After a moment, Rick followed him there.

"Just . . . what are we going to do?" he asked quietly.

Irritably, Kittredge turned on him and fought

184

down an impulse to bare his fangs. This was unreasonable. All these weeks, he had kept them alive, fed them, sheltered them, *worked* for them, taking all the risks. . . .

Now it was going to be up to them. "Survive," he told Rick. "Any way you can."

"Like *them?*" Rick turned his head toward the bodies of the raiders still lying in the woods. "Or the way they did in Danby, locking everyone else out?"

*Or like you.* Kittredge heard, unspoken, in Rick's voice. "Any way," he repeated, "if you want to live."

"Do any of you ever ask yourself if you *deserve* to live? Is it worth it—what you have to do?"

Kittredge caught himself staring back into the long dark years of his existence. Perhaps, in life, he could have asked himself that question. But he was not alive any more, and not human. *Don't mistake me,* he wanted to warn Rick.

"Just what is it you want me to do?" he asked instead.

"I don't know. I was thinking, if we had something they needed, gasoline, food, or drugs— enough of that, and someplace like Green Springs might let us in. If you could . . ."

Kittredge turned away angrily. Did they have any idea what kind of risk he ran every time he went into Danby? No, of course they didn't, he answered himself. He had superhuman powers, he was immortal, invulnerable. They had just seen him blown apart with a shotgun and stand up from it. No, they didn't think he was human.

And Rick was right. It was probably the only chance for them to survive. He thought of a chessboard and swore silently to himself in exasperation. *All right, one more time.*

Kittredge turned away to take off the clothes he had ruined. He called back to Rick, "Did Krusack take all of the guns?"

"I don't know."

"Well, you'd better go out there in the woods and try to find the ones the raiders dropped before it gets any darker. Take a flashlight—don't forget ammunition, either. You'll be needing it. And tell Lorraine and Danny to start packing things up. *Goods,* you understand, things people need. Not makeup and clothes."

"Right," Rick muttered, suddenly overwhelmed with orders. "Are we going to go at night?"

"You can go whenever you want. Once this is finished, it's over, do you understand? You're on your own. I can't keep doing this forever."

*I don't know why I'm doing it now.*

When he came out of the garage, looking as respectable as possible under the circumstances, Lorraine was standing outside. She looked at him dubiously. "You're going to get us some supplies?"

"This once. So you can buy yourself into someplace like Green Springs, you and the kids. Oh, and I suppose—"

"Not *her!*"

"God, Lorraine," Rick started to object.

"No," said Kittredge. "She's right." Mindless, incontinent—no one with any sense would agree to waste food on the nameless victim from the farmhouse. "I'll take care of her."

His look told Rick, *don't ask how.*

He had been thinking while he changed his clothes. With his bad leg, Krusack might have used

186

a rifle or maybe a shotgun as a crutch, but he could never have carried much more than the drugs back to Green Springs, all those miles over snow-covered roads. The Archers were not much better off. Julia would be a burden, and he did not think Lorraine or Danny would be able to pack much of a heavy load. If they could load up a car, it would be different.

What they needed, he concluded, was something on the order of a tractor. There were tractors, all kinds of equipment, parked in Danby. The John Deere place. Gas would be no problem—he had been taking gas all along from the tank at the Texaco station to run the generator. In fact, a few drums of gasoline might make the Archers welcome in a place like Green Springs. If they took gas, it would mean that he wouldn't have to break into one of the shelters again, risking recognition.

"You can drive, can't you?" he asked Rick.

"Yeah, sure."

"Do you think you can handle a tractor?"

"I guess so."

"All right, I'll want you to come with me, then. The rest of you be ready to load your things up and get away fast. They'll probably be coming after you."

Rick was nervous, sweating despite the frigid air, by the time the two of them got to Danby. "I can't see a thing! What about the sentries?" he asked as Kittredge led him down the black, deserted highway directly into the middle of town.

"They don't patrol at night. They can't see a thing, either. Not unless we make a light. So

187

don't."

Rick bit his lip, remembering the fiasco back at the lake house when they had come outside.

He followed Kittredge blindly into the cavern of a large garage.

"Here," Kittredge said finally. "This should do."

He took Rick's hand and pulled him up into a tractor cab, pointed out the instruments by touch. "This has lights," he said, "but you can't risk turning them on until it's time to break out. We'll just have to hope it starts then, too. I'm going to be bringing the drums of gasoline over here. So just sit here and don't make any noise until I get them loaded up."

Rick nodded. His heart was racing, and his hands felt shaky and numb. *I could get killed, doing this. Does he remember that?*

Kittredge left him there, not without some misgivings. He had brought his shotgun so he could cover Rick's escape, but the whole plan would go for nothing if the tractor didn't start or if it got stuck in the snow. Maybe, he started to think, this wasn't such a good idea after all. But he couldn't think of a better.

There was a sentry post with a floodlight that covered the front of the Texaco station. Kittredge used his usual approach, through the back, over the fence, where the old oil drums were stacked. He stared at them dubiously. Normally, he filled up a couple of five-gallon cans. It was going to be quite a task, even for his strength, to manhandle a fifty-gallon drum over that fence. Almost as bad as getting the generator down the side of the church. He hoped Rick wouldn't get impatient, waiting, and do something stupid.

The snow around the tank was thoroughly trampled, his own footprints lost among the rest. Gasoline fumes drowned out the other scents. He took hold of the hatch cover and began, slowly, to turn it, trying to make no sound.

The wire was concealed under the lip of the cover. Kittredge did not see it. He barely heard the slight click of the mechanism that ignited the gas. The loosened hatch cover hit the right side of his chest, knocking him down as a bright orange fireball engulfed him. He was burning!

Frantically, Kittredge put up his arms to protect his face as he threw himself into the snow to try to extinguish the flames. His panic was screaming, *Fire!* Next to sunlight, the element most dreaded by his kind. It was searing his flesh, consuming him! Screaming, he writhed in the snow, hoping the humans would at least give him the mercy of a quick end, a gunshot through the heart or even a stake. He knew he would be begging for it soon.

The floodlight was cutting through the night, targeting him there on the ground by the storage tank. Human voices were shouting, soon they would be here.

Then he heard his own name, someone—*Rick! The fool!* He raised himself up on one elbow and tried to wave him away, screaming, *Go! Run!* There was nothing he could do to help Rick now, there were already men running into the street.

Kittredge saw that the flames had finally gone out. It was only the pain that was burning him now. He could move, though it was agony, every motion. Fighting the pain, he staggered to his feet and started to half stumble, half run—*where?* He couldn't climb the fence. He had to. It was the only way out. They were coming from the front, the floodlight—. A shot rang out, a puff of snow exploded where the bullet hit, too close.

He reached the fence, seized the metal links, and cried out in pain—the palms of both hands were blistered and raw. He was trapped. But beyond the fence was the night, the darkness, safety. With fangs biting into his lips, he grabbed hold of the fence again, taking as much of his weight as possible on his feet as he struggled up, to the top, link by link. He swung one leg up, then another, and fell over into the snow.

He was beyond the reach of the floodlight now. He lay in the cold embrace of the snow, gasping in his agony, inhaling the scent of his own scorched flesh. But the humans behind him were still firing blindly, and he cried out again as shotgun pellets tore into one leg.

*"Got* the bastard!" came a voice. Then the beam of a flashlight hit the fence, and Kittredge forced himself to his feet again. He had not escaped them yet.

## 2

Rick Archer was sitting in the dark, waiting at the controls of the machine Kittredge had showed him, sick in his stomach with apprehension. He could not forget—they shoot people here. His father . . .

He swallowed hard and wished he was back at the house. He wasn't immortal like Kittredge, who could see in the dark, who came in and out of here past the sentries every night. Kittredge . . .

He shuddered, remembering. For so long, the word *vampire* had ceased to mean anything to him. Once a week or so, it was more like a hospital procedure than anything else. But now, after what he'd seen outside the house today, those men—God, he didn't know if he'd be able to let him touch him again! It was a good thing it was over—

Rick gasped as the explosion lit up the night. Then he hesitated. Kittredge had said *stay here*. But he would never have made a light out there. Something must have gone wrong!

Then he heard the screaming. *Oh, God! What am I supposed to do?*

Another light flared into life outside, and the screaming—how long had it been going on? The

191

sound was horrible. Something *was* wrong. He had to go see for himself. Rick jumped down from the cab of the tractor and ran toward the light.

It came from a deserted gas station behind a chain-link fence. Small splashes of fire were burning themselves out in the snow. And among them, writhing on the ground, a human figure, and he had never heard a sound like that screaming oh, God, it was Blaine Kittredge!

Rick was shaking the fence, screaming out Kittredge's name—God, he had to get in there! The figure on the ground inside the fence twisted in his direction, and Rick could see his face, blackened, seared.

*Fire,* he thought. Can fire kill him?

Rick turned his head around and saw lights, men running into the street, men with guns, who would shoot him if they found him here, the way they had shot his father. He looked back to Kittredge, who seemed to be trying to get to his knees, but Rick knew there was no way he could get in there to save him. It would be hard enough to save himself now.

He ran from the floodlight, into the dark shadow of the gas station, pressed himself back against the wall as men came running past him. He flinched at the sound of gunshots. If they found him . . .

They *would* find him if he stayed here much longer. They were running around the other side of the fence now, away from him, yelling, "There he goes!" *"Got* the bastard!"

Rick took a breath and dashed from the cover of the gas station, running across the street in the other direction, heading for the dark. House by house, street by street, he made it out of Danby, with every step afraid that a gunshot would tear through his back. This afternoon—he had seen the explosion of blood and flesh as the shotgun blast hit Kittredge in the gut. And had thought, for a moment, that he was dead, that he had been killed after all. But an instant later the vampire was on his feet again, with a look in his eyes that was even worse than that night up in the hall.

And now, to see him burning like that, his eyes staring in the middle of that horrible, charred face . . .

Rick felt tears stinging his own eyes. There was a time when he would have said he'd be glad to see the vampire dying that way. But Kittredge had been trying to help them.

Now, with his back to a roadside billboard, all that lay ahead of him was the wide-open snow, with no cover but an occasional tree to mark where the road was buried. Rick hesitated. He *had* to get back. Kittredge—even if Kittredge had escaped, they couldn't count on his help anymore.

Those screams! He shuddered again, remembering. Could *anything* have lived through that?

He finally started down the road, but before he had gone more than a few dozen steps, there was the roar of engines. Panicking, Rick dropped down onto his face in the snow. Lights were moving, the headlights of a snowmobile—no, two of them! They were after him!

But as Rick held his breath and prayed, the vehicles moved away across the field to his left. Now he could see—they were heading for the woods! He scrambled to his feet and started to run, guided by the lights and the vague dark shape of the woods that he knew ran down to Sugar Lake. Home.

As the distance between himself and the searchers grew, the light disappeared. Rick found himself groping his way through the dark. It had taken less than an hour to reach Danby with Kittredge leading him. Now, he was afraid he was going to be lost, at least until daybreak. By then, he might freeze. They hadn't brought winter clothes with them to the lake house. It was supposed to be summer!

After he thought he must have gone at least a couple of miles, if he hadn't been wandering in circles in the dark, he began to bear left a little, hoping to run into the woods. Eventually, he found himself encountering trees. He felt as much as saw the dark trunks ahead of him, stumbling with his arms held out like a blind man. Somewhere ahead, he knew, must be the house.

He kept groping forward from tree to tree. How long had it been? Three hours? Four? Five? There was no sign of daybreak yet. He still kept his watch on his wrist, but the battery had run out weeks ago.

Then, suddenly, Rick missed his footing and fell forward, arms flailing the air. He tumbled down, snow flying into his face, before he was brought up short, knocking his head against a tree. Tiny lightnings flashed in his head. He got to his knees. Now he knew where he was! On hands and knees, he crawled back up to the top of the snow-filled gully. He'd played here with Danny when they were kids. Dad had built the house where the ground dropped down, so it would look over the lake.

Rick groped his way from tree to tree until the shape of the house somehow materialized out of the blackness. Sobbing with relief, he ran, groped for the door and fell inside, into warmth and light.

Lorraine—God, he was glad to see her!—rushed at him, grabbed him, looking over his shoulder behind him.

"Where is he?"

"Huh?"

"Him! I thought you were bringing a tractor. Where is he?" She pulled back and looked at him. "You look awful! What's the matter? You were gone so long, I was worried—"

Rick gasped, "Kittredge . . . There was an explosion. I don't know if he got away. I don't think he did. I made it back here in the dark."

She backed away, staring at him, stunned. "Then . . ."

"I think he's dead. Anyway, we can't count on him coming back."

"What do we do?" Lorraine noticed the state of his hands and feet and started to help him pull off his shoes. "You're frozen!"

Rick shook his head. *What do we do?* They were alone now, the way they had been before Kittredge came. On their own. The vampire had saved them. He knew that now. Like Kittredge said, *You survive. Any way you can.*

He looked around the living room. Lorraine and Danny had carried out their job. The room was heaped with supplies—no food, it was true, or drugs. Krusack and the others had taken those. But they still had things that were going to be

195

scarce from now on. Things that were supposed to buy them a place in Green Springs—if they could get there.

Could they still do it? Without Kittredge? On their own?

There was something else. He told Lorraine, "We're going to have to get out of here. They'll be searching."

"For him?"

"I don't know. Maybe for me. I might have been spotted. But we've got this stuff! What happens if they find it here?"

She bit one of her nails. "Green Springs?"

"We'd have to walk."

Their looks at each other were dubious. They had no chance getting into a shelter at a place like Green Springs if they showed up empty handed, like Joe and Connie had. But they could never carry all this stuff, which was why the rest of them had left it here. And there was Julie. Someone would have to carry her.

But if they stayed, even if the searchers from Danby never came here, there was still no food. And those raiders this afternoon, what if more like them showed up? Rick shook his head again. It all kept going around in a circle and coming back to the same place.

He looked at Lorraine. She was standing up, looking at the piles they had made. "We could *pull* this stuff, on a sled," she said. "Through the snow. We might even be able to take it all that way."

"A sled?"

"The doors. We take the doors off their hinges. We've got rope. We could put the stuff on the doors and pull them along after us."

It might work. Rick said slowly, "Three of them—one for you, me, Danny. We could tie all the stuff down with blankets, like a tarp. What about Julie?"

"She could ride. One of us could pull her with the rest of the things."

Rick nodded, stood up. "We wear everything we've got. I almost froze out there. We'll have to wrap up our feet some way. And our hands."

"I'll go wake up the kids."

"What time is it? We should leave as soon as it gets light enough to see. I almost fell into the lake on the way back, it's so dark out there now. . . .

"Oh, wait! Shit!"

"What?"

"What about, you know—her?"

Lorraine's face went hard. "We can't drag her all that way."

"God, Lorraine, she'll *die* if we leave her here!"

"She'd be better off if she was," Lorraine insisted. "We need the space on the sleds. Besides, didn't *he* say he'd take care of her?"

"He's probably dead by now!"

"You said you didn't know. Maybe he got away. Maybe he'll be coming back for her."

"Maybe," he said, turning his head away, knowing he didn't believe the excuse. But they had to be hard now, they had to think of what it would take to survive.

He remembered one more thing. "Where'd you put the guns?"

"Here. Why? Do you think they might follow us from the town?"

That had been Kittredge's warning. "Maybe. Or we may run into some other kind of trouble."

There was more than one kind of reception they might get in Green Springs. Maybe Krusack was right, and the people there were not as bad as in Danby. But from now on, Rick wasn't going to take any more chances than he had to.

Grimly, he picked up a rifle that he had found in the woods next to a corpse with its throat slashed open. "I'd better figure out how to use this thing."

# 3

Kittredge had been a fugitive before. As always, his greatest advantage was the dark that made it impossible for the humans to track him. And this time he would not be forced to go to ground at daybreak. Still, if it was light enough for them to see, he was leaving visible tracks in the snow—bloodstained tracks.

He paused in his flight to rip away a charred fragment of his shirt with his teeth and tie it clumsily around his shot-torn leg to halt the bleeding. It would be slow to heal unless he could kill again tonight. Already, his system was half-depleted. Limping, he started to run again across the frozen fields outside the town, heading for the cover of the woods.

The pain of his burns was still a torment. The one time, so long ago, when the sunlight had struck him was nothing to this. He had heard of human horror-weapons, phosphorus and napalm, that were said to burn inextinguishably through flesh until it was devoured. That was how he burned. He had constantly to force himself to keep moving, to resist the urge to throw himself back down into the cooling snow.

At least the burns were mainly on his upper body, where his jacket had burst into flames, worst of all on his hands and arms. Much of his hair had been singed off, and his face . . . No, he would not think of his face. The important thing was that his legs were unhurt, except for the shotgun wound. He could still run. The woods were just ahead.

He slipped into memory. It had been in the heat of summer, an all-too-short summer night with daybreak no more than an hour away. He was running, not through the snow and the uneven frozen furrows of a cornfield, but the slippery muck of a marshy creek. He could hear them coming behind him, the splashing of the horses' hooves though the water, the deep-throated baying of the hounds—vicious, slave-catcher hounds trained to rip human leg muscles, to hamstring their prey. Their speed matched his own, they had his scent.

Desperate, with the strength of a fresh kill running through him, he had turned on the dogs, seized one of them, grasping upper and lower jaws, the sharp white teeth cutting into his fingers as he ripped the beast's head apart and hurled the body at the rest of the pack. He had only barely escaped that time, had spent the day buried in the swamp mud. But he *had* escaped.

Only then he had not been burned. Limping, he reached the first trees and gave in to the impulse to kneel down and plunge his hands into the snow. The relief was illusory. There would be constant pain, he knew, until the slow healing process had completed its work. He lifted up a hand and turned it, palm to back. The skin was burned through, the flesh charred, red scored, and raw from the chain links of the fence. He tried to flex it, and the pain made him gasp aloud. But he was thinking in terms of survival once again, already ashamed of the moment's impulse, while he was burning, to beg the humans for a stake through his heart. He could endure this, he would eventually heal.

Then the growl of engines broke the night's silence. Kittredge got painfully back up to his feet. The flare of headlights soon appeared from the direction of the town as two snowmobiles raced onto the frozen field that lay between Danby and the woods.

In a panic, Kittredge flung himself back behind the closest tree. The snowmobiles were as fast over the snow as the horses, as the dogs — wounded as he was, they could run him down.

In the open, Kittredge reminded himself. Here in the woods, they would have to go more slowly. He retreated carefully into the shadows, taking care not to be spotted by the damnable headlights. He could do nothing about the tracks he was leaving through the snow, but as long as they had to stop to track him, he could keep ahead.

The ground was starting to drop away sharply now, down to the creek that led to Sugar Lake, and Kittredge began to move more quickly, no need for stealth now that he was out of the reach of the lights. The ravine would slow the machines even more. He stumbled a few times and once slipped headlong into the snow because his hands were useless to break the fall. He struggled up again and kept going.

The creek was frozen. He limped across the ice and began to struggle up the other side of the bank; but it would be even harder for the snowmobiles. The humans might be able to track him on foot if it were day, but they needed the headlights now to find him.

Kittredge paused, gasping from the exertion, halfway up. Downstream, the lake. He did not want to lead them that way, did not want them to find the lake house with everything that he had stolen. And the Archers—but they were going to have to look out for themselves from now on. He wondered if Rick had gotten away, gotten back to the house, then shook his head. They were on their own now.

He began to head upstream, leading any pursuit away from the lake. Later, he would be able to make his way back.

He could still hear the engines coming closer through the woods on the other side of the creek. He hid, motionless, behind a tree as the headlight beams stabbed down the slope opposite, illuminating the frozen creekbed. He held his breath instinctively, hoping they could not make out his footprints crossing the ice. The lights could not reach up the bank to where he was concealed. From where they were, he was effectively invisible.

The engines diminished to an idle as one figure stepped out, gun cradled under his arm, and started to pace forward the length of the headlight beam, searching the snow for tracks.

After a moment, one of the others called out to him, "Come on, Gene, give it up! The bastard's got away!"

*Gene! Gene Solokov!* Kittredge felt a shiver of apprehension as he realized who was pursuing him. Of course it would be Solokov.

"It was *him,* dammit," the man called back. "I *know* it was him. And the bastard was shot, too! He couldn't have gotten away!"

"Maybe he's dead by now, then. Maybe we missed him in the snow. Nobody could have gotten this far."

"Besides," came a different voice, "I don't see how you could have recognized him, all burned up."

"It was *him,*" Solokov insisted. He stood there, staring into the darkness across the creek, and Kittredge could have sworn for an instant that their eyes met. But Solokov turned back to the snowmobile.

Kittredge heard him, faintly, say, "Once it's light . . . tracks . . ."

Then the machines turned around and began to climb back up the slope the way they had come.

Kittredge watched them disappear into the darkness, exhaling in relief. But Solokov was going to be back. He was sure of it. Back to track him down once he could see to make out the trail. The man had held his gun like a hunter. Suddenly Kittredge felt a touch of panic. He was certain there were no hunting dogs left alive in Danby. But he had not known about the snowmobiles, he reminded himself.

Carefully, he began to make his way back down the slope, holding his hands to his chest to keep them from further injury. It was not easy. Several times more he slipped, branches hit his burned, unprotected skin. It was even harder climbing back up the bank on the other side. But finally he came to where Solokov had stood.

He mingled his own footprints with his pursuers'. Then he started to follow the snowmobile tracks back up toward the town, doubling back once or twice, circling around to his original trail, doing whatever he could to confuse the situation. He had at least four hours until the light, he calculated. And here in the woods, it was more than possible that the humans would not, after all, be able to see his trail well enough to follow it.

He tracked back from the woods to the edge of town, where he again found human footprints to add his own to, until he was certain that they would never be able to pick them out. His boots, once the property of a farmer, made tracks indistinguishable from the rest, though smaller than the average. He was cautious, keeping well into the darkness, stopping every few feet to check for human scent.

Finally, while it was still fully night, he limped wearily through the back streets of the town, crossing the highway, and left Danby going north, away from the lake. He badly wanted rest, but he feared that the pain of his burns would not allow it to him. He needed clothes, too, a new shirt and jacket to replace the ones that had been burned away, and gloves, if possible, to protect his hands. His face . . .

Suddenly he stopped, and his hands, heedless of the hurt, flew to his face. How much of it was burned? How badly would it be scarred? He almost howled aloud, knowing he would never be able to see. To be scarred, to be hideous . . .

He wanted to weep with frustration and pain, but that relief was denied him, too. At least, he realized, his eyes had been spared. He could be thankful that the fire had not blinded him. He touched his face again, carefully. The forehead seemed the worst. His nose had not been burned away. Perhaps it was not too bad, after all.

*Please,* he prayed, finding no irony that a being of his kind could pray. That first day of this existence, hiding below the floor of the church where he had been buried, had given him hope that he was not damned. That the alterations in him were merely physical, not touching his soul. If he had ever had a soul. Now, after so many years, his lifetime habits of prayer were nearly lost, but there were times when he still could hope. He did not know what for, except that at some point his existence must end. There were times when he prayed for that.

But now, he thought, he would sell his soul if it would buy him relief from the pain—if he only had one to sell.

He went on, putting distance between himself and Danby, until he finally found a barn where he could lie down in the frozen straw. It was harsh on his blistered skin, and he longed for the soft leather seats of the Archers' station wagon, but he was in no condition to confront any looters who might come into an empty house. As he had feared, rest would not come, and his heartbeat was a metronome that marked every second with a stroke of pain.

The dim light passed slowly across the sky as he

lay there, suffering, waiting for dark to come again. And with the dark, as he had known it would, came true hunger.

He could not hunt, not with his hands this way. His donors were gone from the lake house. At least, if they had any sense at all, they would be gone. He could imagine what would have happened if Solokov, searching for him, had discovered where the stolen supplies had gone. But there was one item, at least, that Lorraine Archer would not have taken with her.

Kittredge felt sudden, fierce hope. *Be there!* he prayed again as he got stiffly to his feet. He took a direct route to the lake house, cutting past the outskirts of Danby in the dark, hunger driving him with an urgency beyond pain. In the rapture of the kill, he knew, he would feel nothing, and he looked forward with pitiful eagerness for that momentary relief.

The house was empty, cold, and dark. He could see no tracks of snowmobiles or dogs, but there were marks as if something had been dragged through the snow. Then the Archers must have gone. They did have some sense, after all.

With as much caution as hunger would allow him, he went inside and down to the basement. He stopped, relief breaking through his anxiety. She was still there in her corner of the laundry room, fouled with her own wastes, whimpering. It must have been well over thirty-six hours since she had been fed or even given water. But her suffering would be over soon.

He knelt next to her, ignoring the filth that dampened the knees of his pants, and brought his mouth to her throat. The dark savor of madness made his senses reel with pleasure, and for a few moments it was enough to obliterate the pain. He drained her as slowly as he could make himself, prolonging it. She slipped away quietly, still so lost in her private mental hell that she could not even sense her own approaching death. The horror faded, the heartbeat faltered and stilled.

Kittredge let her go, looked down for a moment at the emaciated body on the floor, and felt no real regret. The brief time when he had come to know humans again was gone.

He stood up, finding his leg was sound again. He would have to be moving on. It was too dangerous for him to stay here, even in the garage. Eventually, Solokov would find this place.

He took one final look around the basement where he had spent so much time. The Archers had left quite a few things behind. He paused at the table. The chess set was there, abandoned. So they were starting to learn what was essential and what was not. Perhaps they might survive, after all.

Kittredge slid the lid of the box into place with his fingertips. Then, for the last time, he went up the stairs into the night.

# 4

This was the last house he was going to check. Gene Solokov looked back as Jack Rodebaugh stamped his boots in the snow and cupped his hands over his mouth for a moment, breath hanging in the chill air. Jack was a good man. He couldn't afford to bring any more men out on this—people were starting to talk. Even Vonnie didn't seem to understand how important it was to catch this bastard.

There was Earl Thomas's crazy story—not that anyone believed him. How *could* you believe him? Except, you had to admit, Thomas must have been hiding out *someplace* all this time, and he sure as hell hadn't lost any weight. Solokov ground his teeth together and shifted the weight of his gun as he tramped on through the woods, Rodebaugh following. If there was any truth to the story at all, he'd promised to let the damn hoarder come back into the shelter. *Vampires,* for God's sake!

But Solokov could still remember meeting those eyes in the school basement. And seeing them again two nights ago, those same eyes, reflecting the flames . . .

And the screams—inhuman, almost. A hard

thing, to see a man burning like that. How he had managed to escape, burned and shot . . .

It was the bastard's own fault, though, stealing their gas. The damn looters wouldn't be getting any more of it. Solokov had moved the gasoline they had left into storage in the garage. The booby trap had been an afterthought. But it had worked, that was for sure.

He stopped again in front of the big cedar-and-glass house overlooking the lake. His conscience was less easy when he thought of the man who had owned it. But, dammit, it was Archer's own fault, what happened to him, Solokov insisted to himself. Too bad, of course, about his wife and kids, left alone out here to starve. Maybe he should have done something about them, after all. But Thomas said they were still alive. Maybe, if they were still here—

"Gene." Jack Rodebaugh nudged him, pointed. Over in the trees was a familiar-shaped mound of snow. They went up to it, brushed the snow away. Neither of them recognized the man, his skin pallid in death. There were wounds on his throat. He had been quite young. "Raider," said Solokov flatly. He glanced over at the house, saw the door standing open. He flipped the safety off his gun.

"I don't know, Gene. This looks funny," Jack whispered.

"Be careful," Solokov agreed. He looked again at the man's throat, his face. There was something strange about the body, that he couldn't quite put his finger on. It almost made you think Earl Thomas wasn't so crazy, after all.

Their footsteps rang on the bare wood floor of

the front hall, their breath hung in the air. The place looked just about like any deserted house, ransacked, half-empty. The door to the basement was open, too, but they could both see where it had been sealed. Switching on their flashlights, they went down, slowly, a single step at a time.

It was deserted. But walking around, it was evident that the place had once been used as a shelter. Mattresses on the floor, a pile of empty, flattened cans in a corner—*Danby's* cans!

"Gene, look here!"

Solokov came over. It was the generator. The one from the church, he was sure of it.

"Well, this must be it, all right."

"It's him?"

Solokov nodded. "Got to be." The trouble was, this place was cold, obviously deserted. The generator hadn't been running. What had happened to the Archer family, then? The other people Thomas had said were down here? And *him,* the one Solokov wanted? Thomas had given him a name— Blaine Kittredge. Had said things about him . . . The dead raider in the woods, the wounds on his throat—was that his doing? Were there more of them?

Curious, he opened a door to what looked like an empty wine cellar. Another door—the stink made him gag. Then his flashlight picked up the body on the floor. There were dark marks on her throat, small, deep punctures.

"Jesus!" Jack swore, seeing the dead girl's condition.

Solokov turned his head around nervously. He felt an unaccustomed chill in his gut—true fear.

Was this the lawyer's wife? One of his kids? He was seeing the evidence of something—he had never before used the word—*evil*.

*Those eyes.* What Thomas had said . . .

"Like that guy outside," said Jack.

"Yeah."

"Must be some kind of psycho."

"Yeah." Solokov nodded. Jack had heard Thomas's story, too. For a minute there, he had almost been ready to believe . . .

His voice went brisk. "It's starting to get dark outside. We can send someone back out here to get the generator tomorrow." After a pause, "I guess we've got to let Thomas back in."

They started back through the twilit woods. "There could be more bodies out here somewhere," Rodebaugh said nervously, looking around. "Too dark to tell."

*Too dark to see what's right behind you,* thought Blaine Kittredge as he followed them silently through the trees. Solokov had come and gone, but he knew he could never feel safe here again. Too many humans knew he had been here, humans who wanted to destroy him. Solokov, Krusack, maybe some of the others.

It was ironic. He had for so long anticipated this time, when the humans of Danby would come out into the open for him to hunt. But instead, he was their quarry. The human scent of them made a spasm of hunger throb through his system, but with his hands so badly burned, he knew he was helpless. There was no way he could risk taking on

211

two armed men, even from behind. Bitterly now, he regretted not saving the girl for one more night. But no, they would have found her down there just now, even if he had let her live.

He stifled a cry of enraged pain, holding onto the frayed remnants of his control. Why was he still waiting around this house when he knew it was no longer safe? They were gone. They were not coming back. He had let them go. He didn't need them anymore, he reminded himself bitterly.

Briefly, in his desperation, he considered the notion of following them to Green Springs, finding Rick there, and asking him—just one more time. But he did not even know if Rick was still alive. More likely, it was Paul Krusack he would find in Green Springs—Paul Krusack and a sharpened stake.

Kittredge had never before realized how much he depended on his hands. It had been instinct, not good judgment, that made him try to shield his face from the flames. Hunger pulsed through his system. Soon its demands would become urgent, and he did not know how he would satisfy them. An easy victim, one who was alone and could not fight back. But where could he go to find one? Danby? Solokov and his partner were well out of sight by now. He could still hear them, though.

No! The voices were not the same! Suddenly alert, Kittredge strained to catch the scent. Silently, he crept toward the source.

"Come on, Leon, they're gone!" came a hoarse whisper.

"No, man, I can't make it." The second voice was slurred, almost inaudible.

"Sure you can make it! The house is just a few yards down the road. It's empty. That was them we saw yesterday, leaving the place."

Kittredge heard a moan, then saw two figures emerge from behind a fallen tree, one supporting the other, dragging a gun behind him. Hunger surged as he realized that these two were in no condition to resist him.

The weaker human slipped to his knees, dragging the other down with him. The gun dropped into the snow. This was his chance! Kittredge was on them, knocking down the stronger one from behind, kicking the gun away. He fell onto the man to pin him with his body, fangs ready to plunge into his throat—

He twisted away at the last moment, as the scent reached him and he caught the taint of poisoned blood. At the same time, he saw the unhealed wounds on the man's throat and hissed a curse of enraged frustration. *Not again!* He struggled to his feet, over to the other one, but the taint was even stronger. They were the raiders who had attacked the lake house—the contaminated survivors.

And they knew him, too. Kittredge could see the recognition in the first man's eyes as he lay on his back, arms flung up across his throat, mouth open, exhaling a horror almost as dark as madness. Bloodlust responded to the horror-scent, exacerbating Kittredge's frustration. He wanted to hurt them somehow, to make them share his pain.

Then the other one moaned, rolled onto his side. Bloodlust ebbed as Kittredge realized that this one had gone past fear, almost past pain. He stepped closer, felt the fever-heat.

213

His rage died. What was the use? They were all three of them hungry, wounded beings. He looked back to the stronger man, who seemed, somehow, familiar. "Oh, go on into the house," he said. "It's safe now. But they'll be back tomorrow, once it's light."

Kittredge walked away, leaving them to make their way to the house if they could. The weak one would not live out the night. But his own survival was in doubt if he could not take a healthy victim, somewhere.

# 5

Greg Reichler lay in the snow for a long time, shaking. He had wanted to scream, but it was like there was something stuck in his throat, choking him. His throat—he cautiously touched the wounds—they were there, it had really happened, and it had been real just now, bending over him. He whimpered with the memory of fangs tearing into his throat, the cold touch of death. And that other memory, older, even more terrifying: eyes glowing in the darkness of the Wallace farmhouse, those *same* eyes.

He raised himself on an elbow and cried aloud, *"Wait!"* He had to know. His Dad was dead, and Matt Duchon. *Why not me?*

He heard a sound and crawled over to where Leon Pike was curled on his side in the snow, shivering, moaning with fever. Leon hadn't been killed, either. Both of them spared, both times. But not Matt. Why?

It had looked like a man, bending over him. The face, horrible, like something burned. Had it been like that two days ago? Reichler tried to remember, but the vision of eyes filled his memory. *Those* were the same. What *was* he? Reichler shuddered again. There couldn't be two of them, whatever he was.

He looked up toward the house, by now only a darker shape in the growing night. The light was almost gone. He began to pull on Leon's arm, saying, "Come on, Leon. Come on, we're almost there. You gotta get *up*, man."

The black kid, by now even skinnier than ever, was sick. Maybe even dying. Only the two of them left of the gang. Reichler hadn't seen what had happened to Travis Butler, but at least two other guys were killed. One of them Matt Duchon.

He was lost without Butler, he and Leon both. They should never have come back here to this place, where *he* had been waiting for them again. *I saw him kill Matt. I couldn't stop him. I shot him, I hit him, I know I did, but he just kept coming, coming at me!*

Reichler shuddered again, the memory out of control now. The man's shape rushing at him, bloodstained and horrible, those eyes glowing and the fangs, oh, God, the fangs ripping him open, the cold breath. It was going to kill him, he was already half-dead with fear. Then, in the next second, he was on the ground, still alive.

Later he had found Leon, cut up on the throat but still alive, just the same way he was. They were both so weak after what happened that they couldn't get very far. They almost froze that first night, when there was some big commotion in the town—an explosion, guns firing. And then men searching all over the place the next day, so they had to stay put where they were, hiding, while

Leon got more and more fevered, too sick to move on.

This was the closest place there was. He couldn't drag Leon any farther, and he wasn't in much better shape himself. Another night like the last two, and neither of them would make it. He could remember this place, the light shining out the door, the heat almost visible in the air. And he'd seen those people leaving, dragging some kind of sleds. The house was empty. It was their only chance.

At last they were at the door, and he dragged Leon inside. He shoved a couch up close to the fireplace and lifted him onto it, then started to break up some of the tables for firewood. He hardly cared anymore if anybody spotted the smoke. Besides, hadn't . . . *he* said the place would be safe till morning?

Once the fire was going, he went through the house searching out blankets. The bedrooms were empty, but there were some downstairs where it looked like there had been a shelter. He brought them up and wrapped one around Leon, who was trying to talk now.

"I *saw* it," he whispered in a cracked voice. "Out there."

"Yeah, I saw it, too," Reichler reassured him. "You're not crazy. But it's not coming back, all right? You stay here. I'm going to go try to find something we can eat."

There was nothing in either the kitchen or the basement, where the people had been. But there was a pile of cans and stuff. He went through the trash, licking out the empty cans with his tongue and fingers. There was a bad-smelling corpse in the

217

laundry room. One of the guys had said something once, that there were people who got so hungry . . .

He took a closer look at the body. It had been a girl. Then he saw the throat. *He* had been here, all right. It must have been why all those other people had cleared out. His stomach heaved. He couldn't do it. Not with that stink.

He managed to scrape a little more from the garbage onto the flattened side of one can and brought it upstairs to Leon. Then he wrapped himself up in the blanket next to him and fell asleep.


He woke, shivering. The fire was out, but it was light enough that he could make out the room where they were sleeping. Daytime. Time to get out of here. Those guys from the town were supposed to be coming back.

"Hey." He reached over to shake Leon awake, and he knew, the minute he touched his shoulder. The body was already cold, starting to get stiff.

"Oh, God, no," he moaned. First Jake dead, then Matt, now Leon. He was struck then by a thought so horrible that his heart seemed to freeze. He was so scared he couldn't breathe. He turned the dead kid's head with shaking hands, then exhaled in relief. There were no fresh wounds on Leon's throat. *He* hadn't come back under cover of the night and killed him while they both slept.

He started to pull the blanket out from under the body, working numbly. No use leaving anything behind that he might need later on. The nights were going to be colder now, alone.

218

Alone. There was no way a man could survive these days alone. And he had to get out of here now. The men from town were coming back. They'd be able to smell the smoke from the fireplace.

Reichler loaded up his few things, took his gun, and went out into the frozen dead woods. The lake was on one side of him, that damn town behind him. No way he was going back there.

Realistically, he knew that his only chance to stay alive was if he could find some other gang to join up with. There was just the slightest hope that Travis Butler had managed to survive that other night. If he could just find Butler. His life depended on it.

## 6

It was nearly dawn by the time Blaine Kittredge managed to allay his hunger that night. His victim was one of another band of starving looters, four of them in an abandoned house. They had taken no precautions against attack, doubtless, Kittredge assumed, because they had so little left to lose. Except their lives.

By the time he had found the house and had found a way inside, his hunger was a deep compelling need that almost overwhelmed the pain of his burns. The humans slept, unaware of his presence. He crept silently into the living room, where they were gathered around the glowing fireplace, their only source of warmth. The one who lay a little apart—Kittredge drew closer, caught the scent. He was wrenched by a hard spasm of hunger. Uncontaminated!

He held himself back, assessing the situation in the room. This would not be easy, to take one without waking the others. Perversely, the looters' carelessness had made it more difficult. A single, isolated sentry would have been an easier victim than these heedless, clustered sleepers.

He looked down at the one he had chosen. The

man's face was gaunt. Hunger was a universal condition, Kittredge thought dispassionately. But sympathy for his victims was a weakness he must forgo. He had spent too long in that unnatural existence at the lake house.

He flexed his hands, measuring the pain. Would he be able to hold a man down, to choke him into silence? He would struggle. The others would wake, would find him there, and he would be lucky if he managed to escape. The risk was too great. But the hunger was a compulsion he could not resist. Kittredge cursed his nature, that it drove him this way.

The man stirred, mumbled something in his sleep. An idea came, a slight chance. Cautiously, he nudged the sleeper, once, again. The human stirred again and rolled over. Then he sank back into sleep. Next to him, another man stirred, too, and half opened his eyes. Kittredge went still, a shadow in the room, no more. But the second one was getting groggily to his feet and starting to go toward the door of the room. In sudden hope, Kittredge realized his prodding had worked on an unintended subject.

He glanced back at his first-chosen victim reluctantly, then followed the other out to the hall where he was starting sleepily to relieve himself. *If this one is contaminated . . .*

But the scent was clean, and he crept up close behind the man, grabbing him awkwardly in a chokehold with his forearms, bearing him down to the floor and pinning him there with the length of his whole body. He was in agony as hands clawed at the painful blistered skins of his arms, and he fought desperately to keep his victim quiet while

221

his fangs went for the throat-bite.

The man was thrashing, and Kittredge missed the artery, but the blood flow was no less than with the wrist-bite. He clung to his victim, who quieted as terror paralyzed his will, as his blood was drained away. Kittredge felt the pangs of hunger begin to diminish. Bloodlust, sharp and frenzied, pulsed with the heartbeat, as it faltered. . . .

Kittredge jerked his head back, gasping. He looked down at the man, at the rise and fall of his breathing. Even at the throat, now, he was capable of stopping. He had learned that much control. Twice already tonight potential victims had been contaminated. These healthy ones were too rare. He *had* to try to preserve them.

Carefully, he listened. The others were all still asleep. His victim moaned, coughed weakly. Alive. Hunger satisfied, his victim preserved against another night's need, Kittredge backed away and passed into the night.

Dawn was already at the horizon, and he thought he might be able to rest during the day. He felt weary but satisfied, at the end of an ordeal. He would heal now, he thought. He would survive, as one of his kind was intended to exist. That time in the lake house was over. He would have to endure no more of the heat and noise of the quarrelsome humans. No more of the endless work required to keep them alive.

It was the scent, hours later, that roused him. The odor of roasting meat, something almost forgotten in the Nightfall world where humans considered themselves lucky to exist on canned peas. Where would the looters get meat?

There was only one, obvious answer. By the time

222

he reached the house, the origin of the scent was unmistakable. There was no other like it. The carcass was hung up on the back porch, where the cold would keep the rest of it from going bad. Whoever butchered it had done a workmanlike job. The right hindquarter was missing. And the head. But Kittredge knew his own victim.

His first frustrated reaction was to curse the waste. He had left that man *alive*, to come back to another time. But reason objected that blood loss must have killed his victim after he had gone. He had drawn back too late. The waste had been his own. Grimly, he resolved that it would not happen again. But certainly he could not blame the humans for what they had done to survive. This expediency was less of a waste, certainly, than leaving the flesh to rot.

He thought of Rick Archer, who would doubtless insist that he would starve before he would ever come to the point of consuming human flesh. Kittredge wondered, how many of the looters might at one time have said the same? He looked through the window and caught a glimpse of the man he had chosen first last night, the jaws of his lean face working as he chewed the meat. There was still a great deal of it left. The looters would be healthier now that they had sufficient protein food. *I'll be back,* Kittredge promised them silently.

Not tonight, perhaps. They would be alert for a repetition of the attack. But soon. They were his, now.


The raiders, Kittredge discovered over the next few weeks, were predators much like himself, except that they operated most effectively in bands, while his kind was solitary by nature. The difference between wolves and leopards, he thought. But it was no longer easy for any hunter to discover lone and defenseless victims. It was a choice that many survivors had been forced by hunger to make—either join the raiders or fall to them. The earlier marauders had already died out. Increasingly, the raiders Kittredge encountered had spent the fallout months in shelters, emerging to find no other way to survive. Their blood, for the most part, was untainted.

His burns healed, his hands most slowly. He would stare at them sometimes, at the ugliness of the scar tissue. He tried not to wonder what his face looked like. But in his present company, scars were a commonplace.

"You been in a fire?" the raider leader asked.

Kittredge kept his hand from going to his forehead. He was nervous under this close a scrutiny, even though the room was dark. In the raider's eyes, he could virtually read the real questions working in the man's mind—*What things have you done? How far are you willing to go? Are you going to cause trouble around here, challenge my authority? Does it bother you that I'm black and most of the rest of you are white?*

Mutual suspicion was the rule when a stranger was trying to join a band. A man with a gun could be an asset to a gang, but he could also end up with his throat slit. Or worse, if things were hungry enough. They often were.

Kittredge nodded shortly, warily. "Yeah. In Danby," he replied. "It was some kind of gasoline bomb."

"Danby. Good place to stay clear of," the raider commented, drawing out the stranger.

Kittredge agreed. "Too much firepower over there. They've got this pit full of bodies." It was common knowledge among the raiders that Gene Solokov had made Danby into a stronghold that the most cautious gangs avoided. "I don't think the other guy I went in there with ever made it back out," he went on, skirting close to the truth. "He was just a kid, on his own. He told me how they shot his father over there. Both of them are probably in that pit by now."

"Bastards," the raider said offhandedly. Such stories, also, were commonplace. "Well, I guess you can throw your things over there. My name's Travis Butler."

There were over a dozen men already in the house, though it was hard to tell just how many, since they kept coming and going out of the room. Kittredge had caught a faint scent of contamination, but he had not yet been able to isolate which humans were tainted and which were potential victims.

Suddenly he turned his head away from the door to hide his face, wishing the room were a lot darker. The man coming inside now was one he recognized—one of the raiders he had met at the lake house, one of the two contaminated ones. He remembered the man staring up at him, the horrified recognition in his eyes. This one knew him, knew what he was!

Kittredge nervously measured his distance to each of the possible exits from the room. He could not risk staying here. If the raider had not recognized him already, he would, soon.

The man had just glanced back in his direction. A sharp wave of fear-scent increased Kittredge's uneasiness. *Oh, yes—he knows!* Kittredge cursed his earlier impulse to leave this one alive, tainted, useless, familiar with his face. His hands clenched. The terror-scent flooding the house was so strong now that he almost felt the humans must sense it. But it was already near evening, growing darker. Bloodlust and hunger were already awake, at war with the need to get out of this situation before it was too late.

But then Butler came over to him again, and Kittredge learned why the other men had been going back and forth out of the room.

"We got a girl down the hall," the raider told him. "You want a turn?"

Kittredge briefly imagined a creature like the nameless girl he had brought to the lake house. But this was his chance to escape from this trap. He stood up, easily counterfeiting eagerness. "Yeah, sure!"

"It's the door on the right," Butler told him. "Just stand outside and wait your turn." The raider made no comment as Kittredge took his gun and pack along with him. Lack of trust was another commonplace among their kind.

The room was at the end of a corridor with no other way out, but there was no one else waiting outside the door. Kittredge stood for a few minutes in front it, listening to the sounds from inside. He glanced back down the hall, saw that no one was watching, and quietly turned the knob.

The man on the bed jumped half off, enraged at the interruption, but then Kittredge had him on the floor, fangs in his throat. The girl watched it all

226

from a corner of the bed with huge, silent eyes, clutching a scrap of blanket around herself, up to her chin, as if it could protect her. Her fear-scent intensified his bloodlust and made it hard for him to pull back from his victim. When he finally did, she whimpered, shrinking away from him, and her terror drew him closer. But he knew he could not take her. The man on the floor was starting to struggle up to his hands and knees, choking. In a moment he would be able to call out for help.

Kittredge reluctantly drew away from the girl and ran to the window, jerked it open, and leaped to the ground outside, wondering how willing the girl had been, what they would do when they were finished with her. She had been uncontaminated.

He heard the cry when he was halfway to the road and paused for a moment. It came again, a man's voice calling, "Wait!"

He went on without turning back. They had seen his face in that house, and there were three living humans who knew for certain what he was. The next time he met them it would be in the dark.

# 7

It was *him!* Almost as soon as he came back into the room Greg Reichler noticed the blond stranger talking with Butler—the colorless face that turned away from him when he tried to get a better look. His hand went involuntarily to his throat. It was suddenly hard to breathe.

The stranger was making a place for himself in a corner now. Reichler's heartbeat pounded—*it can't be him!* He couldn't be sure. The stranger wouldn't meet his eyes. He looked, now, like any ordinary man. The time before, in the woods, his face had looked burned. Now there seemed to be a fresh scar across his forehead, running into the hairline. Reichler noticed how he kept his face in the shadows.

It was hard to identify this slight, blond stranger with a monster's eyes glowing red in the dark, with gleaming sharp fangs. But Reichler knew, as a terrified sweat broke out deep inside himself, he *knew* that he was in the same cold presence. *What is he? Why is he here?*

But he knew the answer to that, too, if he was right. He hesitated at the thought of going to Butler with his suspicions. Neither of them liked to talk about that day they had tried to take the house by the lake. Reichler's hand went to his throat again, to the scars there. It was shaking.

Butler wanted to pretend that day had never happened. That the guy in the woods had knifed Matt and the rest of them, that all their shots had missed. Christ, he'd *been there!* He *saw* what happened! But Bulter hadn't been there on the ground with *him* bending over him, hadn't felt those fangs ripping into his throat, or lain there afterward knowing he shouldn't still be alive and wondering *why?* Reichler groaned aloud. The killer had followed him all the way from the Wallace house. Three times now he had him in his power. His dad killed, and Matt and the rest of them, but he was still alive, and he didn't know why.

*He's here in the house with us now! I have to tell Butler!* He watched, paralyzed somehow, as Butler came back up to the stranger and said something about the girl in the back room, as the stranger got up and went down the hall.

The girl. Reichler had just come out of that room, where he'd tried, failed, then felt disgusted with himself for even trying. All he could think of in there had been Frieda, the things the raiders did to her in their own house. What was he coming to, that he could be a part of this?

But now the killer was in the room. What was happening in there now? Did the stranger have his fangs in her throat? Would he kill her, or would he leave her alive, too?

Reichler went back down the hall, feeling the same numb sense of dread as the day he walked up to his own house, knowing he would find the raiders inside. Death was behind that door. His hand holding his gun was sweaty. He had shot the killer before. Had hit him, he knew it, but he just got up and kept coming at him. What if it happened again? What if he couldn't be killed?

*They say you can't kill a vampire.*

He stood in front of the door. His hand refused to reach out for the knob. Inside, he could hear harsh gasps of breathing, a female gasp of fear or pain. He couldn't move. He waited, sweating, shaking. Then a man groaned, a different sound that Reichler knew. He kicked open the door, saw Mike Tomek kneeling on the floor, bloody fingers clutching his throat, the girl in the bed, writhing and thrashing, and the window open. He ran to it, leaned out. The light was going, but he could see the stranger running down the driveway, getting away. . . .

He called out desperately, "Wait!"

The thing that looked like a man seemed to pause as if it heard him. He called out again, but the stranger never looked around.

Yet Reichler knew he would be back.


They *had* to believe his story. There was Mike Tomek, for godssake, with his throat torn open, just the way Reichler's had been, and Matt, and the rest of them. And there was the girl, who saw the whole thing, though it was hard to get anything out of her.

He told the whole band all about the big house down by the lake near Danby, the way the vampire came at them, killed Matt and at least one other guy, the way their shots hit him and he never even slowed down.

And Travis, all through it, just stood there with a face like it was carved out of wood—hard. He couldn't deny what Reichler told them, not with Tomek sitting there saying the same thing. But when he was finished, Butler turned on him with a voice like a whip snapping.

"You mean you *recognized* this guy from the house and you didn't *say* nothing?"

Reichler looked at the floor. He couldn't explain, couldn't even understand what made him go to confront the vampire, face to face. It sounded like a crazy thing to do. He mumbled, "It was *dark*, for crissake! I couldn't get a clear look at his face. I *thought* it might be him, and I followed him in there to make sure." He added, looking directly at Mike Tomek, "I scared him off, too, or he'd of killed Mike just like he did Matt."

He exhaled in relief when Tomek gave a grudging nod of agreement. Mike had been pretty groggy, he couldn't remember the whole thing all that clearly. Anyhow, it *could* have been that way.

But Butler wasn't satisfied. "You had a gun. Why didn't you shoot?"

"I *told* you—bullets go right through him! Anyway," he added, "I couldn't shoot without maybe hitting Mike."

Christ, why was Butler trying to make out like it was all his fault? "Hey, you were there, too. How come you didn't know him? You were sitting right there talking to him."

"I wasn't the one saw his *face*," Butler snarled. "That was *you!* I was around the other side of the house, trying to *get* the bastard!"

Reichler shut up. Whatever was wrong with Butler, he didn't want to talk about it. And this was

Butler's band. He would have died by now, he knew, if he hadn't found Butler again and joined him.

Reichler wanted to tell them that the vampire was going to be back, but Butler didn't want to hear it, and he just couldn't explain how he knew it was true.

The dark was getting longer. There were only a few hours of light when you could see. And the vampire was still out there. They liked the dark.

Reichler couldn't sleep, but he wasn't the only one. McNamara, a couple nights after Tomek got it, woke up everybody with his screaming, and his throat was torn open. You could see the blood running down, looking black. The vampire had been right there in the house with them!

They kept watch after that, inside and out, with the fire as bright as they could make it. But it was like the vampire could walk through walls, invisible. McNamara, though he looked like a dead man for days, was still alive. But a few days afterward, they found Zach Poling out by the woodlot, his throat ripped open, his eyes wide, staring in death. The expression on his face—it reminded Reichler of Matt.

The worst thing was, they couldn't do anything about it! Something was stalking them, taking them one by one. But you couldn't see him in the dark, couldn't hear him coming. Worst of all, you couldn't save yourself, couldn't kill him, even with a gun! Everybody felt helpless. Men wouldn't go outside by themselves, were always looking back over their shoulders. The only question was, who was going to be next?

But Reichler knew something none of the rest of them did. It would not be him. Four times now, and he was still alive. He'd started to think of the scars on his throat as something that set him apart, a mark of protection.

But the dark reached out to him again. There were nine of them that day, on the way back from raiding a place over by Green Springs, hauling their loot with them. It wasn't much—hardly worth the effort or the risk, though at least no one got hurt or killed this time. It was already close to night—

In front of Reichler, someone swung a rifle up to his shoulder. Ahead was an abandoned car, the kind of place someone might crawl into to get out of the cold. And next to it, a man-shape was crouching over something, crouching over a body. The shape lifted up his head with a red flash of eyes, and the too-familiar chill hit Reichler's gut.

Mike Tomek was yelling in his hoarse, ruined voice, "There's nine of us, dammit! That's too many for him!" He fired, and there was the ring of metal as the bullet hit the car.

Greg Reichler saw the man-shape straighten up with an inhuman snarl of rage, his fangs . . .

The fangs, the eyes, the blood-streaked face of death that stared back at Reichler did not belong to the blond stranger from the house by the lake. It was the face of Matt Duchon, who had died there.

## 8

It was over six weeks since the fire, and Kittredge continued to lead a feral existence among the raiders, almost as one of them, hunter and victims virtually indistinguishable. By now some of them knew him for what he was. He stalked them unseen in the terror-filled nights as they waited for him to strike. Some bore scars of past encounters on their throats.

The gray pall of radioactive smoke still covered the sun, and as the year progressed toward the solstice, it was as if the world had been condemned to perpetual night. In all that time, Kittredge had not once gone back to Danby, even though he knew from raider reports that the citizens were out on the streets with their guns day and night, accessible. *Soon,* he would promise himself. He had not relinquished his claim on the town. But even the raiders avoided Danby. As the one named Butler had said, it was a good place to stay clear of.

Kittredge knew he would have to go back eventually, to face Gene Solokov again. Soon. But Danby would still be there after one more night. And then another night after that.

And so he was still among the raiders when he

first heard the rumors begin to spread, rumors of something inhuman, a killer that ripped open the throats of its victims like a wild animal.

*Wolves,* some of them speculated, or dogs gone wild. But they all knew how fallout had devastated the animal life of the county. And as the rumors grew, it became clear that whatever the killer was, it went upright on two feet, like a man. And, some reports insisted, bullets could not kill it.

At first, Kittredge was not overly concerned. The bands led an unsettled existence, and it was inevitable that news of his presence would spread among them, rumors distorted by fear. The atmosphere of terror did not displease him.

But too many of the rumors continued to insist: the thing *killed.* The details were too specific, the descriptions of the victims, their names, places where Kittredge knew he had not been, had not killed. Once or twice, it was true, his victims had died. They had been weak from hunger, or had struggled too hard for him to spare them. Then, he remembered, there had been the girl at the lake house, and the raiders he had killed there. . . .

Doubt grew into a certainty, and he knew what must have happened. Which one was it? And how? None of his recent victims had been buried, he was sure of that, not with the ground frozen for so long. Was it possible that in the perpetual darkness of the Nightfall world a body could undergo the metamorphosis without burial?

Rage building, Kittredge cursed his oversight. No matter how it had happened, there was another one of his kind at large in the region, one of his own making.

At the very thought of an intruder in his territory, his vision went red. The rage surging through his system was almost like bloodlust. The other was taking his victims, *his!* He must be destroyed.

Reason struggled for control against this unfamiliar frenzy. He was responsible for the other's existence, after all. He could hardly blame him for killing, for reacting to the same hunger that he knew so well. But nothing could alter the fact that there were not enough living, uncontaminated humans for two of their kind, especially if one of them was not leaving them alive afterward. And instinct insisted, *Every one he kills is mine!*

He began to search, unable to rest, compelled to find traces of the other, or one of his victims, to pick up his scent. Night came when he was close to the lair of a raider band he had been stalking. He waited near their woodpile until one of them came to get more logs to put on the fire. Kittredge seized the man, clamped a choking hand around his throat, and dragged him away a distance from the house. In the dark, he stared into the face. It was one that he recognized from Butler's band.

"You know what I am, don't you?"

He could get no response but strangled sobs and a terror that was almost overwhelming in its intensity. Kittredge held his bloodlust in check, eyes averted from the throat.

He whispered softly, *"Listen* to me. I'm not going to kill you. Do you hear me? You know the one in the room with the girl? The one in the front bedroom a few days later? They didn't die. Neither will you, if you cooperate."

"Dammit, don't be *afraid!"*

He felt a slight ebbing of the incoherent terror and loosened his hold a bit. "All you have to do is tell me what I want to know, and I won't kill you. I'll let you go, alive, like the others. You know

236

them. Nod your head if you understand what I'm saying."

Finally, a response.

"All right. Now, I want to know about the one who kills, who tears open peoples' throats. The *other* one. You know what I'm talking about, don't you?" Even now, he refused to use the word. But there was another nod.

"All right. Have you ever *seen* him?"

The man was trying to answer. Kittredge took his hand an inch away from the throat.

"I . . . today . . ."

*"Today? Where?"*

"Down by . . . Green Springs."

"Was there a kill? A body?"

"Maybe two. Reichler . . . went crazy, he ran off after him. You . . . you . . ."

The fear-scent was still intense. Kittredge could imagine how he must appear to the human. He could feel the frenzy building up in him, close to the breaking point. *Green Springs. Today. So close!*

He did not know if he could trust himself. But he had now another, even more urgent reason why he must not kill. There was no room, in this part of the Nightfall world, for more than one of his kind.

He shifted his grip and pulled the coat sleeve up from the man's wrist. "This won't kill you," he said through clenched teeth. "Just hold still. And it would help if you could relax," he added with no humor at all.

It was over in less than five minutes. Kittredge took only enough of the terror-rich blood to blunt the edge of his hunger, some instinct telling him not to sate himself. By then, he could hear the voices of the men from the house, calling out for

237

the one who was missing. He pulled his victim up to his feet. "Go on back."

Then he was gone, south toward Green Springs, following the tracks that the raiders had left in the snow. It was only a few miles later that he scented blood. The raiders must have been in too much of a panic to carry the body off with them. It was lying sprawled at the side of an abandoned car, and the scent of the other was on it. *This was mine!* Kittredge felt a tingling as the hair rose on the back of his neck, and the world was tinged rage-red.

With the rationality left to him, he deplored the waste. The body was free from the radiation taint. And the wounds on the throat were gaping slashes. There was something repellent about the sight — *was I ever that bestial?* It made him wonder what it must be like for one who had to begin this cursed existence in the Nightfall world, without the regular alternation of sunlight and night. For one who had never known a grave.

Then the air brought him the scent — human-scent, and familiar. Kittredge glanced across the snowfield. This was no place for a human, alone, in the dark, with no shelter from the cold. He went toward the source, found a hollow in front of the windbreak of a fence with a human figure curled up in its slight shelter.

He touched the man — cold, almost as cold as his own flesh. Contaminated scent. Alive, but barely. He recalled his victim's words: *Reichler went crazy. He ran off after him.* Why? Was this man Reichler?

He shook him, harder, and the face slowly turned toward him, then lighted with recognition. The voice was a numb whisper through frostbitten lips. "You . . . not Matt."

Kittredge knew him then, the raider from the lake house, the one in Butler's band who had recognized him from the woods. "Reichler?" he asked. "Who is Matt? Do you know where he is now?"

"*You* . . . killed him!"

"You know me, don't you? Was it Matt who killed that man over by the car? Where is he now?"

Reichler stirred with the effort to speak. "Gone. Ran. I . . ." His voice faded. Kittredge straightened, started to leave. An arm strained to reach out to him. Reichler was struggling desperately to say something. Kittredge bent down again, repressing for a moment the frenzied need to find the one named Matt.

"Why . . . not me?"

Kittredge frowned, perplexed, before he understood what the man was trying to ask him. Well, it would do no harm to tell him the truth.

"Radiation poisoning, in your blood."

Reichler fell back down and shut his eyes. His lips moved again, and Kittredge heard, ". . . die . . ."

He hesitated an instant. Did Reichler want to die? That much mercy was not alien to his nature. If the man's blood had been clean . . .

He grasped the neck and twisted, hard. There was a grating sound, and the body went limp. It was an easier end than the fate that radiation sickness held out for him.

Kittredge left the two bodies behind him. He had a scent now. And a name, Matt. The name meant nothing, only that the other was one of the raiders he had killed by the lake house. The memory of that bloodlust merged with his rage, surged into frenzy. He *knew* that scent!

239

It grew stronger as he came within the limits of Green Springs. The scent of the intruder! And human terror. *He is here!*

A scream came, and a gunshot. Kittredge was running, the hated scent ahead of him, closer. Then he *saw*—the figure running away from one of the buildings, carrying another, struggling with it. He started after them, but just as he was about to pass the building, the door crashed open and he was face to face with Paul Krusack and the barrel of a shotgun.

The shock was enough to jolt Kittredge to a halt, and Krusack saw him, gasped, "You!"

But shock also made Krusack hesitate an instant before he could bring the gun to bear and pull the trigger, an instant when Kittredge could knock it aside. The shot went into the air as the gunburst roared in his ears. Then he wrenched the gun out of the man's grasp and pinned him back against the wall with it. More humans were in the doorway now, halted in their rush after the intruder.

Kittredge spun around, pointing the gun at the figure standing motionless in the street, the light from the open doorway making lurid embers of his eyes. The other had scented him now. The child he had abducted lay forgotten at his feet as the two of them faced each other for a single silent moment. Kittredge threw the gun away into the snow. His vision of the other was crimson. His lips drew back from his fangs in a hiss.

Then they both sprang, straight for each other's throats. They grappled, twisted, and bit, both berserk with a rage soon intensified by the scent and taste of their own blood. The presence of each other had rendered them no more rational than rabid wolves.

Kittredge was the slighter of the two. But there were other factors between them that meant more than physical strength to their kind. Kittredge was the dominant—he had killed the other, and they both knew it. His scent meant death and defeat to the one he had brought into being.

And the other was sated. He had already killed the man by the car earlier in the evening. Kittredge had held back. Now his lust for the other's blood drove him in a final, frenzied lunge to plunge his fangs into the throat. For the first time in his existence, he savored the blood of his own kind.

The other's struggles weakened slowly as Kittredge drained him, savaged him, biting down again and again. The rapture was overwhelming. He could not feel his own wounds. He could not have stopped, even with all his will, until the heartbeat faltered, stilled. Shuddering in a reaction close to shock, he let the body fall away into the snow and blinked, as it if were some object he had never before seen. His vision was clear.

Then he caught a glimpse of movement and turned, fully alert again. The humans, who had stood transfixed in horrified fascination to watch the bloody combat of shadows in the dark, were starting to react. One of them was fumbling a shell into a shotgun—Krusack! Kittredge tensed, ready to dodge the blast as the gun lifted.

"No!" Another man stepped into Krusack's line of fire. "There were *two* of them!"

Kittredge paused, looked again. The other man was Rick Archer, and he was arguing, "It wasn't him! It was the other one!"

Krusack tried to shove him aside to get a clear aim at his target. "Dammit, Archer, get out of my way!"

There was a whimpering sound from the snow — the victim, forgotten in the midst of the conflict. Kittredge looked at her a moment, the child he had taken from the other, saved from the other, still alive. His. He saw Krusack lowering his gun as he stepped closer to her, reached down, and lifted her up. She cried and pulled away from his frigid touch.

Rick Archer was echoing his thoughts, although not as he had meant them. "Look, Patty's still alive! Kittredge *saved* her. God dammit, he saved you once, too!"

The shotgun lowered a fraction of an inch. Rick walked out from the doorway toward Kittredge, and Krusack, after a moment's hesitation, followed, took the child from him. Rick stood there, looked down at the body of the other, up at Kittredge as if he were something he had never before seen. "Why?" he asked.

The mundane matters of existence seemed almost unreal to Kittredge after the heightened sensations of the killing. The world looked colorless and pale. How could he answer? How could he explain the effect of the other's scent, the frenzied compulsion to kill, to defend his territory? But he knew the answer Rick would want to hear.

"He would have killed everyone in the county if I hadn't stopped him. It was the only way."

And it was true, though not true in the way that Rick understood it. But Rick was human, and his kind was not. There could never be complete understanding between them.

"*He* was doing the killing, then, not you?" Rick's voice held the need to believe.

Kittredge could not disabuse him. "That's right."

"I thought you were dead," Rick said apologetically. "Back there in Danby. I *saw* you . . . on fire. I'm sorry, I should have gone back to make sure."

Kittredge shrugged. But Rick had thought he was dead. Had *cared,* at least enough to regret it. Despite himself, Kittredge discovered that it mattered to him. "I wasn't sure whether you'd gotten away, either. It looks like you're doing all right." He was sincere. Rick had grown during the weeks since he had left the lake house. He was no longer just a kid. Perhaps, after all, he might survive.

Paul Krusack had taken the child to the others. Now he was coming back, and Rick told him, "It *was* this one doing the killing. Not Kittredge."

Krusack glared down at the body. "So. How do we know he'll stay dead?"

Kittredge *knew* that the other would never rise again. Yet, to make certain . . .

"Put a stake through his heart. He'll stay dead then. And if you know of any others, do the same thing."

Krusack looked up at him, startled. *Yes,* Kittredge challenged him silently, *now you know.*

"Shit!" the farmer said finally, and he gave a kick to the torn body lying in the snow.

Kittredge shoved him violently backward. "Leave him alone! And his name was Matt. Maybe you can put that on the stake when you bury him."

He wished now that he had asked Reichler for Matt's last name. But it was too late. Reichler was dead, and no one else would ever know who the other had been when he was alive.

# 1833

It was summer when I was killed, that season of brief nights and interminable days. As I began my new existence, it seemed each night that sunrise would be upon me almost as soon as I had left my resting place. I was desperate, in fear that I would not be able to satisfy the demands of hunger before the daylight came to drive me back into hiding.

And afterward would come the endless hours of stifling close confinement, waiting for the all-too-brief moments of freedom once the dark finally came to release me. How I welcomed the coming of the equinox, the lengthening of the nights! How I looked forward to the approaching solstice with a sense of limitless possibilities before me! The winter, the cold, the snow, the long hours of darkness—these have always meant freedom to me.

But mine is not the only kind to be governed by the ceaseless turning of the year. Even as the night was at its longest, I knew that the great solstice feast was at hand, when humanity celebrates the return of the light to the world.

# Stronghold

## 1

The door shut behind Rick Archer, the last one of the humans to go back inside. The building where they sheltered was a large brick church, doubtless one of the most defensible structures in Green Springs. The light from inside was cut off, leaving Blaine Kittredge alone in the cold and the dark.

He considered for a moment following them inside, shocking them with his presence in a holy place. But there was nothing more that he and they had to say to one another. He was evil, a menace, he belonged out here, alone.

But he was not entirely alone. "This is our proper element, you know," he said aloud to the body lying in the snow. One of his own kind.

The compelling rage had washed entirely away, now that the other named Matt was dead. If "dead" was the proper word. Can we die twice? he wondered. No more than twice, certainly. With or without a stake through his heart, Matt would remain in whatever grave they gave him in Green Springs.

Kittredge knelt down again in the snow. He had so rarely met another of his own kind, had learned, early in his existence, to respect another's territory. Matt had never had time to learn—so many things. He was young, hardly older than Rick Archer. Cut off, after so short a time.

Of all his victims, Kittredge had never before encountered one who had undergone the metamorphosis. Was Matt really the first? Were there others, perhaps still existing?

If Eleanora . . . if Eleanora had risen from her grave, would he have felt that same overwhelming lust to kill? And she? Could their wills have overcome the compulsion? Kittredge shook his head. It was best that she had remained as she was. He could not have borne it, to look down on her like this. He gently touched the boy's dead face. The cheeks slightly hollowed by the hunger that had driven him out of shelter to take up a raider's brief life. Eyes already gone dull in death. The sharp tip of a fang barely visible beneath the upper lip. You might not know, Kittredge thought, what he was. The lifeless face looked almost human. Matt would have remained young forever.

*Do I still look as I did at twenty-eight, when I died?* But no, he remembered. There were the scars now.

He pressed the dead eyelids shut regretfully. Had it been necessary? Should he have tried to overcome his rage, to warn the boy out of his territory? But the frenzy had been mutual. Their natures had conspired to eliminate one of them. And so few of his kind ever came into existence. Could it really be, since the Apocalypse, that he was the last? That he would remain the last?

He got up from his knees. This was doing him no good. Whatever might have been, Matt was irrevocably dead, and the citizens of Green Springs would have a good supply of stakes at hand from now on.

Kittredge looked around at the town. Green Springs, unlike Danby, had a town square. Within its perimeters were indistinct mounds that doubtless hid an ancient cannon or a green-bronze statue. A drinking fountain. There would have been trees once, but the humans had cut them down for firewood. His territory, he thought, that he had just defended from the interloper.

He recalled for a moment the words of one of the Stoic philosophers: *For this is your task, to act well the given part, but to choose it belongs to another.* He had not—God knew he had not—chosen this existence. But it was his, as it had been, for such a short time, the boy named Matt's.

He laughed. He could imagine the humans, right now, debating what they were going to do about him, Rick Archer and Paul Krusack arguing. What a disappointment when they discover him gone! Perhaps, some time later, he would come back to Green Springs. But there was another part of his territory, that he had claimed before Green Springs.

It was time to go back to Danby.


The dark shape of the town lay ahead of him, the church spire tall against the flat farmland, thin columns of smoke rising into the frigid air. It felt almost as if he had just come from the lake house to steal supplies again. In fact, on his way back from Green Springs he had stopped for a moment outside the house. It was empty, the door standing open. Deserted. He did not go in.

He stood within sight of Danby, watching the sky darken to black above the church spire. There were barely six hours now of twilight day, this close to solstice time. The hours of night were his alone. Even before Nightfall he had anticipated this season, its long nights of freedom from the sun. Now—he bared his fangs in a smile. He had come through the fallout and the burning. Now it was all his, even the day!

Danby was his. Gene Solokov might think differently, but he would learn. They all would learn. He would not conceal himself any longer. He would hunt, and they would know what he was, as the raiders had learned. And none of them, not even Solokov, would dare to meet his eyes again.

Still, he could not afford to be reckless. Although he had abandoned his shotgun and pack when he went after the interloper, he kept a .38 automatic inside his jacket just in case it might be necessary in an emergency.

And there had been changes in Danby. They were no longer sheltering from the fallout. He could see people out in the open, working, bringing in food and fuel. Kittredge grinned again, thinking of the amount of work necessary to keep humans alive. At least, now, he was not the one who had to do it all.

Raiders were obviously a major concern to the town. He knew, from the raiders, that Danby's defenses were effective. There were sentries, no longer restricted to their shelters, and he took care to locate all of them. There had been no sign of looting as he came into the town, no squatters in the empty houses, even as far away as Sugar Lake. Gene Solokov, he had to assume, was still in charge.

Solokov, who had met his eyes in a challenge of wills, who had rigged the gasoline storage tank to explode in his face. It was time for him to end it, to face Solokov, once and finally. And it had to be a confrontation on equal terms.

Kittredge made his decision. He would let Solokov know, first, that he was back. And what he was. Then they would see whom Danby belonged to.

Under cover of the deepening night, he went into the town to begin his careful stalk of the sentries. He knew which one he wanted.

## 2

Gene Solokov held a recurved hunting bow in one hand and assessed it with the eye of an experienced hunter. He grinned at Ron Meagher. "This looks great!" he told the mechanic. "Can hardly wait till tomorrow to try it."

Ammunition wasn't exactly running out—Danby's defenders had taken almost as much off the bodies of dead raiders as they expended in killing them—but you had to anticipate future needs. Danby wasn't going to be defenseless whether or not they ran out of bullets, not as long as Gene Solokov could help it. If it came down to throwing stones, he was going to have more and better stones on hand than the next guy.

Of course—his conscience twinged—he still had the M-16 with over five thousand rounds cached back at his own place. The pair of Uzis that had given them such a decisive advantage in the early firefights *were* nearly out of ammunition—that was the trouble with automatic weapons, the way they run through it. But the same rule held true for the raiders. And they weren't likely to have the facilities to manufacture a bow like this one. Solokov figured he was still ahead of the game. And he was going to like it a lot better if they could get a few dozen of these things made. Then, of course, there was the question of teaching people to use them effectively—

There was some kind of commotion out in the hall. Then he heard Vonnie's voice, calling, "Gene!"

He jumped up, still holding the bow. Another raid? Now, when it was almost totally dark?

Vonnie came panting into the armory. "They just brought in Dan Erlanger!" she gasped. "Brian has him in the clinic."

"Is it a raid?" He looked down at the bow in his hand, wishing vainly that it was an assault rifle.

"No, they don't think so. But you'd better come and see for yourself."

Dan Erlanger was lying on the couch in what had been the school nurse's office. There was a bloodstained dressing around his neck and he looked as pale as death. Shock, Solokov thought, seeing the tremor that shook him. Brian Mercier was standing protectively next to his patient.

"You should see this," the doctor told Solokov. "All right, Dan?" he asked.

Erlanger gave a nearly imperceptible nod before Mercier moved his hand toward the dressing and lifted it off. He focused the light on Erlanger's throat and Solokov came closer. He saw a pair of wounds spaced about five centimeters apart. There was something about the injuries—not a knife. Animal bite? He remembered now, there had been rumors. . . .

Solokov looked up questioningly at Mercier. The doctor said, "I know Dan's story sounds pretty fantastic, but I can't think of another explanation for these injuries. They're *not* human bites."

He nodded encouragement at Erlanger, who took

251

a painful breath. "I was on patrol. It was getting hard to see. He jumped me. Had a . . . hand around my throat so I couldn't yell. He dragged me . . ."

Erlanger's voice broke, and Solokov looked away as Mercier gave him a sip of water. "Go on, Dan. It's all right."

With another shuddering gasp, Erlanger tried to regain his voice. "He . . . bit me. . . . He . . ."

His hand moved toward his neck, then dropped away. "After, he carried me back into the light. Oh, God! He . . . *wanted* me to see his face. It was *him*. You know—the one who . . ."

The doctor intervened. "Take it *easy*," he whispered.

"You're sure?" Solokov demanded.

"I could never forget that face. He . . . made me look right at him. He said, 'You remember me, don't you, Dan?' He knew my *name!* Then he said, 'Tell Solokov. I'll be back again.' "

*Tell Solokov.* Solokov's fists clenched, white at the knuckles. The bastard *wasn't* dead! He had *known* he shouldn't give up till he found the body!

Against his will, he was totaling up the evidence. There was Earl Thomas's ridiculous story. But—admit it—he'd been right about that house. The generator had been there. And those scars on his wrists . . .

He frowned and looked again at Dan Erlanger's neck, the two marks—of teeth? "Did Earl Thomas ever show you those scars of his?" he asked the doctor.

Mercier's eyes widened. "Oh, by God, yes! I *thought* I'd seen something like this before!"

Solokov shook his head. This was absurd. Only—like Dan, he would never be able to forget

252

the sight of that face, the deathlike paleness of the skin, the way there had been something about the eyes . . .

He shivered, remembering it all once again. The mysterious thefts had all taken place at night, in the dark. What was it they said about vampires: only the sunlight could kill them? And how long since any of them had last seen the sun?

He bent down to Erlanger, whispered, "He said those words? *Tell Solokov?*"

"He made me . . . repeat it."

Gene Solokov straightened. He looked around the room at the others. "I want this kept quiet, do you understand? Even if this . . . story turns out to have some basis in fact, the last thing we need is a bunch of crazy rumors flying around, people panicking. Whatever this bastard is, we'll take care of him."

Grimly, he told himself there was at least one more way you were supposed to be able to kill a vampire—you drive a stake through his heart. So, all right. They had a vampire on their hands. In that case, he was going to be ready when the bastard came back.

"Who brought Dan in?" he demanded. "I want to get this story straight!"

## 3

Blaine Kittredge was quite pleased with the way it had gone. The sentry *had* remembered him from the school basement — the terror flowing through his blood had been exhilarating. And by now Solokov would know that he was back. What he was.

He had discovered by this time that, with the fallout no longer such a hazard, the humans were no longer crowded together in the basement shelters. Each family had at least a room to itself now, somewhere within the fortified inner perimeter of the downtown district on the east side of town. Much more accessible.

Throughout the night he could observe the effects of his message as word passed from one inhabited building to the others, lights flaring on, armed residents searching every possible hiding place, checking and reinforcing all the locks. When day came, with its gray light, Kittredge retreated to his selected observation post in the attic of an ancient three-story white Victorian on the southern outskirts of the town. Today, no one in Danby came outside to work. Instead, small squads of men soon appeared on the streets, extending the search outside the perimeter. Kittredge watched, ready to retreat farther if they came close to his hiding place. He did not dare to rest.

After a few hours, while the searchers were still going from house to house, the sound of an engine broke into life. As Kittredge looked out from the attic window, a snowmobile roared south down the road toward Sugar Lake. One of the men inside, arms folded across some kind of weapon, was Gene Solokov.

Kittredge nodded to himself. As he had figured, Solokov was going back to check out the lake house. And in a hurry, too. Fangs showed in a grin. Solokov probably wanted to make sure to be back before nightfall. It was only too bad about the station wagon in the garage. He was going to miss that resting place.

While there was still some daylight, he climbed down from the attic of the white house, out of sight of the searchers still some blocks away. A barn would serve him well enough to rest for a few hours, as long as it was far enough from Danby.

He waited until well past sunset before he went back to the town. Hunger and tension equally had him on edge. What he was about to do was risky. Foolhardy, his common sense amended. There were easier opportunities to take a victim. Easier victims.

On his way to the school, he paused, catching human scent from a small blue house. A couple of starvelings were huddled inside, keeping out of the cold. Hunger urged how simple it would be to take one of them and forget his chosen target. But Kittredge knew that Danby would never be truly *his* until he had taken Gene Solokov first.

For too long he had avoided the town, making excuses to himself, evading the truth. But no more.

Tonight, at last, Solokov would look into his eyes and be the one to know fear.

Kittredge came into the school through the darkened window of a restroom on the upper floor. There was only minimal lighting in the hallway outside and no sentries patrolling the corridors, only the single post looking out into the street. This would change, once they realized he was stalking them from the inside. But humans had to sleep. Solokov had spent last night awake and searching for him. Odds were, he was sleeping now.

He passed by room after room of humans asleep behind locked doors. He had been uncertain if he would be able to pick out Solokov's scent from among all the others, but they had made it easy for him. Almost every door had a name on it. There was only one name that concerned him.

He found it where he had thought he would. Solokov still lived on the basement level, close to the supplies. Kittredge stood outside the locked door, listening, trying to isolate that single scent. Yes, his victim was there. He started to work on the door, with slow, silent care. The lock clicked open.

He would have been sweating if he could, thinking of traps, a sudden blaze of light or flame as he opened the door. Never had a human intimidated him as this one had. Kittredge touched his tongue to the tip of a fang. Already, he knew this scent, had chosen this victim for his own. *Remember that,* he told himself. *If you can't face him, what are you?*

He stepped soundlessly into the room and closed the door behind him. There were two of them sleeping together, the man and his wife. Kittredge recognized the woman who had been guarding the door during their first encounter and suddenly understood a great deal more about Gene Solokov.

There was a gun next to the man's mattress. He bent down and moved it carefully away out of reach. Then he took hold of the man. Solokov was awake and struggling almost before Kittredge had seized him, but Kittredge's grip was unbreakable. The wife was awake now, too. Her gasp was almost a scream, and Kittredge whispered quickly, "Quiet! Not a sound! I think you know who I am. You just keep still and this will all be over with nobody getting hurt—more than they have to be."

Solokov's hate flared almost painfully as he fought to free himself from Kittredge's grasp. But fear was there, as well. Kittredge willed him to fear. It intensified as he tightened his grip on the man's throat, choking off curses, and said, "On the other hand, if you give me trouble, maybe neither of you will leave this room alive. Think about it. I could kill you in a second and take *her,* instead."

It had occurred to Kittredge that possibly he had chosen the wrong victim. It was his fear for his wife that finally stopped Solokov's struggles. But he was certain that he would never succeed in taking her unless he killed Gene Solokov first, and he did not want to do that. Danby might not survive without him.

Vonnie Solokov's stare was fixed on him in horror as he lowered his head, so slowly, to her husband's throat. Kittredge could feel the man starting to shiver from the chill touch of his undead flesh, the fear-scent intensifying now, sharp and tantalizing, his own bloodlust welling up in response.

The man was no coward. Kittredge had not expected him to be. At the first piercing touch of fangs at his throat, he barely flinched. Kittredge drew out the bloodletting as slowly as he could, in control every instant of it, savoring the bitter mix of hate, anger, and fear. Incredibly, even as he drew his mouth away from the throat, Solokov was still, weakly, testing the strength of his grip.

But Kittredge knew that never again would this human be able to face his eyes without trembling with the memory of how he had been held helpless and fed upon. And spared, to be fed upon again. The thrill of satisfaction was almost as great as the kill would have been.

"There will be another time," he whispered softly, directly into his victim's ear. "I'll be back." Then he let go.

Solokov fell to the floor, but was almost immediately up onto his knees as he and Vonnie both lunged for the gun that Kittredge had set out of their reach. Solokov reached it first and fired through the door that had just shut behind the vampire. He struggled to his feet and flung it open, stood looking up and down the hallway with blood still running down his neck onto his shirt. People came running from their rooms, some of them armed, and stared at him. But the vampire was gone.

# 4

Of course, Kittredge had to see for himself how Solokov would respond to his challenge. He watched the next day from the outskirts of town as the search went from house to house, even more intensive than the day before. Solokov, with a bandage on his throat, was out on the streets directing operations from the first moment of light. Kittredge was forced to admire the man's determination.

Gradually, he moved in, shadowing the searchers from a distance at first. Then, as one group came out of an empty house, he stole up behind them, close enough that he could hear the whispered question, "You just tell me, what are we supposed to do if we find this damn vampire?"

One man spit onto the snow and said, "Shit, you believe that crap?"

The other two glanced nervously at each other. "*Something* got Gene last night. Came right into his room, that's what I hear. Then it just disappeared! And there was Dan Erlanger, night before that."

"OK, so there's some kind of psycho loose around here. Doesn't surprise me—we've got murderers, cannibals, God knows what else." The skeptic snorted. "If you ask me, maybe it's Solokov has got a few gears loose. Couple months ago, he had us chasing around after this guy he says is the one breaking in everywhere. Now we're after the same guy, except now he's supposed to be a *vampire!* Come on!"

"No, *Gene* never said that! Just that he's back, attacking people."

"Yeah," said the nervous one, "but did you see Gene's throat? I heard Vonnie was right next to him when it happened, and she could see the guy's eyes in the dark."

"Well, I heard what Earl Thomas said—"

"Thomas? I don't know why Solokov ever let that little piece of shit back into town."

"All I know is I want to be back inside before it gets dark, just in case."

"What good will that do? I mean, Gene and Vonnie had the door locked on their room last night. And I'll tell you something else. Thomas says a gang of raiders came and shot this guy, shot him right in the gut, and he just got up off the ground and caught them, killed eight or ten men— tore their throats right out!"

The three men looked at each other. Then one said slowly, "It was supposed to be the same guy that burned. Even Gene said he must be dead. But nobody ever found the body."

Grimly, emitting fear-scent, they entered the next house.

Kittredge found it interesting that Solokov was trying to deny the rumors of what he must be. After another night or so, they would all be forced to recognize the truth. He dwelt for a few moments on the image: the whole town waiting in dread and terror for sunset to come, never knowing where or when he would strike next.

The crack of a gunshot interrupted his thoughts, and a moment later the three men came rushing down the stairs of the house and ran toward the sound. Kittredge followed, suddenly angry with himself. Those squatters in the blue house—he had completely forgotten about them!

The two shivering wretches were backed up against one wall of the house by the time Kittredge got close enough to see what was happening. The men surrounding them had already begun to lower their guns. "It's not him!" someone called out to the new arrivals. "Just a couple of Mexes hiding out in here. They got no guns, either."

Kittredge started. *Mexicans?* He strained for a look at the two captured squatters, but they were hidden behind the growing number of searchers. Could it be Joe and Connie Flores? Why of all places would they have come back to Danby? (Back to the shelter of the lake house?)

Then a white-faced Gene Solokov arrived, and the rest of them parted to let him through. He stared hard at the two captives as the others repeated, "It's not him. Might as well give these two a warning and let them go."

"No. Shoot them. Shoot them both."

"What?" Several voices protested at once. "Come on, Gene! They don't even have guns!"

"I said shoot!" Solokov screamed. Wildly, he brought up the Uzi, firing. The two humans against the wall twitched grotesquely as the burst ripped through them at point-blank range.

It was silent as they dropped, broken, into the blood-splattered snow. Solokov lowered the submachine gun, his hands shaking.

Then one man said, "Jesus! You didn't have to

261

do that! One of them was a woman, for chrissake!"

"I . . ." Solokov shook his head and looked down at his weapon in apparent confusion. A few men walked away, disgusted. A couple of others shrugged and bent down to lift the feet of the bodies and drag them away.

"What about the search?" someone asked.

"Oh, the hell with it!"

We're never gonna find that guy, anyway."

*"Vampire!"* one voice said scornfully.

Solokov, after standing there alone for a few moments, followed after the others, the Uzi almost dragging in the snow at his side.

Kittredge watched them disperse, frowning. This turn of events was not so satisfactory. Two lives wasted that could have been his if he hadn't passed them by last night, so anxious to get to Solokov. Or if he'd remembered, afterward, and warned them away. Done something.

But Flores should have *known* better than to risk coming into Danby! If it had been Flores in that house. Kittredge recalled something. But the baby would be dead, too, if that was who the two had been. All three of them dead, now.

Kittredge left the scene. He could not shake the feeling that something had gone wrong, something he should have been able to prevent.


Yet Danby was his, in fact. They could not stop him. That night he took another victim from the town, the next night another, and their blood was untainted. They tried. They locked doors and posted watchers. But Kittredge had known from his experience that they could not guard themselves from all directions at once. Always, there was at least one who was vulnerable.

Gene Solokov was still his greatest danger. He had finally acknowledged what was stalking the town, but this just served to make his traps more canny. Defenses against the menace were not enough for him. Kittredge was well aware that Solokov was determined to trap him, to destroy him once and for all. Certainly, it would have been safer for him in Danby if he had killed the man while he had the opportunity. Yet Kittredge had never wanted to destroy Solokov, only the human's power to intimidate him. And that had been accomplished. And, he admitted to himself, he rather enjoyed the challenge he represented.

After several nights, the futile searches ceased. The humans gradually resumed most of their former routines. There were other hazards still at large to threaten the town. The work of survival was too important to be neglected.

And they had begun to notice something else — none of the victims so far had actually *died*. It was true, they were being taken, one by one, but perhaps the threat was not so serious as people had initially feared. Only Solokov was implacable, still determined to stop at nothing to eliminate the menace.

Kittredge could hear the reaction from the sentries at their posts, from the crews out bringing in wood:

"This thing has really got Solokov spooked."

"It was *his* rule, not to use the Uzi unless it's a raid. There was no call to kill those two."

"He's letting everything else slide. It's an obsession, that's what it is."

"Yeah, it's not like he was the only one."

Kittredge, watching a work party hauling corn from a storage elevator, saw the one who had made that last remark suddenly look embarrassed and the rest of them fall silent, looking away from one particular man whose neck was wrapped in a scarf. Underneath it, Kittredge knew, there were fresh scars.

"Sorry, Dan," the speaker said finally. "But, well, you know what it was like. What *is* this guy—is he human or what?"

Dan Erlanger looked at the ground for a long time before he whispered, "Cold. His breath—it was so cold. . . . No, he's not human. He couldn't be."

He shivered. The others turned their eyes away again. Finally one of them said, "Vampire or not, people still have to eat around here."

"Maybe Solokov should start to remember that," said another, as they went back to their work.

One cold morning shortly afterward, Kittredge observed a distant solitary figure tramping through the snow on the road leading away from Danby. Curious, he followed after it and soon recognized Gene Solokov. Somehow, he wasn't surprised. Was it another trip to check out the lake house again?

No, he was heading more west than south. And he wasn't armed—at least he wasn't carrying a rifle or shotgun. Or the Uzi. That was the most unusual thing of all. No one went out alone and unarmed into the Nightfall world, least of all this man. Once or twice he stopped abruptly and turned around, but Kittredge was careful to follow him at a distance.

Solokov came to a modern red-brick farmhouse,

where he began to check the snow for fresh foot-prints. Apparently satisfied, he went into the house. About fifteen minutes later he came out again, still empty handed, and the lines on his face were even more grim. This was his own house, Kittredge supposed, and looters had been into it.

He followed the man, more closely now, to what looked like a tool and equipment shed. Solokov looked behind him one more time before opening the broken door and going inside. Kittredge waited again, then dared a look. A hatchway in the floor of the shed was standing open. He could see the dim glow from a flashlight from below.

He stepped inside the shed, glanced down the stairs. There was a small, secret bunker hidden beneath the shed, no more than eight feet square, stocked with what Kittredge could recognize as survival supplies. Solokov stood below him with an M-16 assault rifle on the floor at his feet, piling ammunition into a pack.

Kittredge made sure there was no clip in the gun before he said, "Is that intended for me?"

Solokov whirled around, stared upward. There was an intense flare of panic as he dove for the M-16, but Kittredge had moved first. The impact of his body knocked the man to the floor, and by the time he recovered himself Kittredge had the gun and was standing over him.

"Don't," said Kittredge as Solokov started to reach inside his coat. "I'm faster than you. You should know that by now. And besides, haven't you heard? Guns can't kill me."

The human was breathing hard, kneeling on the floor of the bunker, radiating hate and, yes, fear.

"You know," Kittredge went on, "they're saying in town that you're letting things slide. Don't forget, there are still raiders out there. You should stop wasting your time. You're never going to stop me. I don't *want* to kill you people, don't you understand? You're *mine*. There aren't that many humans left."

It was the argument that had worked at the lake house, but not now, not with Gene Solokov. His hand was moving almost imperceptibly toward his coat. "I should add," Kittredge warned him, "that I will kill you if I have to. Don't provoke me, Solokov. Learn to live with it."

Suddenly, he threw the M-16 at the man, who caught the gun instinctively. Before he could reach for a clip to shove into the magazine, Kittredge had jumped up to the top of the stairs and slammed the door down over his head.

Seconds later, as he was running across the yard, he heard a muffled burst of automatic fire, but by the time Solokov came rushing out of the shed after him, he was already out of sight. Panting, the man stood in his yard, searching the half-darkness for a sight of him.

Finally he went back into the shed. When he came out shortly afterward and started the trek back to Danby, he had the M-16 slung over his shoulder and a full pack on his back.

Kittredge, watching him, sighed. He had wasted his time, maybe even made things worse. Solokov was not about to give up. He might have to kill the man one day, after all.

# 5

It was a long, cold, solitary trek back through the snow to Danby. Gene Solokov *knew* the bastard was somewhere behind him out of sight, following him, but he refused to turn around and look back. Not to give him the satisfaction of letting him see how scared he was.

He could admit — to himself — that he was scared. He shivered. God, there was something about the bastard that made his blood turn to ice. *Vampire.* He refused to say the word aloud, but it had to be true. There was something about him, when he had you, that compelled fear. *He wants me to be scared. He enjoys it.*

That was why the bastard had followed him out here, to taunt him. "You can't stop me. Guns can't kill me." *Well,* Solokov thought grimly, *we'll just see about that.* His hand gripped the familiar, reassuring stock of the M-16. Some things you don't forget. Over twenty years since Nam, when one of these things was like an extension of himself, and that hadn't changed a bit. He almost wished the vampire would try it now. Get it over with. Better than waiting, *knowing* he's out there someplace. That's what he wants. Wants me to sweat, wonder when he's going to grab me. Probably wait till I get back to town, just to drag it out.

Days of dark brooding over the attacks had convinced Solokov of one thing at least: no matter what the vampire really was, no matter what he might want them to believe, he was not invulnerable. He had known it instinctively, from the very first, before he knew what the bastard was (yet had *felt,* meeting those eyes, that there was something wrong). Why else, that first time, did he hold a gun on Dan Erlanger? Why else did he always run away?

He could be hurt. Solokov remembered with distinct satisfaction the sight of the flaming figure by the gas tank, writhing in the snow, the sound of his screams. That had been *pain.* Back there in the bunker, he had seen a scar on the pale forehead, like a burn scar. He hoped it came from the gasoline bomb. He hoped he had put it there.

Yet—what was it the bastard had said back there? People were talking about him? He was letting things slide? Reluctantly, he had to admit to himself that it might be true. People *had* complained about the searches, until he had to stop them. There was the bow project, stalled. And the methane digesters—he hadn't done anything about that, lately, either.

With every step, Solokov admitted to himself the truth of the indictment. He was letting things slip. His jaw clenched and he gripped the M-16 even more tightly. *God, what is he waiting for?* Once the damn vampire was out of the way, everything would be all right, he'd get everything back on track again.

\* \* \*

It had taken most of the day to get over to his place and back. Now, approaching the downtown perimeter of Danby, Solokov noticed that something had changed. He glanced instantly toward the nearest sentry post, waved, and saw one of the guards wave in return. Everything must be all right.

He knew what it was the second he came into the school building and caught the evergreen aroma. The tree stood in the middle of the main hall, its top brushing the ceiling. Children were running around, knocking into the boxes piled up on the floor, and someone was up on a ladder, winding a string of lights around the highest branches.

Solokov suddenly felt a great upwelling of sorrow for his daughter and grandchildren, almost certainly dead in the ruins of Indianapolis. Tears filled his eyes, and the figure of Vonnie was blurred as she approached him.

"Gene! Thank God, you're back! We were getting worried." Then her eyes went to the M-16 slung at his side. "Where did you get that?"

He frowned at her. "I had it."

There was a sudden burst of cheering as multicolored lights blazed into life on the tree. Solokov blinked. "Who authorized this?"

"What do you mean, who *authorized* it? Since when do we need permission to put up a Christmas tree? People in town went back to their houses today and brought back the lights and decorations. In fact, if I'd known where you were going . . ."

Looking at his face, she sighed without finishing what she was going to say. Gene Solokov's eyes were fixed on the tree. They had done all this without consulting him, without even letting him know what they planned. Even Vonnie! Half of them would be dead by now if it weren't for him, but now they all thought he was losing it.

He stamped out of the hall, ignored by the celebrating crowd. Vonnie followed him down into the basement. "Where are you taking that thing?"

"To the room." Not the armory. And let somebody try to make something of it!

His wife sighed again. She turned around and went back up the stairs to the brightly lit hall.

Alone in their room, Solokov stowed away the ammunition for the M-16. He kept a few clips, put them in the pocket of his coat, and added a strip of jerky from the supply at the bunker. Somewhere, he knew, he had a spare pair of gloves. His hands were numb after the long day outside in the cold. His feet were hardly better off. He knew he wouldn't be able to last the night out if he didn't get something hot inside him.

The kitchen was open, and he ladled out a bowl of the hot corn-and-pea mash that was what they were subsisting on these days. Animal feed, sure enough. Animal feed that the raiders were trying to kill them for, the way he'd predicted from the first. He sat with the gun on the table next to his bowl and spooned the slop down, nursing his grievances, longing for a hot cup of unobtainable coffee.

Finally he stood up again, felt that his feet had come back to life, and picked up the M-16 from the table. He went out the back way so he would not have to look at the Christmas tree. At least there was a guard on duty at the door, and he logged out, ignoring the glance of curiosity directed at the assault rifle.

There was a utility garage at the rear of the school, and Solokov hunkered down in the doorway, wrapping a blanket around himself. He lifted the M-16 and sighted through its night-scope. *Now,* he thought, *now let the bastard try to get past me. We'll see whether guns can kill him or not!*

Uneasily, he recalled what the vampire had said to him, about not wanting to kill anyone. It was true, nobody *had* been killed. Not yet. He shook the thought away. He waited.

Well after midnight, the door of the school opened and someone came out. "Gene, are you out here?"

He tried to stand, was too stiff and numb. "Over here," he called out as low as he could. When she was closer, he added, "What is it? Can't you keep it quiet? He can probably hear everything we say."

"Gene, for heaven's sake, come inside to bed. It's Christmas Eve."

"And what kind of a Christmas will it be if *he* kills someone tonight? What if it's a kid?"

"You'll freeze to death out here all night! Can't you forget about it, just this once?"

"Just go back inside! This is something I've got to do."

Vonnie shook her head. She looked at him for a moment and then went back inside the school.

Her brother's room was on the first floor, close to the nurse's office where they had moved his clinic. Vonnie knocked softly. It was after midnight. In a moment her sister-in-law Beth came to the door, wearing a flannel bathrobe.

"Is Brian still awake? I have to talk to him."

"Come in."

Vonnie came into the room, quiet so as not to wake the children sleeping, wrapped up in blankets at the back. She thought suddenly of how many times Beth had welcomed her into her house, always with a fresh cup of coffee and a piece of

271

homemade cake. Would they ever know that life again?

Brian sat up. "Vonnie? What's wrong?"

She went to kneel down next to him. "It's Gene. I'm so worried. All he can think about now, the only thing that matters to him is that . . . monster. He's outside now with a gun, waiting for him. I think he's going to stay out there all night! . . . Tell me, do you think he's losing his mind?"

Her brother grasped her shoulders. "He's had a shock. He's not the only one. It must have been horrible to wake up like that, to find him bending over him."

Vonnie shuddered, nodded.

"I'd prescribe a tranquilizer if I could, but . . ." The doctor shrugged. "It would be hardest for someone like Gene, a man who always thought of himself in control of everything. You know, Vonnie, I didn't think much of all this business at first — survivalists and everything — but I've had to admit, Gene was right about more than I gave him credit for. The people in this town owe him a lot. I don't like to see what's happening to him, either. We *need* Gene."

"I've heard some of the things they're saying. But, oh, Brian, he came in today, with that gun, and the way he looked when he saw the Christmas tree, and everyone so happy for a change — do you know what he said? 'Who authorized this?' He wasn't *like* that before . . . everything happened.

"Do you think if he finally catches, or kills this vampire, he'll get over this?"

Her brother shook his head. He didn't know. "I hope so."

They held each other. It was all they could do.

\* \* \*

Gene Solokov waited out the night in the doorway, stirring only when he had to get his blood moving again. By the time dawn came and he could hear the squeals of children from inside, he could barely get up to his feet. And the vampire had never appeared.

## 6

Blaine Kittredge saw Solokov begin the long walk back to Danby, watched the stubborn, stolid figure until it disappeared into the shadows. He did not follow. Gene Solokov feared him now. But Kittredge felt that he had mismanaged things, coming here. He shook his head — managing humans. Now Solokov was even more determined to destroy him. Perhaps it was inevitable, that one of the two of them must be destroyed, as the interloper Matt had been.

It was wrong to feel personal enmity for a human. He should be trying to find a way to keep Solokov alive, protecting Danby from the raiders. Instead, the man was obsessed with his destruction. Kittredge went back into the shed and cautiously eased open the hatch. The bunker was too small for a shelter, but it was stocked with enough emergency supplies to enable a man to survive for months. A single man.

Solokov would have made a formidable raider. He was certainly well equipped for it. Was he keeping this cache of supplies for that contingency? But something had come along that he hadn't planned for, something that made him break that gun out of storage. Thoughtfully, Kittredge lowered the hatch, concealing what was hidden below.

That night he hunted outside of Danby.

For the next two days a blizzard complicated Kittredge's existence. He preferred to take his victims while they were outside, in the dark, but even the raiders were not venturing out into the wind-lashed snow of the storm. They would have been lost within minutes. Kittredge himself found it hard to see more than a few yards, and he spent most of the time resting inside the white Victorian house, confident that for once not even Solokov would be pursuing him.

Then the storm passed, leaving behind a frigid polar icescape. The thermometer dipped below minus twenty. Few of the humans ventured outside, and the ones who did were continually stamping their feet, cupping their hands around their faces, breaking off their work to warm themselves for a while.

They were careful to lock themselves in at night before it got entirely dark. But locks had been no barrier to Kittredge for well over a century. Indeed, their false sense of security was an asset to his purpose. All he needed was to find one of them alone.

That night it was a woman. He carried her to a garage just a few blocks outside the downtown perimeter, where she could see the lights to make her way back.

Less than an hour later, though, a search began, armed men with flashlights out in the streets, calling out a woman's name. Solokov was among them, carrying the M-16 from the bunker, glancing into every shadow. He, alone among the others, was not searching solely for the missing victim.

Concerned, Kittredge backtracked to where he

had left her, just five hundred yards from the shelter of the Elks Lodge. But it had not been close enough. The woman lay on her side, arms wrapped around her body. He touched her, seeking heat, a heartbeat, but she had already frozen to death. The cold had been too much after the blood loss.

Kittredge cursed, fangs biting down on his own lip. Another one wasted! It was his own carelessness, not to see that she had gotten back to safety. His victim was dead and he had not even had the satisfaction of the kill.

He looked down at the body. Just three days ago he had told Solokov that he had no intention of killing any of his people. Now this. And there was another complication he had to consider. In Green Springs, they would have known what to do, but he could not count on the humans of Danby.

The chances of it happening were minimal. But if she did rise to ravage the town in the frenzy of her first hunger, with no sunrise in this endless night to bring it to an end . . . His imagination made the scene all too clear. He could feel the response begin to stir within his own system, a wash of red across his vision.

No, he could not take the risk. Kittredge looked around the garage for a moment, then tore loose a cracked plank of siding. One end terminated in a sharp point. He turned over the body onto its back, pulled away the coat and sweater, exposing the location of the heart. He held the stake poised, hands unsteady.

He could not do it. It was *wrong.* He was not human, to do this to one of his own kind. It was the equivalent of murder, not in a frenzy, but with all the deliberation of cold blood. Never before, in all of his existence, had he felt this way, not even

276

at Eleanora's death, not even when he had killed the one named Matt.

But she was not, almost certainly not of his own kind. And if she were, it would be another case like Matt, all over again. He wished, in all his loneliness, that it need not be so. But it was, and it was not in his power to alter the fact.

He took a breath, and with all of his inhuman strength he plunged the sharp wood through the ribs, through the heart, until the point splintered on the cement floor of the garage.

He exhaled, shaking. Lifeless blood welled slowly from the corpse, and he turned away from the scent of it. Outside, barely a block away, he could hear the voices of the searchers. It might be hours until they could find her in the dark.

Kittredge took the feet of the corpse and dragged it outside, down the driveway and into the street. He wondered—when they found it, would they understand what he had done? Would they understand why?

## 1833

Although I was never a regular churchgoer, as Eleanora was, while I lived, I had been in the habit of prayer. Yet what Deity would heed the prayers of a being such as I had become?

Often, in those first months of my existence, I would creep silently into some church to touch the altar and the holy objects in an attempt to reassure myself that I might indeed not be damned. Once or twice I considered seeking the judgement of a priest. But what would they have known of my kind? Their opinions would have been no more informed than my own. And, as well, I did not wish to bring further risk upon my soul with the sacrilege of spilling blood within the precincts of a church.

There seemed to be no possibility of redemption. I must be damned, if not by my nature, then by the deeds it demanded of me. My only hope: that the soul was an illusion, damnation only a myth. Who, after all, had ever proved the existence of the soul?

I have long since accepted this as the most rational conclusion. After so many years, I am accustomed to the being what I am, to the exigencies of this existence. Yet why else have I been so willing to prolong it, if I did not dread the aftermath?

# Midnight

## 1

His eyes flew open at the sound of a single shot. Blaine Kittredge struggled to bring himself out of rest. There seemed to be no reason to panic. The sound had come from Danby, over a mile away, a single shot only. By the time he left his resting place, he was certain it had only been an alarm.

Still, he approached the town with more than his usual care. He could discover no signs of raiders in the vicinity, but something was happening. There were no workers out in the streets, and the visible sentries were doubled.

Kittredge waited. After nearly an hour he observed four figures leaving the school building. They went past the sentries and headed out of Danby, going south through the deep drifts of snow.

He moved to intercept them where the road went past the woods near Sugar Lake. All four men were armed with hunting weapons and alert to possible dangers. Not likely victims.

As he watched from the trees, they stopped, just where the drive led down to the Archers' lake house. The four of them seemed to be arguing about something. Some of the voices were familiar.

Kittredge came closer and recognized Rick Archer and Paul Krusack, with two other men who must have come with them from Green Springs.

A voice said angrily, ". . . can't even find him!"

Rick answered, the words muffled by a scarf around his face. Who was he trying to find? Kittredge hesitated within the concealment of the bare-branched trees. This could, somehow, be a trap. He could possibly trust Rick, he thought, if he had been alone. But Krusack? And he knew nothing of these other two.

Now they had turned off the road to Green Springs and were heading through the woods toward the house. Were they thinking to look for supplies the looters from Danby might have missed? Maybe they just wanted a chance to warm up. There was no other shelter for miles on the way to Green Springs. Kittredge shadowed them.

The four humans went into the house, and soon smoke started to rise from the fireplace chimney. Through a window, Kittredge could see that they had laid their guns aside and clustered near the fire. He made up his mind and silently went in through the back door.

Their voices were still angry. One of them was asking how long they were supposed to wait around here—until the smoke brought every raider in the county down on their heads?

"Just who are you waiting for?" he asked.

"Kittredge?" Rick's voice held an unmistakable tone of relief.

"You came out here to look for me?"

"We came out here to try to talk sense to those bastards in Danby!" snapped Krusack.

Kittredge stepped out into the open, on the edge of the firelight's shadows. "You talked to Solokov?" He ignored the slight scent of fear from the other two.

"We talked to him, all right!"

Rick explained, "A few of the towns — Green Springs, Granger, Edwardsburg — we're trying to put together some kind of a defense against these raids. Everybody knows about the kind of weapons they've got in Danby."

Kittredge nodded. "And Solokov told you to go to hell, didn't he?"

"Sounds like you know the bastard," said Krusack.

"We've met, in a way. He wasn't going to share the food, before. What made you think he'd share his guns?"

One of the others burst out, "We offered to trade — whatever they asked for."

Kittredge shook his head. What did Green Springs have that Danby might need that badly? "He said he didn't need anything you could offer, right?"

"I'll tell you what he *said*," Krusack snarled. "He said we were mixed up with *you!* He almost had us *shot!* The bastard's crazy!"

Rick explained again, "He recognized me. I guess he must have traced you to this house and figured out who was stealing the stuff. Does he . . . know about you?"

"He knows. They all do."

"Shit!" muttered Krusack.

"If you're thinking I could explain things to Solokov, I'm afraid anything I did would do more harm than good," Kittredge said.

"I . . . we thought maybe you could do something. About the raiders, I mean," Rick stammered uncertainly.

"Do what?"

"We've heard rumors."

"I think," said Kittredge slowly, "it was the other one who was the cause of most of those rumors. He was a raider, once."

"Well," said Krusack, glaring at Kittredge as if to blame him for the raids, "couldn't you do the same thing? Wouldn't bother you, would it?"

Kittredge stiffened. "You mean kill? If I wanted to, why shouldn't I just start with you? What difference should it make to me?"

"We had a deal once," said Rick desperately.

"An agreement is supposed to work in both directions. What would I need from you if I were killing the raiders?" Kittredge faced Krusack, who moved back a step as he drew back his lips from his fangs. "You want the same arrangement we had before? Well?"

The man went pale, shut his eyes for an instant. Then he opened them. "If that's what it takes. Go ahead."

Kittredge turned away, disappointed. "No. No, I told you before, it doesn't make sense for me to kill humans now." He looked back to Rick. "You know what you're asking, don't you? You want me to kill someone else so you can survive."

He thought of something else. "And have you considered what might happen if I do? Do you want another one on your hands—like the one I destroyed?"

"We figured you could take care of that."

"Oh, you don't ask much, do you?"

"Goddammit!" Rick cried out. "These are *murderers*! They killed *Danny* yesterday!"

Kittredge stared at him in shock. "Danny?"

"That's right! They hit us again yesterday, killed

my brother and three other people. And they took Lorraine."

Kittredge looked out the window into the darkness, confused. He owed these humans nothing. If anything, it was the other way around. And he was incapable of judging the raiders, who were only trying to survive in their way, not so much unlike his own. Any of them, even Rick, might have taken that way themselves if things had gone differently.

He thought of Solokov. "I think I can show you something that might help," he said slowly. "I know where some supplies are hidden. I can take you there."

"What kind of supplies?" asked Krusack scornfully. "Are there any guns, at least?"

"A couple. And ammunition."

One of the other men said, "Well, it's a better offer than we could get from Danby."

"Oh," Kittredge said with grim humor, "you'll be getting it from Danby. Do you want to know whose supplies they are?"

# 2

The cache was a lot more than the men from Green Springs had expected it would be. They instantly started cramming supplies into their packs, regardless that there was more in the bunker than the four of them could carry back with them. Kittredge stood guard at the door of the shed. Paul Krusack came up the steps with a hunting rifle and a heavy pack. He sighted down the gun and grinned with malicious pleasure. "Solokov's, huh?"

Kittredge did not respond. There was no question—Solokov would know who had led the looters here, where they had come from. But things had already gone past the point where they could get any worse with him.

The strangers from Green Springs emerged from the bunker after Krusack, and one of them glanced at him uneasily and mumbled, "Well, thanks."

Rick came out last and stopped at the door of the shed. "This stuff is great," he said. "But are you sure you can't . . ."

Kittredge was shaking his head. Quietly, he said, "Has it ever occurred to you that if I started to kill again it might not be so easy to stop? Then what happens when the raiders are all gone?"

"I guess I hadn't thought of that." Rick looked at him directly. "I guess I don't really understand how it is."

"Well, you probably never will. It's starting to get darker. You'd better go."

"You're going to stay here?"

*Why? Were you going to invite me inside this time?* "I have other plans."

He watched them go, glad to be alone for the moment in the cold air that held no human scent to stir his hunger. He had considered Krusack's offer, but after so many months of short rations the four of them would need all their strength to make it back to their town with those packs. Yet they were not so hungry as the raiders.

*They killed Danny.*

Kittredge put his hands to his head. Under other circumstances, *he* might have killed Danny Archer, with no regret whatsoever. Humans were mortal, after all. There was no way he could stop them from killing each other if reality dictated that there was not enough food for all to survive.

And besides, he argued with himself, killing the raiders would not bring Danny back to life. But he could not forget that there was still Lorraine.

Without conscious decision, he was walking through the snowfield in the general direction of Green Springs. If they had abducted her yesterday, she could still be alive. He remembered the wide-eyed girl in the bed when he had first come to Butler's house. They liked to use their women first. And Butler's band was still the closest to Green Springs.

He plowed through the drifts, deliberately trying not to consider his motives, which he suspected would not stand close examination. Perhaps it was because both Danny and Lorraine had been *his* for so long. But Paul Krusack had been in the lake house, too, and he could not imagine himself going off to rescue Krusack from the raiders. Or maybe he was getting to be demented enough to do just that.

He considered the patterns of the raider gangs' operations. They were a mobile, fluid presence in the county, but they had roughly defined territories, much like his own kind. Perhaps the fact would serve to explain what he was doing. Butler's group controlled the Green Springs region, south of Danby. There were a couple of other gangs that operated closer to Granger, the Fulham County seat.

Butler's band still occupied the same house, and Kittredge laughed when he caught sight of it. Since his last visit, they had boarded up the windows — on the lower floor. There were some things that humans never seemed to learn. But they had been spared trouble of his kind since he had eliminated the one named Matt.

As he approached the house, the human scent brought his hunger to life. He fought it down. First, he had to discover if they were the group holding Lorraine, if she was still alive. It would simplify matters, he thought, if she were dead. Then he would be able to tell himself — well, he had tried. That would be the end of it. It would have been different, he thought, if it had been Danny.

They were still awake in the house, and he did not want to wait, not with hunger starting to build in him. It was a simple matter to check each room — the lights were on inside, and none of the windows was completely boarded over. In a second-story bedroom he saw a woman tied spread-eagled to the posts of a bed, one of the raiders heaving on top of her. Whoever she was, she had not been compliant. Kittredge could not see the woman's face, but beneath the rapist, the hair on the mattress was blond.

He observed the animal phenomenon for a few moments, repelled. Never had he felt more remote from living beings. That he had once, in life, responded to such urges, performed such acts . . . His cherished memories of Eleanora were of a different kind. Or—had he simply forgotten?

The man lifted himself off and Kittredge could finally get a clear look at the woman's face. It was Lorraine, her elegant features marred with bruises, her nose and lips swollen, bleeding. She had not given in easily. But how she would hate it if she could see herself now! He could see no remaining trace of her resemblance to Eleanora. For that, he was grateful.

The raider was leaving the room, and Kittredge tried the window. It was locked or nailed shut—he was not sure which. He had to get in quickly, but breaking the glass could be heard from the inside. Shifting his grip, he forced the sash slowly, stripping the turnbuckle's screws from the wood.

Lorraine heard the sound. As he came in through the window, she recognized him and twisted frantically, the ropes digging into her swollen wrists and ankles.

"Quiet!" he whispered. There was a blood scent in the room that sent hunger spasms through his system. Resisting it, he went to the bed, snapped the ropes. Freed, she turned immediately on her side and rolled herself into a ball. Her naked skin was dark blue with cold. He suspected she would have no feeling in her hands and feet, would not be able to stand, even if she were capable of walking any distance after the multiple rapes. He knew nothing of such things, did not care to know. He looked around for something to warm her, but the room was empty, all the sheets and blankets gone. There were no clothes. He took off his own jacket to put over her, but it was completely inadequate to warm a living human. He could never take her outside into this cold with no more protection than that.

He turned away from the sight of her on the bed — the only mercy he could afford her right now — and went over to the door. It had only been two minutes since the raider had left. When would the next one come for his turn?

Kittredge waited until he heard a man's step in the hallway. His plan was simple. He would take this one, satisfy his hunger, then strip off the man's clothes for Lorraine to wear while he took her back to Green Springs.

The door opened, the man came into the room, and Kittredge seized him, ready to plunge his fangs into the throat. Instead, he drew back abruptly, hissing a curse. This one was contaminated!

Keeping his grip on the man so he could not cry out, Kittredge shoved him against the wall and recognized his captive. It was Butler. His eyes were wide open in horror, the scent of it making Kittredge's hunger throb sharply, despite the radiation taint.

Now what would he do? How long did he have before the others would wonder what was happening inside the room? He might at least use the time he had. Bringing his face close to Butler's, he whispered, "You know what I am?"

He had dealt with this band often enough in the past. At the nod, he went on, "If you want to live, keep quiet. You understand? All right, now I want you to take off your clothes."

He eased his grip away from Butler's throat. The man choked. Kittredge said impatiently, "Go on, take them off. Hurry up."

The man's hands worked clumsily. He could not keep his eyes from staring at Kittredge. Finally the clothes were on the floor and he was standing, naked, shivering in the chilly room.

Kittredge scooped them up and threw them across to the bed. "Go on, Lorraine, put these things on." When she did not move, he whispered more urgently, "Hurry up! I can't take you out of here like that! You'd freeze!"

As she stirred on the bed, Butler stood, braced against the wall for what he obviously thought was going to happen next. His fear was turning to bewilderment. Kittredge was thinking of some way to dispose of the man quietly, breaking his neck, when Butler whispered, "Shit, get it over with, why don't you?"

Annoyed, Kittredge shook his head. Butler put his hands to his throat, not understanding.

"Radiation," Kittredge said curtly, and at the look of incomprehension, "Your blood is poisoned. I can't use it."

Shock wiped out much of the human's fear. "You know that?" he asked unbelievingly.

Kittredge glanced to see how fast Lorraine was getting dressed. "It's the scent," he said absently.

"Reichler kept trying to say—"

The name caught Kittredge's attention. "Who? Reichler? Were you one of them, by the lake house? Did you know the one named Matt? What his last name was?"

Butler shook his head. "No, I don't remember. Reichler just called him Matt. Reichler said he was dead. He told me . . ."

Butler's voice seized up as he saw Kittredge pick up one of the ropes he had torn from the bedposts. "What you . . . gonna do?"

"Nothing." Kittredge grasped the man's wrists, pulled them behind his back. "Matt *was* dead. Reichler died, too. He froze to death, out in the cold running after Matt. That's who it was, doing all the killing a month or so ago. Not me."

*"No! He was dead! I saw . . ."*

"Yes." Kittredge pulled the knot tight, felt Butler flinch. "I killed him. He turned into . . . one of my kind. There's no need to worry about him anymore, though. This time, he's dead for good."

He glanced back, saw Lorraine standing up, slowly pulling on Butler's coat. Finally, she was finished. Now all he needed was to finish tying the man, then wait for the next one. . . .

Lorraine had finally seen Butler. She came closer, not taking her eyes off of him. Suddenly, without a warning, she screamed, launched herself at the bound man, tearing at his face with her fingernails, trying to drive her knees into his groin. Tainted blood scent filled the air.

Kittredge seized her flailing, twisting body, put a hand over her mouth to stop her screams. They must have heard that! Although, considering the circumstances, a woman screaming in this room might not arouse too much attention—

The door opened. Butler, his hands still tied, had managed to turn the knob, was running from the room, calling for help.

*"Damn!"* He *knew* he should have killed the man! Now he only had seconds. Lifting Lorraine, Kittredge went to the window, kicked out the glass, and jumped with her down into the snow. The drop—fortunately—stunned her into silence. There were shouts coming from the house. He looked back up and saw armed men starting to enter the room he had just left. He started to run, Lorraine's slight

290

weight slowing him down as he went through the deeper drifts, but it was soon clear that they would not be coming after them.

Now all of his instincts were urging, demanding that he take her to satisfy the torment of his hunger. He paused. She was clinging to him for human warmth, but his undead flesh had none to offer. He looked down at the battered human he was holding. After that ordeal—beaten up, repeatedly raped, tied naked in the frigid bedroom without food—Lorraine would never survive the long miles to Green Springs if he took her blood. He had a vivid memory of how quickly his last victim in Danby had died, the body frozen in less than an hour.

But the pulse in her throat, the hot, rich blood flow within his reach, tantalizing.

With an effort of will, Kittredge shifted his grip and went on. Why had he come all this way, made this effort, if he were just going to end up killing her? He might as well have let the raiders have her. When he came to Green Springs . . . He quickened his pace through the snow.

Lorraine had not made a sound since the house, although her breathing was steady enough. He supposed she was in some state of shock or hypothermia—humans were fragile beings, after all, and she was a woman.

He recalled that in these days that remark would be considered a sexist insult. But Kittredge had not lived during times when women demanded liberation from male protection. Eleanora—well, it simply seemed natural to him that the role of the male was to shelter and protect the female, the strong to defend the weak.

Of course, now, in the Nightfall world, it was the strong who would survive, the weak who would die.

It was what he had tried to make Rick Archer understand. There were women in Green Springs. Women, children, the old and the weak. In Danby, as well. Among the raiders, how long had it been since he had seen a woman, except like Lorraine, tied to a bed? The demands of survival were selecting for ruthlessness. Too many raider males saw women simply as prey. Butler was far from being the worst of them, and he was a murderer, thief, kidnapper, rapist, cannibal, and doubtless more. Gene Solokov, Kittredge thought, was ruthless, too, but there was a difference. He tried to articulate it to himself as a purely practical calculation, that a species concerned with survival does not kill off its females.

Lorraine, in his arms, stirred, murmured something. Blood oozed through a split in her lip, and his hunger spasmed. Clenching his teeth so that his fangs drew his own blood, Kittredge kept walking. Surely he must be almost to Green Springs by now!

He thought Lorraine must be unconscious. She was not heavy—nowhere near as heavy as Paul Krusack had been—but the long trek through the drifts had drained him. With every step his hunger pangs grew sharper. He knew that if she woke, if she showed even the slightest fear, his control would break. He would—he could admit it—regret it if he killed Lorraine. Not because she resembled Eleanora. He had rid himself of that fantasy. But possibly he had judged her too harshly because of that resemblance. It had taken a kind of courage to face him as she had done and demand that he fulfill his bargain with them. To look directly into his eyes.

Ahead, he could see Green Springs. He fixed his eyes on the town, each step bringing him closer to the moment he could put down his burden. The snow grew firmer where human boots had trampled it down. The town square was just ahead. He came closer, wondering if he should try to take Lorraine into the church. He couldn't hold out much longer, not with all the control in the world, but he couldn't just drop her out here, either, in her condition, not in this cold.

A shot rang out, startling him, overcoming the hunger for an instant. He called out, "Don't shoot! I've got Lorraine Archer out here!"

There was a silence. Then, "Don't you try anything, you hear? Don't even move!"

A pair of armed sentries came out from the door of a building. One of them shone a light and caught the figures standing near the square, one holding the other in his arms. They approached, and the light revealed Lorraine's face. "Damn!" the man swore at the sight of her; then, as he caught sight of the other face, "Damn!" in a very different tone.

"Here," said the other one, "can she stand?"

"I don't know." As Kittredge relinquished her, other humans came running up, Rick Archer one of them, to his intense relief.

Kittredge held himself rigid as his senses reeled with human scent and his hunger gnawed at him from within, devouring. They were taking Lorraine away, Rick was going with them. . . .

"Wait!" he called out. The strain in his voice made it harsh.

Rick stopped, looked at him. Kittredge's hands were curled into fists, the nails scoring the burn scars on his palms.

"I need . . ."

Rick's face went stiff. Then he said slowly, "Of course."

People were starting to look their way. "Better not right here," Rick said. As they walked together into

293

the shadow of a doorway, he started to pull up the sleeve of his coat.

Kittredge leaned back against the wall, relief flowing through him. And Rick's blood. It occurred to him that perhaps only with Rick, whom he could trust not to be afraid, he could have done this tonight and left the donor living. Or Danny, if Danny had still been alive.

"I'm sorry about your brother," he said.

Rick was wrapping his own wrist. "He missed your games together." He looked over at Kittredge. "I want to thank you, for Lorraine."

Kittredge nodded. He still was not quite certain why he had done it. Rick was shivering hard. "I'd better get you back inside." He helped him up.

In the light from the open door, he paused for a moment. "Rick? Could I ask you . . ."

"Sure. What?"

"The fire. Well, I know it left scars. But, could you tell me, just how bad they are?"

Rick frowned, puzzled. "Not so bad. With your hair longer, you'd hardly notice it. You'd look . . ."

"Almost human?"

## 3

Travis Butler didn't feel too much like talking. Jesus, everybody already knew what happened — *he* showed up again. Lucky that nobody got killed, even hurt. He took the bitch with him, was all, and nobody minded that too much, except for maybe a couple guys who'd been waiting their turn on her.

So he'd gotten into some different clothes — clothes at least were easier come by than food — and kind of mumbled an explanation that the bitch had gone crazy and let him get away while *he* was pulling her off.

What he hadn't said was the rest of what happened in there — how Reichler was right all along, that he *was* the same *thing* that jumped them in the woods by the lake and killed Leon, the kid named Matt, the rest of them. Butler could still remember the sight of those eyes glowing — and how he'd pissed his pants, then turned tail to get out of there as fast as he could, not even looking back for the others. Some Marine! But when you put a hole in a man's gut and he just gets up and keeps coming . . .

Reichler at least had tried to save Leon. He was

dead, now, too. And Matt, who'd been on the ground with his throat torn out, was the one running around biting out other people's throats. Whole damn world gone crazy.

Butler turned over on his bed and hid his face. And he was going to die, too. Die hard, of radiation poisoning. The vampire had no reason to lie, not about that. He said he could smell it on him. *Jesus! I don't want to go that way!*

But Butler's own body knew—those places on his skin that never seemed to heal, starting to bleed lately—that was cancer, wasn't it? From the fallout.

He remembered bitterly the way he'd gone around from place to place, looking for food, looking for a shelter that would take him, those first few months when the fallout was bad. Joliet should have been safe, far enough from Chicago, but it turned out no place was safe if the cops took one look at the color of your face and wouldn't let you inside.

Now he was dying, and over in towns like Danby they stayed safe, locking everyone else out. Plenty to eat over at Danby, too. Fuckers shoot everyone comes into sight.

Travis Butler lay with his arms around his face. He hadn't planned to end up like this. Shit, the killing, chopping up some dude for meat? You took off the head first so it wouldn't be staring at you, sliced open the belly and all that shit comes falling out, the guts. Jesus, the first time he saw that, he just about puked. Those guys who were farmers, like Reichler was, they were used to that kind of thing. Just pretend it was a pig or something.

He thought he'd see a lot when he was a Marine, but not like this. His dad had been a Marine, too — over in Nam, back then. He still used to have these two shriveled black things he said were gooks' ears. Get a dozen beers in him, the old man would tell how they'd cut off a guy's prick over there, stuff it in his mouth. And he could remember how he'd think — Jesus, I could never do something like that.

Now look at him! But you got to eat. That's what it comes down to. You got to eat something to stay alive. Only now, he was going to die, no matter. It was fuckers like over in Danby, who wouldn't let outsiders into their shelter. Especially not black outsiders from the South Side of Chicago.

Butler lay on his bed, staring into the dark. He could hear the rest of them talking about how now they were going to have to go out in the cold on another raid. But there was plenty of food in Danby.

Show them. Show the fuckers what it was like. Their turn now. Let them be the ones to feel it for a change.

# 4

Blaine Kittredge had not stayed for too long in Green Springs. After he brought Rick back to the church, he tried, fitfully, to rest for a while in an isolated part of the village, but there were too many humans close by who knew what he was and, worse, how he could be killed.

He could not trust their kind, not even the ones who seemed to be harboring some unrealistic expectations that he was now going to take on the raider bands and wipe them out, one by one. Like some kind of vampire Rambo, as Danny Archer might have said.

Rick had asked him outright one more time. "Look, you know, people here do understand that you're different—from that other one. I mean, nobody'd . . . bother you if you stayed around here."

"What do they expect—the next time the raiders show up, should I turn into a wolf and scare them away? I can't *do* that kind of thing!"

"Well, I suppose it's really our problem, not yours. We'll have to find some way to handle it ourselves."

It was the same advice Kittredge had given Rick three months ago at the lake house. Somehow, though, it sounded different coming back at him now. He tried to explain as well as he could. "I'm not . . . completely invulnerable. You remember the fire. I admit I misled you about some things, back there. I thought it would make things go more smoothly if you thought I was more than I really am."

He stared down at his hands, the long, slender, white fingers, the disfiguring scars. "Look, maybe I might be able to do something, but my own way. Besides," he tried to make a joke out of it, "I wouldn't want to find out if Paul Krusack has been sharpening any more stakes."

"He wouldn't . . ." Then Rick understood. "I suppose not," he said. "Well, maybe I'll see you again some time, then. Maybe we can have a game of chess."

"Maybe."

And Rick had gone inside, shutting the door behind him.

Talk in Danby generally supported Gene Solokov's decision not to join the defensive coalition with the nearby towns in the county.

"Why should we risk our skins?" Kittredge overheard them saying. "Let them fight their own battles, like we do."

"Yeah, do you think any of them would show up to help us?"

"Ammunition's low, anyhow. We can't afford to waste it."

"Besides, weren't those the same guys who came around earlier, trying to steal supplies?"

"Yeah, and did you see who was with them? That vampire kid!"

Solokov had been generous, was the prevailing opinion, letting those bastards from Green Springs walk out of here. Maybe Gene wasn't so crazy after all, about that vampire thing.

Kittredge was fascinated by the continual metamorphosis of the rumors. The Archers' lake house was by now supposed to have been a den of vampires, with dozens of humans kidnapped and held captive for their blood. Their bodies had been found everywhere, in and around the house. Earl Thomas, according to his own stories, was lucky he had finally managed, after great danger and hardship, to escape.

Kittredge had to laugh. As long as the fallout lasted and they had supplies down in the shelter, you couldn't have moved Earl Thomas out of the lake house with high explosives. But he did not mind the rumors. It was normal, and somewhat reassuring, for humans to hate and fear him for what he was.

On the other hand, he was not excessively gentle with Earl Thomas when he took the grocery store clerk in his bed the night after he came back from Green Springs. But that would only serve to lend verisimilitude to his account of the way things had been. And the fear-savor was quite intense.

Danby was functioning more normally now. The citizens were united behind their leader once again. Those individuals who tried to argue in favor of cooperation with the other towns were a distinct minority. Danby was safe. Let the others look out for themselves.

The towns. If it came down to the towns or the raiders, Kittredge knew he had only one conceivable choice. There was no sense in allowing a contaminated human like Travis Butler to kill off a dozen healthy ones to keep himself alive. The raiders were predators, too much like his own kind. And this was his territory.

Thus it was disturbing, as he approached the region of Granger, the Fulham County seat, that the entire countryside seemed empty. The snow blew across the fields under the gray sky, over a landscape totally barren of life. It was an emptiness profound and terrifying, a portent to Kittredge of the way the world must become if humans were to vanish entirely.

It was true, the raiders led unsettled lives. There had been two gangs established close to Granger. Perhaps they had simply moved on, out of the county altogether. But that seemed unlikely. From the stories he heard, things were no better anywhere else, and most places worse. And, though gangs had been known to war on each other in territorial disputes, he could detect no sign of a conflict, no snow-mounded bodies, no hint of blood scent in the air. He passed the lifeless, burned-out village of Merton—but that had happened over a month ago. The gangs were simply, mysteriously, not where they had been.

Night came, and Kittredge went into the town of Granger to locate a victim. He questioned the man first, who was well aware of what he was. He knew nothing of what had happened to the raider bands, where they might have gone. He was simply glad they hadn't been around lately—no sign of them for the last two or three days. Though why should they bother coming around, when there was nothing left to take, anyway? People were starving everywhere, except for maybe over at Danby.

Danby. The man realized the implication of what he had said almost as soon as Kittredge. Danby had stores. They had the canning plant. They had enough food locked up to feed the whole county. Kittredge knew how far the rumors were from the truth. But truth would never stop the raiders.

And how many raiders were there in Fulham County? How many could they assemble together for a single, massive attack on the only target that would make such an enterprise worthwhile?

# 5

It was all very easy to say: hurry back to Danby and take care of everything. But what could he actually *do* to stop an attack by . . . how many bands? Kittredge counted them mentally: the one around Edwardsburg, Butler's band near Green Springs—he knew of at least six in this county alone. If they were all in this, how many men altogether?

Wait—was he letting his imagination run away with him? He had no real proof. But it had only been a matter of time before the raiders were desperate enough to turn on Danby. None of them was strong enough individually to take on the stronghold by itself.

Kittredge paused just outside of Granger. Danby was about fifteen miles away. Green Springs was half that distance, though a few miles out of the way. They had been talking about a militia, a protective association, in Green Springs. This could be the opportunity to crush all the raider bands in the county between such a force and Danby's defenses. Kittredge turned away from Danby and went south the few miles to Green Springs, where he knew he could find Rick Archer, the one human who would listen to him.

Rick came awake with a sudden start as the cold hand shook his shoulder. "Oh, Christ, it's you! I thought . . . What is it?" he asked, sitting up.

"Raiders. No, not here. I think they've gone to attack Danby, at least five bands together, maybe more. Didn't you tell me there was a defense association you were setting up to deal with the raids?"

Rick shook his head, still half-asleep. "Yeah, but Danby wouldn't go along with it. You know that."

"You mean your towns would rather wait until it's their turn?"

"Shit!" Rick exclaimed softly as he realized what Kittredge was telling him. "Five bands? That could be . . . God! We'd be wiped out! Are you sure?"

"Not entirely. I haven't seen them yet—"

"But—"

"But it's the only logical explanation. They aren't *anywhere else.*"

"Look, I'm not in charge of anything around here. I was only along that one time we went to Danby in case we ran into you."

"Well, tell them, then, whoever is in charge. They can do something about it or not."

"If you talk to them yourself, explain . . ."

"No. There might not be time. If I'm wrong, if I find out anything for certain, I might come back. Right now, I'm going there myself."

"Why? I mean, what can you do?"

"I don't know. I'll see when I get there." Because Danby is *mine,* he added to himself.

The detour had taken time. As Kittredge grew close to Danby he could sense the presence of the sun at the world's horizon, still undetectable to human eyes. But soon the raiders would have enough light to make their move. Unless—he broke into a

304

run—they had attacked in the dark.

His eyes swept over the flat gray snow plain, but there was no fighting, no raider band advancing. Either they had not yet arrived—or his conjectures had been all wrong.

So, what could he do now? Walk into town and talk the problem over with Gene Solokov?

Then Kittredge blinked. Something, in the fields ahead of him, had moved. He looked again. The wind had contoured the snow into drifts and hollows. Men could have hidden themselves in those hollows to wait for enough light to attack.

He hesitated. From the viewpoints of the church steeple and the water tower Solokov's sentries would spot a raider band approaching. If they were alert. If there was enough light.

But he could see the attackers now, digging themselves out, shaking off the snow, checking their weapons. Watching, Kittredge started to count. There were at least two hundred men about to advance on Danby from all sides through the snow-covered fields. It was a matter of minutes before it was too late, and now the question he had been asking himself became urgent: what, really, could he do to stop them?

There were men out there who were terrified of him, on whom he had fed his hunger. But that was an effect he could only produce at close range, alone with a human in the dark. It would do little good under these circumstances. At the lake house, he had taken on six or seven armed men, but then he was out of his mind with the frenzy. It was only luck that one of their shots had not hit his heart. It was not the kind of luck he wanted to count on again.

He glanced up to the height of the steeple, silently urging the sentry to be there and open up his eyes before the raiders got into position. Already, some of them were only a few hundred yards from the cover of an abandoned store on the highway. Then he thought, why keep silent?

Reaching into his pocket for the .38 he still carried, Kittredge fired a shot into the air.

At once, the advancing raiders froze into place, and he could hear a voice cursing, "Goddammit, who did that?"

But it was too late. The town was already alerted. A rifle shot came from a sentry post. Soon, Kittredge knew, every armed citizen of Danby would be running onto the streets. Belatedly, it occurred to him that he might have fired to better effect.

The raiders were running now, their leaders shouting for them to make it into the streets before they were pinned down in the open. That threat decided a few who had been hanging back. Gradually the fire from the town grew heavier as the defenders took their positions and their enemies came into range. But both sides, Kittredge noticed, were being sparing with their ammunition.

He looked again at the .38 in his hand, checked the magazine. Five shots left. All right. He had already alerted the town, robbed the attackers of the element of surprise. Now he supposed he could account for a few of them. It was absurd, now, to be concerned about wasting lives. Too many lives were going to be lost in the next hours. He reminded himself again: better to shoot a blood-tainted raider than let his kind lay waste the whole town. It was the only practical alternative.

But even with his inexperience, Kittredge knew he would have to get closer to the fighting to have any effect. Already there had been casualties. Blood scent grew stronger as he came up unseen behind the raiders. A man was kneeling behind the corner of a house, two others standing next to him. Kittredge aimed, pulled the trigger, and his target fell, face forward in the snow.

Not so hard, he was thinking, but one of the others turned to the threat from their backs as Kittredge fired the .38 again. His shot missed. Both of them were shooting at him now, and he dropped to the snow. Three rounds left. Maybe not so easy, after all. They had him outgunned, each with a hunting rifle, though at this range a shotgun would have had a more lethal effect.

Or a submachine gun. From the center of the town came the fast sputter of automatic fire. It had better be in Solokov's hands than a raider's, Kittredge thought to himself. The blood scent grew more intense. He fired again, missing again and bringing more return fire in his direction. The odds were distinctly unfavorable, but he was feeling more angry than afraid, thinking it would be his own stupid damned fault if he got himself killed out here, involved in something he knew nothing about. He should have learned this lesson back at the lake house. It was a good thing the raiders were no better shots than he was.

Another shot came over his head, and a curse from the same direction, "Goddammit, where *is* that bastard?"

Kittredge wanted to kick himself. It was still barely light! Because they couldn't *see* their target, that was why they hadn't been able to hit him! Why did he start thinking like a human the minute he put a gun in his hand? All he had to do was run.

Quickly, he sprinted to the cover of a tree, then around a corner. He looked down at the gun he was still holding and wanted to throw the thing away. But there were still two more rounds, two more raiders it could account for if he could get close enough once again not to miss.

Again he crept around the backs of the houses, behind the raiders' positions, until he found one of them by himself with his back turned. A single shot from behind was effective. The same thing worked again, and finally the gun was empty.

Kittredge felt profound relief. He did not have to keep this up any longer. The relief faded abruptly as he saw the raider's gun beside his body. He went slowly to the weapon, searched the corpse for more ammunition, recoiling only a little from the taint of its poisoned blood. He could go on almost indefinitely like this, he realized, working the bolt of the rifle and wondering if he could hit anything with it. He was going to have to keep getting in close to have any kind of a chance.

As the battle went on, and the raiders advanced steadily toward the central stronghold of the town, Kittredge continued to circle around the periphery, sniping away at them from their rear. There was a kind of strange, cold bloodlust beginning to take hold of him, and he no longer could feel regret for the lives he was wasting. One fell, another, and he would crawl in close enough to take that one's weapon, then move on to find another target.

He figured he had accounted for at least twenty of the enemy when he noticed a subtle change in the sound of the fighting. Gunshots were coming less frequently now. Ammunition must be running short.

Carrying his current weapon, a shotgun, Kittredge started to make his way closer to the center of the fighting. It was not difficult to move among the raiders, who came from different bands and could not easily recognize each other. Doubtless they thought he was one of their own.

The defenders had retreated or been driven back to their fortified strongpoints. Most of the fighting was now in the street between the canning plant and the school. Here, bodies littered the streets. Intermittent fire came from the buildings as raiders broke from cover. It appeared that both sides were having to pick their targets. The attackers had lost at least a quarter of their number already, but they kept coming. This was not a quick snatch-and-grab operation, as Kittredge already knew. The raiders had confederated to stake everything they had on this one attempt—they meant to *take* Danby and all its rumored riches.

Kittredge could have laughed. What if they knew that they were dying for nothing more than shell corn and canned peas? But to men who were reduced to subsisting on human flesh, perhaps it would be worth it. He glanced at the still forms lying in the streets. Human flesh in plenty.

At first, he could not see how the raiders thought they could win. The defenders seemed to have all the advantages. But as he watched, he realized that by constantly feigning and threatening attack, they were forcing their opponents to exhaust their own ammunition. The defenders were aware of the tactic, shooting only when necessary to keep the assailants back. Occasional short bursts of semiautomatic fire still came from the school, but when Solokov's weapon was empty, then, Kittredge figured, the raiders would rush the building. By the end, it might come down to knives and bare hands.

Even teeth. At that prospect, his bloodlust flared hot.

There was another possibility, he realized, turning his head to the south, to the snow-covered Route 59. How far could the sound of the gunfire carry? All the way to Green Springs? Had they taken his warning seriously? Would they come to Danby's relief? He had told Rick that he would—no, might—come back if he was wrong. But how long would it take, just to get the forces of the several towns together?

And how long could this battle last? Should he consider going back to Green Springs now and telling them that the opportunity they needed was finally here?

But the raiders were clearly not inclined to let things drag out that long. Kittredge recognized Travis Butler as he began to give new orders, waving men around to the other sides of the school building. He watched, appalled, as the attackers sprinted past the defenders' line of fire, men falling, kicking, crawling. How could mortal beings risk their whole existence like this? Butler, perhaps, he could understand. The man had death in him already, and he knew it. But the rest of them?

Within the school, someone noticed the change in tactics. Suddenly Gene Solokov came rushing out of the door with three others. Under covering fire from the school's interior, they sprinted across the front of the building and around the corner, cutting down the raiders. Seeing him vulnerable, Travis Butler burst from cover and charged across the street in a frontal assault with about twenty others, firing as they ran, but Solokov spun around, the M-16 spurting death, and shotguns fired from the windows, leaving more than half of the raiders with their blood seeping into the snow.

Kittredge, without realizing what he was doing, had stepped out into the open, overwhelmed at the scale of the carnage in front of him, by the blood-saturated air. As the surviving raiders retreated back across the street, Gene Solokov saw him.

The man's eyes met his and went instantly wide with maddened recognition. In the center of the street, Solokov stood motionless, firing the assault rifle on full automatic, bullets spraying the raiders' position as he sought to obliterate his nemesis. Even for a few seconds after his ammunition was exhausted, he kept firing the empty weapon, oblivious to his danger. Then he looked down at it in shock and began to fumble for a full clip.

But the raiders were more quick to react. A single shot sent Solokov jerking backward to the ground. Yelling in triumph, Travis Butler dashed forward from cover to snatch the M-16 from the snow.

With that weapon in the raiders' hands, the entire situation was altered in a single instant. Blaine Kittredge did not stop to calculate this as he got to his feet and launched himself with inhuman speed toward the place where Butler lay prone in the snow behind Solokov's body, reaching for the full clip of ammunition. There was no time for calculation, only scant seconds to make it to the gun.

With practiced movements, the ex-Marine jammed the clip into the M-16 as the warning cries of his men alerted him. Twisting onto his back, he brought the weapon up to fire just as Kittredge's body fell onto his.

There was a moment when the motion of the world seemed to stop as the pain gathered itself. Then it struck Kittredge with the first surge of his heart, a wave of blood-red pain like magma erupting within him. The entire lower part of his body ribs, gut, legs—everything was shattered, ruptured. Blood and tissue were splattered onto the trampled, filthy snow. Another heartpulse convulsed him, the torment even worse as his system began to function again, and another. Screaming, wracked by the spasms, he writhed, made it to his knees, fell, lurched up again, conscious only of the overwhelming need driving him to seek blood.

And blood was everywhere. The air thick with the scent of it, the snow stained dark with it, and blood flowed, hot and irresistible, within the flesh surrounding him. Veins and arteries gushed blood as he tore into them. The whole world had turned crimson, but could there ever be enough to drown the pain?

## 6

They had been pounding on the door, kicking it. Now it sounded like they were trying to ram it in.

Brian Mercier winced at the noise. His eyes were bloodshot with fatigue, and his hands were not quite steady after the long night of trying to repair damaged bodies. Dark, dried blood was visible in the creases of his fingers. His shirt was stiff with it and some of the stains were still bright.

"Go away!" he shouted to the door. "Get out of here! Or, so help me, I'll smash every instrument in the room! I'll run the medicine down the sink! I mean it!"

The crashing at the door stopped. Good, they must have heard him.

"Come on, Doc!" came a voice from the other side. Hank Daschle. "Be reasonable. Let us in."

"Forget it."

"Doc, those are raiders. Murderers. God knows what else. You've got people out here need your help."

"I've got two men in here need my help. I've already done what I can for the rest. You want me to do more, get out of here and let me do what I have to."

There was silence again from the other side of the door. Then, "All right, Doc, we're going. We'll be back in a while, see if we can talk about this some more."

"I meant what I said," Mercier warned. "Nobody touches these men. Not if you want a doctor around here anymore."

"Okay, Doc. Just take it easy, all right?"

Silence. Mercier exhaled, went back to the tables where the two men were lying. His knees felt weak, shaky. He had given each of them at least a pint of his own, type-O blood.

Raiders. Murderers. God knows what else. The one with the sucking chest wound was quiet now. Mercier checked his pulse. He was hoping there hadn't been internal bleeding that he'd missed. The other, a Mexican-looking kid, was tossing around weakly, moaning. Mercier hoped he wasn't going to rip out the tubes draining his abdomen. He wasn't a surgeon. It had been the worst job of his life, single-handedly sewing the kid's gut back together, and it was still an uphill fight coming on, against the infection that was sure to set in.

Worriedly, he turned his eyes back to the locked door. There were people in the other room who would be needing more help. But if he opened the door, the men outside would come rushing in, drag his patients out, and shoot them. And he wasn't going to let them do that.

The banging came again. Not so loud this time. "I told you, get out of here!"

"Brian. It's me."

"Vonnie? Is there anyone else out there with you? Hank Daschle?"

"No, they're all gone. Brian, I have to talk with you."

"I'm not going to let them kill these men, Vonnie."

"I know that. It's all right, I understand. Just let me in, all right?"


Danby's police chief left the school building, frustrated. How long before they could get Doc out of there? He sure hoped Vonnie could talk some sense into him.

"Hey! Someone coming!" came a sentry's shout. Hank Daschle flipped the safety off his gun. *Not again,* he was hoping.

They were coming up Route 59, about thirty armed men from Granger, Green Springs, and other towns in Fulham County, including ten from the county seat who had been sheriff's deputies and still remembered that something like this had once been their duty.

Daschle and the other people of Danby stopped their work and watched the strangers approach, saw them slow and stare at the signs of the carnage. Finally Daschle stepped forward to meet them.

"What the hell do you want here?"

One of the deputies was shaking his head as he looked from the stack of stiff, frozen corpses to the half dozen men standing behind Daschle, guns ready. "We . . . heard there might be some trouble around here," he said lamely.

Daschle spit into the snow. "Too bad you showed up a little late. The show was a lot better yesterday."

"Hey," said the deputy, "we thought we might be able to help, that's all."

"Help! Shit, the goddamn *vampire* was more

315

help than you. At least he was *here!*"

"Look," the deputy bristled, "if you bastards had wanted help—"

He was interrupted by another man who elbowed his way forward. "Where *is* Kittredge?" Rick Archer demanded. "What did you do to him?"

"Huh?" Daschle was confused. "You mean the vampire? I dunno. Things were busy, you know?" The Danby police chief exhaled. "Hey, look, sorry. It was kind of bad here yesterday."

"Yeah," said the deputy, still with half an eye on the piled-up bodies. "Shit, how many *were* there?"

"Must be about eighty bodies we found so far. I'd say that was at least half of them. God, the way they came at us . . ."

"Yeah," said the deputy. He squatted for a closer look at one corpse. "The, uh, vampire do that? We had one guy attacked in Granger two nights ago, but—Jesus!"

Daschle glanced, then averted his eyes. "Yeah. Never saw anything like it. This one bastard empties an M-16 into him. A minute later, he's up again. Those guys ran, but it didn't do them any good. Lucky he couldn't get at any of our own men. Or maybe he could have, I don't know."

"What about Gene Solokov?" asked a deputy who had known him.

"Dead. We lost thirty-eight killed. Some more, hurt."

"Well," said another man, "I can help with that. Jim Polk—I'm a doctor in Granger."

"Thanks," said Daschle, his gratitude more sincere. "We do have a kind of a problem. Brian Mercier—you know him? He's got two of those bastards in the clinic, all shot up, and he won't let us get at them. To tell you the truth, I think he

316

may be a little bit . . . you know. Cracking up."

"Why not just let them live?"

The eyes of every human in the street turned to the shadowy figure standing in the mouth of an alley. Some of them lifted their guns reflexively.

"Let them live," said Blaine Kittredge again. "They were trying to stay alive. The same as you."

They were staring at him. He knew how he must look. But he was beyond caring how he appeared to humans. He ignored the guns pointed in his direction. Let them shoot. Let them face the consequences if they failed to destroy him.

Toward morning his mind had slowly begun to come out of the frenzy. Images of blood clouded all his memories since the moment he had lunged for the weapon in Butler's hands. Blood, dried stiff and frozen, caked his shredded clothes.

Eventually he had spotted the line of men traveling from Granger toward Danby and followed behind them. Had Danby survived? He had to know what had happened. The raiders—he had dim, red-tinged memories of encountering raiders throughout the night.

But now he knew that Danby had prevailed. On its own. Gene Solokov was right. They hadn't needed help, after all.

Kittredge limped out into the street. The damage to his legs had been beyond even his powers of recovery. They still ached.

"For God's sake, don't shoot!" a voice exclaimed. Rick Archer. So Rick was with them, Kittredge observed.

Hank Daschle gripped the deputy from Granger tight by the wrist. "Don't *ever* shoot at him!" he hissed. "Do you want to end up like *that?*"

The deputy glanced downward to the mutilated

corpse at his feet and went pale. Kittredge managed a laugh. "Don't worry," he said, "I don't plan to stay for long."

"Wait!" Kittredge recognized the voice of the one human he did not really wish to face. But he waited for the crowd in front of him to part.

He held his head up while Vonnie Solokov stared at him, at the bloodstains, the scars. Up this close, she would be able to see what he was, his fangs. She reached out a hand to touch the chill of his skin, and he flinched slightly. The street was utterly silent.

"You're real, then."

Kittredge nodded. He felt compelled to say something to this woman, but he could not think of what. One thing seemed to sum up Gene Solokov, what had been between them. "He had less fear than any man I have known."

Vonnie shook her head. She had never really expected an explanation. But there was the Archer boy standing a few yards away to remind her of explanations Gene had never made, either.

Her eyes went from Kittredge to the remains of the carnage still visible in the street. "At least it's over now."

"No," he said. "No, it isn't over. Those men are gone, but there will always be more of them. Nothing has really changed. Not for any of us."

For a moment, there was no difference among them: the people of Danby, the outsiders, the one standing with them who was no longer human—even the dead raiders. A few flakes of snow appeared from the darkness overhead and began to drift down upon the town.

# Dawn

There are still a few raiders, desperate men roaming the countryside like wolves. But fewer since the towns began to cooperate, finally, as they realized that their common need for survival outweighed their differences.

There is also a persistent rumor in the region that bad things happen to strangers who come into Fulham County.

The gray snow began to melt last April, and by July the ground had thawed enough that the farmers could get in a quick, cool-season crop. The winter ahead will be hard, but most of us should survive it. And after the winter will finally come the true spring.

Nightfall is coming to a close.

Already the sky is starting to clear. There are days now when I cannot endure the touch of the daylight. The old rhythms of my existence are beginning to reassert themselves.

I have a new resting place, hidden from the knowledge of humans. Soon, they may no longer see any advantage in my presence among them.

It will be hard to give up the day. But I must acknowledge the necessity. None of us could have survived through another black year of winter and night.

Rick told me last night, while we set up the chessboard, that he had even caught a glimpse of blue in the sky yesterday, through a break in the clouds.

I almost wish I could have been alive to see it.